AN INSTRUMENT OF THE GODS
and
OTHER STORIES OF THE SEA

AN INSTRUMENT OF THE GODS

and

Other Stories of the Sea

BY

LINCOLN COLCORD

"Of all fabricks, a ship is the most excellent, requiring
more art in building, rigging, sayling, trimming, defend-
ing, and mooring, with such a number of severall termes
and names in continuall motion, not understood of any
landman, as none would thinke of, but some few that
know them."

CAPTAIN JOHN SMITH.

Short Story Index Reprint Series

BOOKS FOR LIBRARIES PRESS
FREEPORT, NEW YORK

First Published 1922
Reprinted 1972

Library of Congress Cataloging in Publication Data

Colcord, Lincoln, 1883-1947.
    An instrument of the gods.

    (Short story index reprint series)
    Reprint of the 1922 ed.
    CONTENTS: An instrument of the gods.--Outward bound.
--The uncharted isle. [etc.]
    I.   Title.
PZ3.C6725In7   [PS1358.C35]   813'.5'2   72-5863
ISBN 0-8369-4202-7

TO MY

MOTHER

PREFACE

In making another selection of stories for publication, I have been led to inquire more closely than ever before into the essential nature of nautical fiction. It was the sub-title to the present volume which, as it were, brought me up with a round turn. " . . . And Other Stories of the Sea"—the caption went down naturally, almost without thought. Why, certainly, stories of the sea! What else, if you please? I am accustomed to regard myself as a sailor, and what I write as being more or less directly the product of seafaring. The sea is my ground and origin; I have no other point of departure. I am a native of a latitude and longitude. The other day in the attic, overhauling a chest of old letters, I ran across a small pasteboard box containing a piece of shell-encrusted seaweed; it was one of the mementoes that came home among my father's effects when he died on board his vessel in Bremerhaven the year before the war. On the box, in his handwriting, was this inscription: "A bit of weed from L——'s birthplace, washed on board the S. S. *American* on June 2nd, 1905, in 44° south latitude, South Atlantic Ocean, in the same kind of a S.W. gale in which he was born; picked up and salted down by his father, this being the first that any of the family ever have seen of that country."

Thus, although I live ashore, ostensibly engaged
in terrene projects and relations, I find that in
all matters which seem to me of importance I am
sailing still. I measure conduct in terms of seamanship; I pass my days in the condition of a man
waiting for the next voyage to begin. The land
seems alien to me, and fixed life an enigma, strangely
complicated by motives which I lack, strangely bar-
ren of what intrigues and sustains me. "We live
in manhood," says Thoreau, "to fulfil the dreams of
our boyhood." He meant more. We live in manhood to explore and circumnavigate our boyhood;
it is the only world we ever know.

But when I scanned my table of contents, it occurred to me to wonder if I were playing fair with
my readers in the promise of the sub-title. What
constitutes a sea story? Because I was born in a
gale of wind in the region of Cape Horn, because I
was brought up on the quarter-deck of a sailing ship,
am I at liberty to call anything I may choose to
write a sea story? Hardly. Yet, on the other hand,
may it not be possible that certain pieces extraneous
to the sea derive a nautical aspect from the very
hopelessness of my maritime preoccupation? Is it
no licence that a man views the world through
sailor's eyes?

Sailors themselves have strict ideas of the legality
of nautical fiction; they might be among the first to
call some of my stories before the bar. Yet, all else
being equal, I would rest my case on the factor of
nautical verisimilitude. In sea literature, as in the
kindred matter of the nautical painting, it is this
question of the accuracy of the picture which above

all others concerns the sailor. Life has overwhelmed
him with lessons of the value of spiritual integrity;
the dominating note of sea experience is that inac-
curacy, incompetency, insincerity, spell danger, ruin,
defeat, and even death. All slipshod work at sea
is inartistic; the inexorable criticism of the free-
spirited ocean affords no margin of safety. Thus
seamanship, to those who understand it, acquires,
like engineering, an application beyond the technical field. It means the attitude and way of life which
faces facts, which deals in realities without evasion,
which knows that the only failure is dishonesty and
that error is truth betrayed.

In the matter of reading, then, the sailor is well
aware that the stalls are filled with sea books written
by landlubbers. Rarely, indeed, does he find a work
which bears the authentic stamp of seamanship.
How vividly I recall my father's scorn at an incident in one of the novels of a famous writer of nautical fiction. He was reading the book aloud one
evening, on board the bark *Harvard*, going up the
China Sea. The tale had arrived at the point of
love-making; the scene was set on the quarter-deck
of a sixteen hundred ton sailing packet. The hero-
ine reclined in a deck-chair against the lee rail; a
gentle air from the spanker wafted down upon her,
for they were sailing sunny seas. The hero whispered his message; and while she listened, turning
her face away, she trailed her hand idly in the
water. "Ha!" snorted my father, when he reached
this passage. "That fellow had better look out for
himself—she has long arms." An incident like this
will ruin a book for a sailor. And why not? The

distance from the rail of a sixteen hundred ton
packet to the water would be something like twenty
feet. The author obviously was thinking of punting
on the Thames. He had confessed himself a landlubber. How, then, could anything he had to say
of the sea be taken seriously? This particular writer
had produced a formidable array of sea volumes,
some of them regarded as classics by a landlubber
standard; the whole set thereafter was damned and
doubly damned in my father's eyes.

I must confess that I entirely sympathize with
this point of view. The landlubberly sea story is an
inartistic product; no man can tell a true tale of
something which he does not know. The high degree
of specialization in the craftsmanship of the sea,
and of differentiation between it and anything to be
found on land, alike make the writing of true nautical literature a task for seamen alone. For only
through a knowledge of the craftsmanship may one
arrive at a sense and appraisement of the under-
lying values, the secret urgent sentiments, which are
the unique characteristics of seafaring—all that we
mean when we speak of the "feeling of the sea."

On the score of nautical verisimilitude, also, the
sailor has a criticism of the daily press which, to
my mind, cuts well below the surface. The press, as
everyone must recognize, has developed a distinc-
tive style for handling news with a sea flavor, a style
compounded of equal parts of mild facetiousness
and smart romanticism. It carries a great deal of
this material, the most of it topical or feature stuff;
tales of strange happenings beyond the horizon,
tales of terror or crime or mutiny, tales of trivial

humor, tales of disaster or miraculous escape. To
the landsman, these may serve their ostensible purpose of entertainment; but the sailor writhes and
curses as he reads them, for almost invariably they
are nautical monstrosities. They are untrue to the
sea; and this, to him, is sacrilege. Even when a
straightforward news report of some maritime
event needs to be written, it suffers from the same
fatal injection of landlubberism.

Every sailor, at some time in his career, has met
with the experience of participating in such an event,
and of reading the newspaper accounts of it afterward. Oftentimes he was the man who gave the
story at first hand to the reporter, who pointed out
the facts, who explained the technical situation, who
warned against certain obvious pitfalls. And when
he sees the story in print, a bitter laugh is all that
remains to him. Every pitfall has been tumbled
into; the technical situation has been rendered unintelligible to a seaman; the facts have been juggled to
suit an imaginery taste, to conform to a professional
technique; everything about the job serves only to
confirm a strong impression which this sailor has
acquired through a lifetime of observation—an impression of the general incompetency of the press in
his own special field. He makes a saying of it, a
saying known to seamen everywhere about the world.
He says: ''If the newspapers so badly misrepresent
this event in which I participated, and so ignorantly
treat of this life which I know, what shall I think
of their report and treatment of things which I do
not know?''

The sailor's demand for accuracy, however, like

any other virtue, may easily be driven too far. Indeed, it cannot be denied that the constant pressure
of this demand, coupled with an arbitrary superi-
ority of special knowledge, tends to create in him
an attitude of extreme literalness, if not of rigidity,
toward the broader problems of literary creation.
I prize, in this connection, an incident of my first
reading of Conrad's "Lord Jim." I was fresh from
the sea at the time, fresh from Singapore and China
waters as well; and the book, as was to have been
expected, struck me flat aback. (I still maintain that
"Lord Jim," when all is said and done, will live as
Conrad's masterpiece.) In the fervor of my enthusiasm, after that first reading, I forwarded the book
at once to a shipmaster with whom I was in close
relation. He sent it back, after some months, with
a criticism and a comment. The criticism ran:
"This man Conrad backs and fills too much." The
comment said: "He has tried to tell the story of
W——, but has made a poor job of it. I know
W——; his wheels don't go around that way. He
didn't give a damn."

It is necessary to explain this comment at some
length. The original of Conrad's character, Lord
Jim—that is to say, the fellow who did go mate of
an old steamer carrying native pilgrims from Singapore to Mecca, who did, along with the rest of her
officers, abandon this steamer somewhere in the Indian Ocean, leaving the pilgrims to their fate, and
who did return from this despicable adventure to
become a runner in the ship-chandlery business on
the China coast—this fellow is, or was, an individual
well known to all seafaring men whose courses used

to lead them to Eastern waters. His name is
W——, if he is still alive.

This man actually did, as I have stated, undergo
the initial set of experiences out of which Conrad
developed the story of "Lord Jim"; but there the
resemblance ends. For the sentient and palpable
W—— was not in any degree the sort of chap to
follow Jim's romantic and tragic destiny. In the
phrase of my shipmaster friend, he didn't give a
damn for the loss of reputation involved in the
abandonment of the steamer; he used to treat the
matter as a broad joke. As I recall him twenty-
five years ago, located in the cosmopolitan center of
the East as runner for the firm of McA——'s, living the life of a European renegade, he was a man
of gross and materialistic parts, a man without conscience, I should say, and with very little principle.
He lacked every quality which brought to Lord Jim
the refinement of life's cruelty; he was everything
in life that Jim would have abhorred. In short,
W—— himself was more like the man Brown, who
finally drove fate home to Jim in Patusan, than he
was like the character reared on a foundation of his
own experience.

Knowing the facts, it is plain to see what Conrad
did. The incidents of W——'s story, familiar to
everyone in the East, kindled his creative imagination; he saw in them a powerful motive for a tale of
human weakness and divine fatalism. W——, he
felt acutely, ought to have suffered, his conscience
ought to have driven him from the world, his life
ought to have sunk in retribution. The next step
was to make things as they should be; that is, to

create a character with the proper temperament, and
put him in W——'s shoes. That W—— himself
lacked a conscience, of course made no difference;
from the point of view of creative genius he had
lived inartistically, and had wasted marvellous romantic opportunities. But the literalness of my
seafaring friend would not permit him to bridge
the gap of literary creation. This book, "Lord
Jim," by one Conrad, was nothing but W——'s
story in much-garbled form; he knew W——, who
wasn't that sort of a character at all. In fact, I
think he loathed W——, and took this as an
effort to whitewash the rascal. He never could forgive Conrad for what seemed to him a lapse in
veracity.

But we have not yet defined the sea story. The
loose popular definition, I take it, would be a story
of the sea, about the sea, or situated on the sea,
This is at the same time too broad and too narrow a
ruling. It admits, on the one hand, that vast body
of landlubberly sea fiction which I have instanced;
for this material is just as truly of the sea, about
the sea, or situated on the sea, as that of the most
legitimate nautical production. On the other hand,
it would exclude the authentic works of sea fiction
primarily concerned with the development of character, perhaps with the character of landsmen, but
presented through a nautical atmosphere; those
land books, in short, which have suffered a sea
change. It would exclude "Lord Jim," for instance,
or "Captain Macedoine's Daughter." Neither of
these books is primarily of the sea, or about the sea,
or situated on the sea; both are studies in human

psychology, thrown against a background of sea experience—they are life looked at through sailor's eyes. As such, they are works of unimpeachable nautical realism.

It is this matter of characterization, I believe, which more than any other leads to confusion in the real measure of the sea story. The sea in fiction has been looked upon almost exclusively in the past as a source of romantic plot material; and the great reading public ashore has become thoroughly familiarized with, if not educated to, this aspect of nautical literature. It expects unusual and exciting happenings in its sea tales, scenes of elemental struggle, of broad comedy or tragedy. It scarcely realizes that it has formed the habit of regarding the sea too narrowly with a plot motive, and that its estimate of the sea story is unconsciously cast in this plane.

But the sailor himself, the native of the wilderness of waters, quite as unconsciously thinks of the sea in the plane of characterization. He thinks of it as a place where life goes on. He thinks of it as he knows it, and wins his way across it, and freights on its broad bosom the precious cargo of his own particular life problem, the simple and universal problem of human enterprise and aspiration. To him, in consequence, a sea story is a story of life touched by the influence of the sea; and a true sea story is such a story told by one who understands.

For my own part, the definition must forever be paradoxical; there are no categories. This work is authentic, that is spurious; the ruling is wholly arbitrary. I must submit each case to my own judg-

ment, with the candor and responsibility of a man
alone on the quarter-deck, bringing his ship through
perilous waters. The integrity of true criticism is
no less than the integrity of creative art, its nearest
point of reckoning the sun and the stars.

The sea herself is a character in a stirring tale.
As a child, I knew that she lived about me. I was
taught at my father's knee that, notwithstanding
the countless disasters of the deep, the gruesome
record of maritime adventure, the sea had no harm
or terror for those who loved her—for those who
found it in their hearts to be faithful to her stern
but generous decrees. I have been afraid of the
land many times, but never of the sea. The dangers
of life ashore are insidious; afloat, one sees what
comes and reaches where one steers. We who have
come up to the land cannot in nature think of the sea
alone as wind and water, silence and solitude, the
materials for romanticists to make their tales a little
more romantic; rather, we think of her always as
part and symbol of our better selves, a creature of
light and color, of pain and joy and love, a spirit of
proud endeavor and conscious humanity. We have
learned from her the meaning of truth. We know
no aim but that of fidelity to her character.

LINCOLN COLCORD.

Searsport, Maine,
    March, 1922.

CONTENTS

AN INSTRUMENT OF
THE GODS

I

"THE longer I live," said Nichols from the darkness of his corner, "the less of difference I see between the East and the West. I've been listening
closely to you fellows. We are fond of saying that
we don't understand the Oriental; but, let me ask
you, do we fully understand our best friends—even
ourselves? Whose fault is it? Or, failing to understand the Oriental, is it logical for us to consign him
to a different sphere of human nature? Of course,
it's the easiest way to dodge the real answer. . . ."

The old *Omega* had drifted past Green Island that
morning, dropping anchor a little later among the
fleet off Stonecutter's; and after dinner, moved by
a common impulse, we had called our sampans and
joined Nichols under her spacious after awning.
There, with the broad land-locked harbor of Hong
Kong under a half moon reflecting the perfect outline of the Peak, talk had wandered lazily along the
range of our shipping activities, to reach at last, as it
always did in such company, that world-old problem
of the races of men.

"I think that I know the race of Chinamen,"

1

Nichols went on, while grunts of assent from several quarters of the deck gave testimony of his reputation. "Oh, yes, I know them. They are made of flesh and blood, if you'll believe me; they eat with their mouths, and think in the recesses of their skulls, just as we do. They marry, beget children, and pass through life. They love, fight, strive for gain, sin, suffer, learn lessons, regret, make restitution, are tempted by devils, struggle and triumph, or give up in despair, and finally die with their years and their secrets on their heads. The same old conscience pursues them. Yes, they are eaten up, like us, by the savage and devastating contest with self, the flesh and the spirit striving for the mastery; and out of the contest, like fire struck from clashing swords, come the sparks of ideas, of aspirations, of creative efforts, of wonder and joy, pain and fear, of all the infinite play of this star-spangled life of ours against the soft darkness of the unknown sky. . . . . You fellows have been discussing only superficialities. At heart, you and the Oriental are the same. The Chinese are romantic, I tell you; they are heroic, they are incorrigibly imaginative. You think not? Let me tell you a tale."

Suddenly Nichols laughed, a snort that might have been of self-derision. "You won't be convinced," he chuckled. "I see it already. You'll derive from this tale, no doubt, only further confirmation of the unlikeness which you imagine. So be it. I merely warn you not to be too sure. Strip my friend Lee Fu Chang naked, for instance, destroy and forget about that long silken coat of his, embroidered so wonderfully with hills and trees and dragons, dress

him in a cowboy's suit and locate him in the Rocky
Mountain region of fifty years ago, and the game
he played with Captain Wilbur won't seem so inap-
propriate. It's only that you won't expect a man-
darin Chinaman to play it. You'll feel that China
is too old and civilized for what he did.

II

"Some of you fellows must remember the notorious case of Captain Wilbur and the ship *Speedwell*,"
Nichols began. "For years it was spoken of among
sailors as a classic instance of nautical perfidy; and
this was the port, you know, where Wilbur first
brought the ship after he'd stolen her, and settled
down to brazen out his crime. But few men have
heard how he lost her in the end, or why he disappeared forever from the life of the sea.

"Perhaps I'd better refresh your memories; let's
go back a matter of forty years. Captain Wilbur
was a well-known shipmaster of those palmy days.
He had commanded the *Speedwell* for a decade, and
possessed a reputation for sterling seamanship and
unblemished integrity. His vessel was one of the
finest moderate clippers ever launched on the shores
of New England. But she was growing old; and
Wilbur himself had suffered serious financial reverses, although this fact wasn't known till after
the escapade that estranged his friends and set our
little world by the ears. He seems to have been
something of a gambler in investments, and by bad
judgment or ill luck had brought his fortune to the

verge of ruin if not of actual disgrace. This, so far as I know, stands as the sole explanation of his amazing downfall. There was nothing else the matter with him, physically or mentally, as you shall hear.

"Out of a clear sky, this was what he did: he deliberately put the *Speedwell* ashore in Ombay Pass, on a voyage home from Singapore to New York with a light general cargo, and abandoned her as she lay. I say he did it deliberately; this is the common surmise, and subsequent developments lend point to the accusation. It may have been, however, that she actually drifted ashore, and that he didn't try at the time to get her off. Whether he planned the disaster, or whether he succumbed to a temptation thrust in his face by the devil of chance, makes little difference. His plans were deliberate enough after the event.

"Within a month after sailing for home, he was back again in Singapore with his ship's company in three longboats and a tale of a lost vessel. There he remained for three months, cleaning up the business. No breath of scandal was raised against him; Ombay Pass on the turn of the monsoon had caught many a fine vessel before this one, and the account rendered by his officers and crew was straightforward and consistent. The *Speedwell,* according to the official record, had drifted ashore in a light breeze, before the unmanageable currents of that region, and had lodged on a coral reef at the top of the tide in such a position that she couldn't be got off. It was another case of total loss of ship and cargo; in those days there were no steam craft in the East to send on a mission of salvage, and the Eastern Passages were forbidden hunting ground. What they caught they were allowed to keep, with no words said and the page closed. The insurance companies stood the gaff, the ship's affairs were settled without a hitch, and the name of the *Speedwell* passed simultaneously from the Maritime Register and from the books of her owners in America. Captain Wilbur let it be known that he was going home, and left Singapore.

"It was his remarkable destiny to be the revealer of his own perfidy; he made no bones about the job. Instead of going home, he went to Batavia, and there hired a schooner and crew with the proceeds of his personal holdings in the *Speedwell*. This schooner and crew he took immediately to Ombay Pass. They found the ship still resting in the same position. What they did there must remain a mystery; I have the tale only in fragmentary form from the Lascar who was serang of Wilbur's native crew.

"He, it would seem, was overawed by the extent of the engineering operations in which he participated; his description partook of the color and extravagance of a myth. Alone in distant waters they had wrestled like heroes with a monstrous task; day had followed day, while the great ship remained motionless and the elements paused to observe the stupendous effort. They had unloaded the cargo; they had sent down the top-hamper and rafted it alongside; they had patched and pumped, and Wilbur himself had dived in the lower hold and under the bows to place the stoppers in their proper location. So far as I can reckon, it took them a couple

of months to get her off; but, by Jove, they floated
her—a magnificent feat of sailorizing. Then they
loaded the cargo again, and came away.

"When Captain Wilbur appeared one morning
off Batavia roadstead with the *Speedwell* under top-
gallantsails, towing the schooner, it was the sensation of the port; a sensation that flew like wildfire
about the China Sea, as it transpired what he
intended to do with her. For he proposed, incredible
and wanton as it seems, to hold the ship and cargo
as salvage; and nothing, apparently, could be done
about it. She actually was the property of himself
and the Lascar crew.

"The crowd alongshore, everyone interested in
shipping, of course turned violently against him; for
a time there was wild talk of extra-legal proceedings, and Wilbur might have fared ill had he
attempted to frequent his old haunts just then. But
he snapped his fingers at them all. He found plenty
of men who were willing to advance him credit on
the security of the ship; he bought off his crew with
liberal allowances, took the *Speedwell* to Hong
Kong and put her in drydock, and soon was ready
for business with a fine vessel of his own. Well he
knew that personal repugnance wouldn't be carried
to commercial lengths; that he and the ship, by cutting freights a little, could find plenty to do. As
for the rest of it, the moral score, he seemed cheer-
fully prepared to face the music, and probably foresaw that with the passage of time he would be able
to live the record down.

"The old *Omega* and I were down the China Sea
on a trading voyage while these events were taking

place. When we got back to Hong Kong, Wilbur had already sailed for Antwerp, leaving his story to swell the scandal and fire the indignation of the water-front. I heard it first from my friend, Lee Fu Chang.

"'An extraordinary incident, is it not?' exclaimed Lee Fu in conclusion. 'Extraordinary! I am deeply interested. First of all, I am interested in your laws. Here is a man who has stolen a ship; and your laws, it is discovered, support him in the act. But the man himself is the most interesting. It is a crowning stroke, Captain Nichols, that he has not seen fit to change the name of the vessel. Consider this fact. All is as it was before, when the well-known and reputable Captain Wilbur commanded the fine ship *Speedwell* on voyages to the East.'

"'Can it be possible?' I said. 'Isn't there some mistake? The man must have the gall of a highway robber! Does the crowd have anything to do with him?'

"'None of his old associates speak in passing; they cross the street to avoid him. He goes about like one afflicted with a pestilence. But the wonder is that he is not disturbed by this treatment. That makes it very extraordinary. He is neither cringing nor brazen; he makes no protest, offers no excuse, and takes no notice. In the face of outrageous insult, Captain, he maintains an air of dignity and reserve, like a man conscious of inner rectitude.'

"'Did you talk with him, Lee Fu?' I asked.

"'Oh, yes. In fact, I cultivated his acquaintance. The study fascinated me; it relieved, as it were, the daily monotony of virtue. In him there is no trace of humbug or humility. Do not think that he is a simple man. His heart in this matter is unfathomable . . . well worth sounding.'

" 'By Jove, I believe you liked him!' I exclaimed.

" 'No, not that.' Lee Fu folded his hands within the long sleeves of his embroidered coat and rested them across his stomach in a characteristic attitude of meditation. 'No, quite the opposite. I abhorred him. He seemed to me unnatural, monstrous, beyond the range of common measure. Captain, there are crimes and crimes, and it has been my lot to know men who have committed many of them. There are murder, theft, arson, treason, infidelity, and all the rest; and these, in a manner of speaking, are natural crimes. Shall we define it thus: a natural crime is one which eventually brings its own retribution? Sooner or later, if justice is not done, the natural crime works havoc with its perpetrator; it plagues his conscience, it fastens like a fungus on his soul. Through lust or passion, natural impulses, he has committed error; but he cannot escape the final payment of the price. On the other hand, there are unnatural crimes, crimes for which there is no reason, crimes requiring no liquidation; and there are unnatural criminals, feeling no remorse. Such a criminal, I take it, is this Captain Wilbur, who goes his way in peace from the betrayal of a sacred trust.'

" 'Aren't you drawing it a little strong?' I laughed. 'It isn't exactly a crime . . .'

"Lee Fu smiled quietly, giving me a glance that was a mere flicker of the eyelids. 'Perhaps not to you,' he said. 'Fixed in the mind of your race is

a scale of violence by which to measure the errors of
men; if no blood flows, then it is not so bad. Your
justice is still a barbarian. Thus you constantly
underestimate the deeper crimes, allowing your master criminals to go scathless, or even, in some
instances, to prosper and win repute by their
machinations. But, let me tell you, Captain, murder is brave and honorable compared to this. Consider what he did. Trained to the sea and ships,
after a lifetime of honorable service to his traditions, he suddenly forsakes them utterly. Because
the matter rests with him alone, because there is
nothing in it for him to fear, his serenity condemns
his very soul. He has fallen from heaven to hell;
flagrantly, remorselessly, and without attempt at
concealment or evasion, he has played false with
sacred honor and holy life. It is blasphemy which
he has committed; when the master of the ship
is not to be trusted, the gods tremble in the sky. So
I abhor him—and am fascinated. He does not speak
of his crime, of course, yet I find myself waiting and
watching for a hint, an explanation. Believe me,
Captain, when I tell you, that in all my talk with him
I have received not a single flash of illumination;
no, not one! There is no key to his design. He
speaks of his ship and her affairs as other captains
do. He is a tall, jovial, healthy man, with frank
glances and open speech. For all that seems, he
might have forgotten what went on at Ombay Pass.
I swear to you that his heart is untroubled. As
you would say, he does not give a damn. . . . And
that is horrible.'

"A little amused at my friend's moral fervor, I

adopted a bantering tone. 'Perhaps the man is innocent,' I said. 'Perhaps there's something unexplained. . . .'

"'You forget that he holds the vessel as his property—the same vessel that he himself ran on shore,' Lee Fu reminded me. 'You still are thinking, Captain of violence and blood. No one was lost, no shots were fired . . . so, never mind. It is not vital to you that a strong man within your circle has murdered the spirit; you refuse to become excited or alarmed. . . . Wait then till actual blood flows.'

"'What do you mean by that, Lee Fu? You think . . . ?'

"'I think that Captain Wilbur will bear watching. In the meantime, take my advice, and study him when opportunity offers. Thus we learn of heaven and hell.'

III

"A few years went by, while the case of Captain Wilbur and the *Speedwell* passed through its initial stages of being forgotten. Nothing succeeds like success; the man owned a fine ship, and those who did business with him soon came to take the situation for granted. Wilbur made fast passages, kept the *Speedwell* in excellent trim, and paid his bills promptly; rumor of course had it that he was growing rich. In all probability it was true. After a while, some of his old friends were willing to let bygones be bygones; there were many more to whom the possession of a fine piece of property seemed of enough importance to cover a multitude of sins. The new fellows who came to the East and heard the tale for the first time, couldn't credit it after meeting Wilbur in the flesh. Little by little one began to see him again on the quarter-deck at the evening gatherings of the fleet, or among sea-faring men ashore at tiffin. When, in time, it became unwise to start the story against him, for fear of misconstruction of one's motive, it was evident that he had well-nigh won his nefarious match against society.

"I'd met him a number of times, of course, during this interval, and had come to understand Lee Fu's urgent advice. Indeed, to one curious as to the habits of the human species, Wilbur compelled attention. That perfect urbanity, that air of unfailing dignity and confidence, that aura of a commanding personality, of an able ship-master among his brethren, of a man whose position in the world was secure beyond peradventure: all this could spring from but two only spiritual conditions—either from a quiet and innocent conscience, or from a heart perfectly attuned to villainy. As he sat among us, taking up his proper word in the conversation, assuming no mask, showing no concern, it was with the utmost difficulty that one placed him as a man with a dark past, with a damnable blot on his escutcheon. So unconscious was his poise that one often doubted the evidence of memory, and found oneself going back over the record, only to fetch up point-blank against the incontestable fact that he had stolen his ship and betrayed his profession. By Jove, it seemed fantastic! Here he was, to all intents and purposes a gentleman; a likeable fellow, too, in many ways. He talked well, was positive without being arbitrary, usually had a fair and generous word for the issue under discussion, never indulged in criticism; and above all, damn him, he sustained a reputation for expert mastery over this profession to which he'd dealt so foul a blow.

" 'It is a triumph of character!' Lee Fu used to repeat, as we compared notes on the case from time to time. 'I think that he has not been guilty of a single minor error. His correctness is nothing short of diabolical. It presages disaster, like too much fair weather in the typhoon season. Wait and watch; mark my word, Captain, when the major error comes it will be a great tragedy.'

" 'Must there be a major error?' I asked, falling into the mood of Lee Fu's exaggerated concern. 'He's carried it off so far with the greatest ease.'

" 'Yes, with the greatest ease,' said Lee Fu thoughtfully. 'Yet I begin to wonder if he properly has been put to the test. See how the world protects him! Sometimes, I am appalled. It is as if we wrapped the doers of evil in cotton wool. so that not even rudeness might disturb them. He merely has maintained a perfect silence, and the world has done the rest. It has seemed more anxious to forget his crime than he to have it forgotten. So he lives with impunity, as it were. But he is not invulnerable. Life will challenge him yet . . . it must be . . . life, which is truth, and not the world. Can a man escape the anger and justice of the gods? That is why I concern myself with him—to know his final destiny.'

" 'You admit, then, that he's not the incarnate criminal you once thought him,' I chaffed, unable to take the matter so deeply to heart. 'He may be only a stupid fool with a wooden face and naturally good manners. . . .'

" 'Not stupid,' Lee Fu interrupted. 'Yet, on the other hand, not exceptional, not superior to life. Such faultless power of will is in itself no mean part of ability. He is, as you might say, self-centered—most accurately self-centered. But the challenge of the gods displaces the center of all. He will be like a top that is done spinning. A little breath may topple him at last. Wait and see. . . . But, for the present, it is evident that there is nothing more to be learned. The mask is inscrutable.'

"Thinking the case over at sea, I often laughed to myself over Lee Fu's intensity. Voyage followed voyage; one time when I had just come in from Bankok and was on my way from the Jetty to Lee Fu's office, I passed Captain Wilbur on the opposite side of Queen's Road. He waved a hand to me as he turned the corner; at once it flashed across my mind that I hadn't observed the *Speedwell* in the roadstead as I came in. When I had finished my business with Lee Fu, I asked him for an explanation of Wilbur's presence in Hong Kong without his vessel.

" 'You are mistaken, Captain—it has little significance,' he answered with a quizzical smile. 'So, after all, you pay a little attention? The fact is, the successful Captain Wilbur has retired from active service on the sea. He is now a ship owner, nothing

more, and has favored Hong Kong above all other
ports as the seat of his retirement. He resides in a
fine house on Graham Terrace, and has three chair-
men in white livery edged with crimson. . . . Captain Nichols, you should steal a ship.'

" 'Who has gone in the *Speedwell?*' I inquired.

" 'An old friend of ours, one Captain Turner,'
said Lee Fu slowly, glancing in my direction.

" 'Not Will Turner?'

" 'The same.'

"I pursed up my mouth in a silent whistle. Will
Turner in the *Speedwell!* Poor fellow, he must have
lost another of his ill-starred vessels. Hard luck
seemed to pursue him. One ship would be sold from
under his command; several he had lost in deep
water, by fire, storm or old age; another had sprung
a leak in the Java Sea, to be condemned a little later
when he had worked her into Batavia. A capable
sailor and an honest man; yet life had afforded him
nothing but a succession of hard blows and heavy
falls. Death and sorrow, too; he had buried a wife
and child, swept off by cholera, in the Bay of Bengal.
A dozen years before, Turner and I had landed
together in the China Sea, and were thrown much
in each other's company; I knew his heart, his history, some of his secrets, and liked him tremen-
dously for the man he was.

"Watching Lee Fu in silence, I thought again of
the relationship between Will Turner and this
extraordinary Chinaman. I won't go into that story
now, but there were overwhelming reasons why
these two should think well of each other; why Lee
Fu should respect and honor Captain Turner, and

why Turner should consider Lee Fu his best friend. It had come about as the result of an incident of Turner's early days in the East; an incident of a ship, a rascal and a doctored charter-party, that might have turned into an ugly business save for the conduct and perspicacity of the two chief victims. It had thrown them violently together; ever since, they had kept the bond close and hidden, as became men of reserve. Probably I was the only man in the world who knew how strong it was.

"And now Turner had taken Wilbur's ship. Strange how this new development seemed to impinge on Lee Fu's fancy, how it brought the Wilbur case nearer home. The next moment, of course, the impression had passed; and I saw that, instead of marking another stroke of ill-luck for Turner, it might spell the beginning of good fortune.

" 'What happened to the old *Altair?*' I asked. Turner had commanded a trading packet by that name three months before.

" 'She was bought by certain parties for a store-ship, and now lies moored on Kowloon-side,' answered Lee Fu. 'I was about to make a proposal to Captain Turner, when this plan came forward,' he went on, as if excusing himself. 'I did not know of it until he actually had accepted. I said everything in my power to dissuade him . . .'

" 'What's the trouble? Didn't Wilbur do the right thing by him?' I asked.

" 'Captain, you are perverse. The business arrangement is immaterial. It is unthinkable that our friend should command a ship for such a man. The jealous gods have not yet shown their hand.'

" 'Nonsense, Lee Fu!' I exclaimed, finding myself irritated at the out-cropping of the old conceit. 'Since the thing is done, hadn't we better try to be practical in our attitude?'

" 'Exactly,' said Lee Fu. 'Let us be practical. . . . Captain Nichols, is it impossible for the Caucasian to reason from cause to effect? There seems to be no logic in your design—which explains many curious facts of history. I merely have insisted, in our consideration of this case, that a man who would do one thing would do another, and that sooner or later life inevitably would present him with another thing to do.'

" 'But I've known too many men to escape what you call destiny,' I argued peevishly.

" 'Have you?' inquired Lee Fu.

"He said no more, and we went out to tiffin.

IV

"That year I plunged into the Malay Archipelago for an extended cruise, was gone seven months among the islands, and wasted another month coming up the China Sea in order to dodge the tail-end of the typhoon season. But luck favored me, of course, since I wasn't in a hurry; and so it happened that for the last three hundred miles across from Luzon I raced with a typhoon after all, beating it to an anchorage in Hong Kong by a margin of twelve hours. It was an exceptionally late storm; and the late ones, you know, are the least dependable in their action. Typhoon signals were flying from the Peak as I came in; before the *Omega's* sails were furled the sky to the eastward had lowered and darkened like a shutter, and the wind had begun to whip in vicious gusts across the harbor.

I went ashore at once, for I carried important papers from Lee Fu's chief agent in the islands. When I reached his outer office, I found it full of gathering gloom, although it still was early afternoon. Sing Toy immediately took in my name. In a moment I was ushered into the familiar room where my friend sat beside a shaded lamp, facing a teakwood desk inlaid with ivory and invariably bare, save for a priceless Ming vase and an ornament of old green bronze.

" 'Back again, Lee Fu,' I said, placing the island letters on the desk before him. 'And just in time, it seems.' A rising gust outside whined along the street.

"He paid no attention to my greeting or the letters. 'Sit down, Captain,' he said. 'I have bad news.'

" 'Yes?' I queried, somewhat alarmed at the vagueness of the announcement. So far as I was aware, no matter that we shared between us could result in 'bad news,' said in such a tone.

"Folding his hands across his stomach and slightly bowing his head, he gazed at me with a level up-turned glance that without betraying expression carried by its very immobility a hint of deep emotion.

" 'It is as I told you,' he said at last. 'Now, perhaps, you will believe.'

" 'For Heaven's sake, what are you talking

about?' I demanded. 'Tell me instantly what is wrong.'

"He nodded slowly. 'There is plenty of time—and I will tell. It often is said that the season which brings a late typhoon, as now, also is ushered in by an early typhoon. So it was this season. A very severe storm came down before its time, and almost without warning. . . . It was this storm into whose face our late friend Captain Turner took his ship, the *Speedwell,* sailing from Hong Kong for New York some four months ago.'

" 'You don't mean that Turner has lost her?'

" 'I regret to inform you, yes. Also, he has lost himself. Three days after sailing, he met the typhoon outside, and was blown upon a lee shore two hundred miles along the China Coast. In this predicament, he cut away his masts and came to anchor. But his ship would not float, and accordingly sunk at her anchors. . . .'

" 'Sunk at her anchors!' I exclaimed. 'How could that be? A tight ship never did such a thing.'

" 'Nevertheless, she sunk there in the midst of the storm, and all on board perished. Afterwards, the news was reported from shore, and the hull of the *Speedwell* was discovered in ten fathoms of water. There has been talk of trying to save the ship; and Captain Wilbur himself, her owner, in a diver's suit, has inspected the wreck. Surely, he should be well-fitted to save her again, if it were possible! He says no, and it is reported that the insurance companies are in agreement with him. That is, they have decided that he cannot turn the trick a second time.' Lee Fu's voice dropped to a rasping tone. 'The lives, likewise, cannot be saved.'

"I sat for some moments in silence, gazing at the green bronze dragon on the desk. Turner gone? A friend's death is shocking, even though it makes so little difference. And between us, too, there had been a bond. . . . I was thinking of the personal loss, and had missed the significance of Lee Fu's phraseology. I looked up at him blankly; found him still regarding me with up-turned eyes, his chin sunk lower on his breast.

" 'That is not all,' he said suddenly.

"I sat up as if under the impact of a blow. Across my mind raced thoughts of all that might happen to a man on that abandoned coast. 'What more?' I asked.

" 'Listen, Captain, and pay close attention. I have investigated with great care, and am fully satisfied that no mistake has been made. You must believe me. . . . Some weeks after the departure and loss of the *Speedwell*, word came to my ears that a man had a tale worth hearing. You know how information reaches me, and that my sources run through unexpected channels among my people. This man was brought; he proved to be a common coolie, a lighter-man who had been employed in the loading of the *Speedwell*. Note how a slight chance may lead to serious occasions. This coolie had been gambling during the dinner hour, and had lost the small sum that he should have taken home as the product of several days' labor. Like many, he feared his wife, and particularly her mother, who was a shrew. In a moment of desperation, as the lighter was preparing to leave the vessel for the night, he escaped from the others and secreted himself in the *Speedwell's* lower hold, among the bales of merchandise. What he planned is hard to tell; it does not matter.

" 'This happened while yet the ship's lower hold was not quite filled,' Lee Fu went on after a pause. 'The coolie, as I said, secreted himself in the cargo, well forward, for he had entered by the fore hatch. There he remained many hours, sleeping, and when he awoke, quietness had descended on the deck above. He was about to climb into the between-decks, the air below being heavy with the odors of the cargo, when he heard a sound on the ladder which led down from the upper deck. It was a sound of quiet steps, mingled with a faint metallic rattling. In a moment a foot descended on the floor of the between-decks, and a lantern was cautiously lighted. The coolie retreated quickly to his former hiding place, from which post he was able to see all that went on.'

"Again Lee Fu paused, as if lingering in imagination over the scene. 'It seems that this late and secret comer into the hold of the *Speedwell* was none other than her owner, Captain Wilbur,' he slowly resumed. 'The coolie knew him by face; a distant cousin once had been in the employ of the Wilbur household, and the man already was aware whose ship it was. Most of the inner facts of life are disseminated through the gossip of servants, and are known to a wide circle. Furthermore, as the lighter had been preparing to depart that evening, this coolie had seen the owner come on board in his own sampan. Afterwards, through my inquiries among sampan-men and others, I learned that Captain Turner had spent that night on shore. It was Captain Wilbur's custom, it seems, frequently to sleep on board his ship when she lay here in port; the starboard stateroom was kept in readiness for him. So he had done this night—and he had been alone in the cabin.'

" 'What was he doing in the hold with a lantern?' I asked, unable to restrain my impatience.

" 'Exactly . . . you shall hear. I was obliged to make certain deductions from the story of the coolie, for he was not technically acquainted with the internal construction of a vessel. Yet what he saw was perfectly obvious to the most ignorant eye. . . . Have you ever been in the lower hold of the *Speedwell,* Captain Nichols?'

" 'No, I haven't.'

" 'But you recall the famous matter of her bow-ports, do you not?'

" 'Yes, indeed. I was in Singapore when they were cut.'

"The incident came back to me at once, in full detail. There had been a cargo of ironwood on the beach, destined for the repair of a temple somewhere up the Yang-tsi-kiang; among it were seven magnificent sticks of timber, each over a hundred feet in length and forty inches square at the butt— these were for columns, I suppose. It had been necessary to find a large ship to take this cargo from Singapore to Shanghai; the *Speedwell* finally had accepted the charter. In order to load the immense column-timbers, she had been obliged to cut bow-ports of extraordinary size; fifty inches in depth, they were, and nearly seven feet in width, according to my recollection—the biggest bow-ports on record.

" 'It has been my privilege,' Lee Fu went on, 'to examine the fore-peak of the *Speedwell* when these ports were in and her hold was empty. I once had chartered the ship, and felt alarmed for her safety until I had seen the interior fastenings of those great windows which, when she was loaded, looked out into the deep sea. But my alarm was groundless. There was a most ingenious device for strengthening the bows where they had been weakened by the cutting of the ports. Four or five timbers had been severed; but these had been reproduced on the port itself, and the whole was fashioned like a massive door. It lifted upward on immense wrought iron hinges, a hinge to every timber; when it was lowered in place, gigantic bars of iron, fitted into brackets on the adjoining timbers, stretched across its inner face to hold it against the impact of the waves. At the bottom there were additional fastenings. Thus the port, when tightly caulked from without, became an integral part of the hull; I was told, and could believe it, that there never had been a trace of leakage from her bows. Most remarkable of all, I was told, when it became necessary to lift these ports for use, the task could easily be accomplished by two or three men and a stout watch-tackle. . . . This, also, I am prepared to believe.'

"There seemed to be a general drift to Lee Fu's rambling narrative, but I hadn't yet caught sight of a logical *dénouement*. 'To resume the story of the coolie,' he continued, with exasperating deliberation. 'This, in plain language, is what he saw. Our friend, Captain Wilbur, descended into the lower hold, and worked his way forward to the fore-peak, where there was little cargo. There he labored with great effort for several hours; you will recall that he is a vigorous man. He had equipped himself with a short crowbar, and carried a light tackle wrapped about his body beneath the coat. The tackle he loosened and hung to a hook above the middle of the port; I take it that he had brought this gear merely for the purpose of lowering easily the iron cross bars, so that they would make no noise. Had one fallen . . .'

" 'Good God, Lee Fu, what are you trying to tell me?'

" 'Merely occurrences. Many quite impossible things, Captain, nevertheless get themselves done in the dark, in secret places, out of sight and mind. . . . So, with the short crowbar he little by little pried loose the iron braces to the port, slinging them in his tackle and dropping them softly one by one into the ship's bottom. It was a heavy task; the coolie said that sweat poured from the big man like rain. Yet he was bent upon accomplishment, and persevered until he had done the job. Later he removed all the additional port fastenings; last of all he covered the cross-bars with dunnage, and rolled against the bow several bulky bales of matting to conceal the crime. . . . Captain, when the *Speedwell* sailed from Hong Kong on her last voyage in command of our honored friend, one of her

great bowports below the water hung on its hinges
without internal fastenings, held in place only by the
tightness of the caulking. The first heavy sea . . .'
    " 'Can it be possible?' I said through clenched
teeth.
    " 'Oh, yes, so easily. It happened, and has be-
come a part of life. As I told you, I have investigated with scrupulous care; my men dare not bring
me lies.'
    "I still was trying to get my bearings, to grasp a
clew. 'But why should he do it, Lee Fu? Had he
anything against Turner?'
    " 'Not at all. You do not seem to understand.
He was tired of the vessel, and freights were becoming very poor. He wanted the insurance. He now
assures himself that he had no thought of disaster;
one hardly could foresee an early typhoon. He had
it in mind for the ship to sink discreetly, in pleasant
weather, so that all hands might escape. . . . Yet
he was willing to run the chance of wholesale murder. Remember how he sweat at the task, there in
the fetid air of the lower hold. It was absentee murder, if you will; he did not contemplate, he was not
forced to contemplate, the possible results of his
act on the lives of others. . . . What do you think
now, Captain, of a man who will betray his profession?'
    "I got up abruptly and began pacing the floor.
The damnable affair had made me sick at heart, and
a little sick at the stomach. What to think?—what
to believe? It seemed incredible, fantastic; there
must be some mistake. . . . While I was pacing,
Lee Fu changed his position. He faced the desk,

stretched out an arm, and put his palm flat down on the polished surface.

" 'Thus the gods have struck,' he said, in that changeless voice that seemed an echo of the ages. 'There is blood at last, Captain—twenty-seven lives, and among them one dear to us—enough even to convince one of your race that a crime had been committed. But my analysis was seriously in error. The criminal, it seems, is destined not to suffer. He continues to go about carried by three men in white and crimson livery, his belly full of food and wine. Others have paid the price. Instead of toppling, his life spins on with renewed momentum. My query has been answered; he has escaped the gods.'

" 'Can't you rip the case open, jostle his security? Isn't there some way . . .?'

" 'No way,' said Lee Fu with a shake of the head. 'You forget the fine principle of extra-territoriality, which you have so kindly imposed on us by force of arms. Captain Wilbur is not subject to Chinese justice; your own courts have exclusive jurisdiction over him, his kind, and all their works. No, Captain, he is amply protected. What would I accomplish in your courts with this fanciful accusation, and for witnesses a coolie and a sampan-man?'

"I continued to pace the floor, thinking dark thoughts. There was a way, of course . . . between man and man; but such things aren't done any longer by civilized people. We're supposed not to go about with firearms, privately meting out justice. We are domesticated. Whatever the thoughts I might have harbored, in the first anger of the realization of wrong, I knew very well that I wouldn't act on them. Lee Fu was right, there was nothing to be done; the man had made good his escape from the hand of destiny.

"Pacing rapidly, as if pursued by a veritable phantom of crime, and oblivious to everything but the four walls of the room, I nearly floored the chief clerk, Sing Toy, as he pattered in with a message from the outer office. He ducked, slipped behind the lamp, and began whispering in Lee Fu's ear.

" '*Ah!*' exclaimed Lee Fu sharply.

"I started, whirled around in my tracks. His voice had lost the level, passive tone; it had taken on the timbre of action. Suddenly, with a quick rustle of silken garments, he stood up behind the desk; the abrupt motion threw his shadow across the floor and up the opposite wall. With a subtle thrill of anticipation, I felt the profound psychic change that had come over my friend. The very air of the room had quickened before that single exclamation, as if a cold breeze had blown through. . . . A breeze, indeed, was at that moment trying hard to find an entrance; the absolute silence of the room brought out in sharp relief the tumult outside, the hoarse voice of the rising gale. We stood as if listening. I looked at Lee Fu, caught his eye. It was charged with energy and purpose, with something like relief —like the eye of a man who has made up his mind after a long period of bewilderment, who begins to understand. . . .

" 'Send him in, alone,' he said in Chinese to Sing Toy, now at the outer door.

" 'Who is it?' I asked hoarsely.

" 'The man we have been speaking of.'

" 'Wilbur? What the devil . . .?'

" 'He merely dropped in as he was passing, to make a call,' said Lee Fu, speaking rapidly. 'So he thinks—but I think otherwise.' Leaning forward across the desk, he fixed me with an extended arm that trembled slightly before it found its aim. 'Keep silence,' he commanded. 'Beware of word or glance. This chanced by predestination. We are on the threshold of the gods.'

V

"Lee Fu remained standing as Captain Wilbur entered the room. His hurried admonition still rang in my ears: 'Keep silence—beware of word or glance!' But I couldn't have spoken; had I opened my mouth just then, it would have been only to emit a snarl of anger. To beware of glances was a different matter. The task might be easy enough for Lee Fu, with that perfect self-control of his that extended to the last nerve of his eyelids and the last muscle of his finger-tips; but for my part I was spiritually incapable, as it were, of keeping rage and abomination out of my eyes. I stood as if rooted to the floor, gazing point-blank at Wilbur with a stare that must have made him wonder as to my sanity. For, of course, he hadn't the slightest suspicion that we knew what we knew.

" 'Good afternoon, Captain Wilbur,' said Lee Fu blandly. 'Do you seek refuge from the storm? . . . I think you are acquainted with Captain Nichols, of the bark *Omega*. He arrived this morning from the Celebes.'

" 'Oh, how do you do, Nichols,' said Wilbur, advancing down the room. 'I've missed you around town for a good while, it seems to me. So you've been off on one of your famous exploring trips? Then you'll have a lot to tell us. I suppose you had the usual assortment of romantic and tragic adventures?'

"I drew back behind the desk, to escape shaking his hand. 'No,' I answered, 'nothing like the adventure that awaited me here.'

"He settled himself in a chair, directly in range of the light; smiled, and lifted his eyebrows. 'So? Well, I can believe you. This office, you know, is the heart of all adventure. The most romantic room in the East—presided over by the very genius of romance.' He bowed toward Lee Fu, and touched a match to a long Manila. 'Genius, or demon, which is it, now?' he chuckled, his eyes twinkling from Lee Fu to me.

"'You honor me, Captain,' interposed Lee Fu quickly, cutting me off from the necessity of speaking. 'If, indeed, you do not flatter. I merely observe and live. It is life which may be called the heart of all adventure—life, with its amazing secrets that one by one transpire into the day, and with its enormous burden of evil that weighs us down like slaves.'

"Wilbur laughed. 'Yes, that's it, no doubt. But there's some good, too, Lee Fu—plenty of good. Don't be a pessimist. Yet you're right enough in a way; the evil always does manage to be more romantic.'

" 'Much more romantic,' observed Lee Fu. 'And

the secrets are more romantic still. Consider, for instance, the case of a man with a dark secret which by chance has become known, though he is not aware of the fact. How infinitely romantic! He feels secure; yet inevitably it will be disclosed. When, and how? Such a case would be well worth watching . . . as the great poet had in mind when he wrote, ''Murder will out.'' '

''The winged words made no impression on their mark. Wilbur met Lee Fu's glance frankly, innocently, with interest and even with a trace of amusement at the other's flight of fancy. The full light of the lamp illuminated his features, the least fleeting expression couldn't have escaped us. By Jove, he was superb; the damned rascal hadn't a nerve in his body. To be sure, he still had no suspicion, and attributed Lee Fu's shaft to a mere chance; yet this very factor of safety lent additional point to the finish of his dissimulation. He might at least have indulged himself in a start, a glance, a knitting of the eyebrows; his conscience, or his memory if he hadn't a conscience, might have received a faint surprise. But his watchfulness must have been unfailing, automatic. Or was it that a reminder of his appalling crime woke no echo at all in his breast?

''I examined him closely. Above a trimmed brown beard his cheeks showed the ruddy color of health and energy; his eyes were steady, his mouth was strong and clean, a head of fine gray hair surmounted a high forehead; the whole aspect of his countenance was pleasing and dignified. He had good hands, broad yet closely knit, and ruddy with the same glow of health that rose in his face. He was dressed neatly in a plain blue serge suit, with square-toed russet shoes encasing small feet, a dark bow-tie at his throat, and a narrow gold watch chain strung across his vest. Sitting at ease, with an arm thrown over the chair-back and one ankle resting on the other knee, he presented a fine figure of a man, a figure that might have been that of a prosperous and benevolent merchant, a man who had passed through the world with merit and integrity, and now was enjoying his just reward.

"He gave a hearty laugh. 'For the Lord's sake, you fellows, come on out of the gloom!' he cried. 'A pretty state of mind you seem to have worked yourselves into, hobnobbing here behind closed doors. I drop in for a chat, and find a couple of blue devils up to their ears in the sins of humanity. Nichols, over there, is just as bad as the other; he's scarcely opened his mouth since I came in. What's the matter? . . . You have to fight these moods, you know,' he quizzed. 'It doesn't do to let them get the upper hands.'

" 'It is the mood of the approaching storm,' said Lee Fu quietly. 'We have been speaking of typhoons, and of the fate which they sometimes bring to men.'

"A fiercer squall than the last shook the building; it passed in a moment, ceasing suddenly, as if dropping us somewhere in mid-air. Wilbur was the first to speak after the uproar.

" 'Yes, it's going to be another terror, I'm afraid. A bad night to be on the water, gentlemen. I wouldn't care to be threshing around outside, now, as poor Turner was such a short time ago.'

"I could have struck him across the mouth for the shocking callousness of the words. A bad night outside! He dared to speak of it; he, sitting there so comfortably, so correctly, alive and well, glad to be safe in port and sorry for those afloat—the same remorseless devil who had sent Turner to his doom.

"Lee Fu's voice fell like oil on a breaking sea. 'All signs point to another severe typhoon. But, as I was telling Captain Nichols, these late storms often are irregular—like the early ones. . . . It happened, Captain Wilbur, that the loss of the *Speedwell* was the subject which we were discussing when you came in.'

"'Too bad—too bad,' said Wilbur soberly, as if overcome by thoughts of the disaster. 'You were away, Nichols, weren't you? Of course!—then you've just heard of it. It was a bad week here, I can tell you, after the news came in. I never shall forget it. . . . Well, we take our chances. . . .'

"'Some of us do, and some of us don't,' I snapped.

"'That's just the way I felt about it, at the time,' he said simply. 'I didn't feel right, to have both feet on the ground. Seemed as if there must have been something we could have done, something we had neglected. It came home hard to me.'

"My jaw fairly dropped as I listened to the man. Something he had neglected? . . . Was it possible that he liked to talk about the affair? He didn't seem anxious to turn the conversation.

"'Captain Nichols and I were wondering,' observed Lee Fu, 'why it was that the *Speedwell* did not remain afloat, after she had cast her anchors.

Neither of us can recall another incident of the kind. What is your opinion, Captain Wilbur; you have examined the hull, as it lies on the bottom.'

" 'It isn't a matter of opinion,' Wilbur answered. 'Haven't I told you?—I thought I'd seen you since the inspection. I put on a diver's suit, you know, Nichols, and went down. . . . Why, the simple explanation is, her starboard bow-port in the lower hold is stove in. It must have happened after she came to anchor. She lay there just scooping up water at every plunge—filled and sank as she lay. I've always been afraid of those big bow-ports; the moment I heard of the peculiar circumstances of the disaster, I knew in my heart what had happened.'

" 'Did you?' inquired Lee Fu, with a slight hardening of the voice. 'Strange—but so did I.'

"Wilbur gazed at him questioningly, knitting his brows. 'Oh, yes, I remember. I was wondering how you happened to think of her bow-ports. But you told me that you had examined them. . . .'

" 'Yes, I examined them. . . . Captain Wilbur, have you collected your insurance money?' The question came with an abruptness that marked a change of tactics; to me, who knew Lee Fu so well, it obviously marked the first turning point in some as yet impenetrable plan.

"Wilbur frowned and glanced up sharply, very properly offended. The next moment he had decided to pass it off as an instance of alien manners. 'As a matter of fact, I've just cleaned up today,' he replied brusquely. 'Had my final settlement with Lloyd's this morning—and did a silly thing, as a fellow will sometimes. You know, they had a package of large denomination bank notes in the office, crisp, wonderful looking fellows; I took a sudden fancy for them, and in a moment of childishness asked to have my money in that form. They chaffed me a good deal, but I stuck to it. You'd hardly believe, would you, that a fellow would be such a fool? I can prove it to you, though; I've got those bills in my pocket now. By Jove, that reminds me— what time is it getting to be? I must leave them at the bank before it closes.'

" 'What is the total amount of the bank notes which you have in your possession?' asked Lee Fu in a level tone that carried its own insult.

Wilbur plainly showed his astonishment now. 'The total amount? . . . Well, if you want all the details, I have about forty thousand dollars in my pocket. I'm not aware, however, that it's any concern of yours. . . .'

"Lee Fu shot at me a stare full of meaning; it might have been a look of caution, or a glance of triumph. I was expected to understand something; but for the life of me I couldn't catch the drift of the situation. Confused by the terrific struggle to keep my mouth shut, I only sensed that a crisis was impending.

" 'As I was saying, I once examined the bow-ports of the *Speedwell*,' Lee Fu calmly resumed. 'At that time, I satisfied myself as to their construction; unlike you, Captain Wilbur, I could not be afraid of them. When properly fastened, they were impregnable to any danger of the sea. . . . And I remember, Captain, that it occurred to me, as I examined their fastenings, how easily these ports could be loosened from within, by one desiring to sink the vessel. The iron cross-bars could be lifted from their brackets by a single strong man; with a small tackle they could be dropped without noise into the bottom. No one need know of it; and, lo, the ship would sail to meet her destiny riding on the waves. Has the thought ever occurred to you, Captain Wilbur?'

"Wilbur's air of mingled repugnance and perplexity was innocence itself. 'I can't say that it has,' he answered shortly. 'Your imagination is a little morbid, Lee Fu—I won't say worse. Who would want to sink the *Speedwell,* I'd like to know?'

" 'Who, indeed?' observed Lee Fu, staring at Wilbur with a steady, biting gaze. As he stared, he reached out slowly with his right hand and opened the top drawer of the desk. Suddenly he stood up. The hand held a revolver, which pointed with an unwavering aim at Wilbur's breast.

" 'If you move from your chair, Captain, I will shoot you dead, and your end will never be known,' he said rapidly, throwing a cold determination into his voice. 'It is time we came to an understanding, for the day wanes.'

"Wilbur uncrossed his legs, leaned forward, and looked at Lee Fu narrowly. 'What's the joke?' he demanded.

" 'A joke that will be clear as time goes on—like one you played with bow-ports on my friend. . . . Captain, we are about to go on a journey. Will you join us, Captain Nichols, or will you remain on shore?'

"The question was perfunctory; whatever was in the wind, Lee Fu knew that my decision rested in his hands. I stood up—for until now I'd been chained to my chair by the amazing turn of the moment.

" 'Bow-ports? . . .' Wilbur was saying. 'Put that gun down. What in hell do you mean?' He started to rise.

" 'Sit down!' commanded Lee Fu. 'I mean that I will shoot. This is not play.' Their eyes met in a sharp struggle, which Lee Fu won. Wilbur sank back, angry and confused.

" 'Are you crazy, Lee Fu?' he growled. 'What is it—do you want to rob me? What's the meaning of this nonsense, Nichols? Have both of you gone mad?'

" 'No, Captain,' interposed Lee Fu. 'But we have found a man who wanted to sink the *Speedwell,* and we wish to observe him under certain conditions. . . . Is it possible that you do not as yet comprehend that I share your secret? You were seen, Captain, that black and cruel night in the forepeak; and those details, also, are known to me. It is needless to dissemble longer.'

" 'That night in the forepeak? . . . For God's sake, Lee Fu, what are you talking about? Nichols, this is too ridiculous! Tell me the answer, and get it over with.'

" 'Ah!' exclaimed Lee Fu with something like satisfaction. 'You are worthy of the occasion, Captain. It will be most interesting.'

"He slapped his palm sharply on the desk; Sing Toy appeared at the door as if by a mechanical arrangement. 'Bring oilskin coats and hats for three,' Lee Fu commanded. 'Also send in haste to my cruising sampan, with orders to prepare for an immediate journey. Have water and food supplied for a week. We come within the half-hour, and will sail without delay.'

" 'Master!' protested Sing Toy breathlessly— their words, in rapid Chinese, were wholly unintelligible to Wilbur. 'Master, the typhoon!' He glanced at the revolver in Lee Fu's hand, then raised his eyes to the wall that smothered the tumult of the gale.

" 'I know, fool,' answered Lee Fu. 'I am neither deaf nor blind. But is it necessary to sail. Go, quickly, do as I say.'

"He sat down, resting the revolver on the corner of the desk, and resumed his former tone of bland conversation. 'I am sorry, gentlemen, that the rain already has come; but there is water also below, as Captain Wilbur should be well aware. Yes, it was destined from the first that this should be a wet journey. Yet it will be possible still to breathe; not quite so bad as solid water all around, where after a grim struggle one lies at rest, neither caring nor remembering. . . . Captain Wilbur, attend to what I say. We go from this office to my sampan, which lies moored at the bulkhead, not far away. During the walk, you will precede us. I will hold my revolver in my hand—and I am an excellent shot. If you attempt to escape, or to communicate with any passerby—if you call for help, or even disclose by your manner the strangeness of the occasion— you will immediately be dead. Bear this in mind.

And do not think that I would fear the consequences;
we will pass through Chinese streets, where action
of mine would not be questioned.'

" 'Damn you!' Wilbur burst out. 'What crazy
nonsense are you up to? Nichols, will you permit
this? Where are you taking me?'

" 'Never mind,' replied Lee Fu. 'As for Captain
Nichols, he knows, if anything, less than you do
about it. He, also, is at my mercy. . . . Ah, here
are the raincoats. Put one on, Captain Wilbur; you
will need it sorely before your return. Now we must
hurry. I would be clear of the harbor before darkness entirely falls.'

VI

"Issuing from the doorway, the gale caught us
with a swirl that carried us around the corner and
down a side street before we could get our breath.
'To the right,' Lee Fu shouted. Wilbur, lurching
ahead, obeyed sullenly. We came about and made
for the water front through the fringe of the Chinese
quarter—the most remarkable trio, perhaps, that
ever had threaded those familiar thoroughfares.
Few people were abroad; a Chinaman now and then
scurried to cover in our path, and more infrequently
we caught sight of a stray European in the distance, called out somewhere by the exigencies of
business.

"Overhead, the sky had settled low on the slope of
the Peak, cutting off the heights from view; it presented the aspect of a heavy leaden roof, spreading

above the mainland to northward, fitting tight along
the horizon, and seeming to compress the whole
atmosphere. Torrents of rain fell from the frequent
squalls; the running water in the streets spurted
about our ankles. We floundered on, enveloped in a
sort of gray gloom like that of an eclipse. When we
reached the harbor, the face of the bay had under-
gone a sinister change; its yellow-green waters were
lashed into sickly foam, and shrouded by an unnatural gleaming darkness. A distant moaning
sound ran through the upper air, vague yet distinctly
audible. It was evident to the practiced eye that
the southern margin of the typhoon wasn't far away;
with the wind in this quarter, its center was headed
straight in our direction.

"As we staggered along the quay, my thoughts
worked rapidly. The wind and the open had cleared
my mind as to the swift events of the last half-hour;
I began to sense the plan, now, and immediately
recognized the dangerous nature of the undertaking
on which we'd embarked. It was to be a game of
bluff, in which we would have to risk our lives if the
other held his grounds. I'd seen Lee Fu in action; I
knew that he would hesitate at nothing, since his
face was committed to the enterprise.

"I edged towards him. 'Will you go on the water?'
I asked close to his ear.

"He nodded, keeping his eyes fixed on Wilbur.

"'But it can't be done,' I told him. 'A boat
won't live. . . .'

"'There always is a definite alternative,' he
replied.

" 'Yes, that she sinks.'

" 'Exactly.'

"I drew away, reviewing the details once more. All at once, in a flash of enlightenment, the greatness of the occasion came to me. By Jove!—Lee Fu had taken the matter into his own hands, he had stepped in where the gods were impotent. But not rudely, as men are apt to do in sudden passion; not with blood and vengeance, an eye for an eye, and a tooth for a tooth. No, he had observed the divine proprieties; had recognized that if he presumed to act for the gods, he must throw his own life as well into the balance. He himself must run every risk. It was for them, after all, to make the final choice. His part was to force action on the gods.

"I gazed at him in wonder—and with more than a flurry of alarm. He advanced stiffly against the storm, walking like an automaton; his expression was absolutely inscrutable. Beneath the close-pulled rim of a black sou'wester his smooth, oval countenance looked ridiculously vacant, like the face of a placid moon. He was the only calm object in earth, sea, or sky; against the lashing rain, the dancing boats, the scudding clouds, the hurried shadows of appearing and vanishing men, he stood out solidly, a different essence, the embodiment of mind and will. Only these could have been superior to the grosser temptation; only these could have met the test, and risen to the awful stratagem.

"And how was it with Wilbur, off there in the lead? He, too, walked stiffly, wrapped in thought. Once he turned around, as if to come back and speak to us; then whirled with a violent movement of decision and plunged on into the rain. He must have known, by now, what it was all about, if not what to expect. He must have known that his crime had been discovered. Yet he had made no break; in no particular had he given himself away. What had he been about to say?—what had he decided? To hold on, of course, maintain the bluff—for he could not believe that we knew all. Would he confess, when he faced death on the water? How long would he hold on?

"Observing his broad back, his commanding figure, that looked thoroughly at home in its oilskin coat and leaning against the storm, it came to me that he would put up a desperate defense before he succumbed. He, too, was a strong man, and no part of a coward; he, too, in a different way, was a superior being, the embodiment of mind and will. I didn't under-estimate him. Indeed, he was worthy of the occasion and of his adversary. It was to be a battle of the giants, with typhoon for background and accompaniment.

"Then, for an instant, my own spirit went slump with the realization of what might lie ahead, and a great weakness overcame me. I edged again toward Lee Fu.

" 'My God, suppose the man really is innocent?' I cried. 'He hasn't turned a hair. . . .'

"Lee Fu gave me a flash of the moon-face beneath the sou'wester.

" 'Have no fear, my friend,' he said. 'I am completely satisfied, in regions where the soul dwells. It has begun very well.'

VII

"When we reached the sampan, lying under a weather shore beneath the bulkhead, we found a scene of consternation. Lee Fu's orders had arrived and been executed; yet the men couldn't believe that he actually meant to sail. Gathered in a panic-stricken group on the fore deck of the sampan, they chattered like a flock of magpies; their gleaming wet bodies writhed in wild gestures under the half-light. As they caught sight of us, they swarmed across the bulkhead and fell at Lee Fu's feet, begging for mercy.

" 'Up, dogs!' he cried. 'There is no danger. I shall steer; and it is necessary that we go. If any would remain, let them depart now, with no tale to tell. Let those who stay prepare at once for sea.'

"Not a man made a move to go; the presence and voice of the master had reassured them. Without another word, they rose and filed on board.

"I found Wilbur beside me. 'What is this madness, Nichols?' he demanded for the last time. 'Are you fool enough to go on the water in that craft? What has that lunatic been saying to the men?—I don't understand their damned lingo.'

" 'He told his crew to prepare for sea,' I answered shortly. 'If he goes, we all go. He says there is no danger.'

" 'Huh! You're a bigger fool than I took you for.'

"A moment later we stood together on the quarter-deck of the cruising sampan. Lee Fu took his station at the great tiller, that archaic steering arrangement worked by blocks and tackles which the Chinese cherish like the precepts of Confucius in the face of mechanical invention. The wind lulled for a moment, as the trough of a squall passed over. Lee Fu gave a few sharp orders. Moorings were cast off, a pinch of sail was lifted forward. The big craft found her freedom with a lurch and a stagger; then pulled herself together and left the land with a steady rush, skimming dead before the wind across the smooth weather reach of the harbor, quickly losing herself in the murk and spray that hung off Kowloon Point. If we were sighted from the fleet, which is extremely doubtful, we were put down as a junk that had broken adrift. Somehow Lee Fu managed to avoid the ships at anchor off Wanchi. Straight down the length of the bay he struck; in an incredibly short time we had left the harbor behind, and were whirling through the narrow gut of Lymoon Pass before a terrific squall, bound for the open sea.

"I watched Captain Wilbur. He stood in a careless attitude at the rail in our race down the harbor, scanning the boat and the water with an air of confidence and unconcern. A slight sneer curled his lip; he had made up his mind to see the nonsense through. The sailor in him had quickly recognized that the craft would stand the weather, so long as she remained in quiet water. Probably he expected every minute that Lee Fu would change his tactics and put into some sheltered cove. . . . But when we shot through Lymoon Pass, I saw him turn and scrutinize the Chinaman closely. Darkness was falling behind the murk, the real night now; ahead of us

lay a widening reach among the islands, that opened
abruptly on the main body of the China Sea. We
were rapidly leaving the protection of Victoria
Island. Soon we would be unable to see our way.
Ten miles outside a high sea was running. And with
every blast of wind that held in the same quarter,
the center of the typhoon was bearing down on us
with unerring aim.

"These facts were as patent to Wilbur as to any
of us. It was his knowledge, of course, that finally
was his undoing; had he been less of a sailor, or had
he been entirely ignorant of the sea, he could have
resigned himself to the situation, on the assumption
that those who were sailing the craft wouldn't put
themselves in actual danger. Perhaps Lee Fu had
realized this when he'd chosen the sea as the
medium of justice; perhaps he had glimpsed the profound and subtle truth that Wilbur couldn't properly be broken save in his native environment. He
knew the sea, he had trifled with it; then let him face
the sea.

"The time came, just before we lost the loom of
the land, when Wilbur could stand it no longer; as a
sailor, used to responsibility and authority, he had
to speak his mind. He knew that the situation was
growing very dangerous. . . . For my part, I had
become convinced by now that it was irretrievable;
it began to look as if we'd burned our last bridge
behind us. I didn't pretend to understand; Lee Fu
seemed reckless beyond measure, he apparently had
given away his cards without trying to play them.
One thing was certain—if some way couldn't be
found to hold up this mad race immediately, we

would be forced in the next five minutes to run the gauntlet of the typhoon in open water.

"Wilbur dropped aft beside Lee Fu, and made a funnel of his hands.

" 'You're running to your death!' he shouted. 'Do you realize what you're doing? You've already lost Pootoy. If you can't haul up and make the lee of the Lema Islands . . .'

" 'I intend to pass nowhere near them—and I know exactly what I am doing,' answered Lee Fu, keeping his eyes on the yawing bow of the sampan.

" 'There's nothing to the eastward . . . no more shelter . . .

" 'Of that I am aware.'

" 'Do you know the meaning of *that?*' Wilbur pointed wildly above the stern rail, into the face of the onrushing storm.

" 'I think that we will get the center of the typhoon, Captain, by noon of tomorrow.'

"Wilbur made a move as if to grasp the tiller. 'Haul up, you fool! . . .'

"A stray gleam in the gathering darkness caught the barrel of the revolver, as Lee Fu steered for a moment with one hand.

" 'Beware, Captain! You are the fool; would you broach us to, and end it now? One thing alone will send me to seek the last shelter; and for that thing I think you are not ready.'

" 'What?'

" 'To say that you sunk the *Speedwell,* as I have indicated.'

"Wilbur gathered his strength as if to strike; his face was distorted with passion.

" 'You lie, you yellow hound!'

" 'Exactly. . . . Captain, be careful—come no nearer! Also, leave me now, and go away, for I have work to do. If you value your life, you will keep silence, and stay a little forward. Go, quickly! Here I could shoot you with even greater impunity.'

VIII

Nichols paused. "It may be that some of you fellows have never seen Lee Fu's cruising sampan,' he remarked. 'In reality she is more of a junk than a sampan; a sizeable craft of over a hundred tons, the best product of the Chinese shipyard. Lee Fu built her for trips along the coast, where conditions of wind and weather are likely to be severe; many of his own ideas, born of an expert knowledge of ships of every rig and nationality, entered into her construction. The result distinctly is a Chinese creation, a craft that in some unaccountable way seems to reflect his own personality, that responds to his touch and works mysteriously for him. She's higher in the bows than an ordinary junk, and a trifle lower in the stern; a broad, shallow hull, requiring a centerboard on the wind. She is completely decked over for heavy weather. In charge of any one of us, perhaps, she would be fairly unmanageable; but in Lee Fu's hands, I can assure you, she's a sea-boat of remarkable attainments and a yacht of no insignificant speed.

"I had seen him handle her under difficult conditions, but never in such a pass as this. How he

accomplished it, was inconceivable to me. The last
I saw of him that evening, he had called two men to
help him at the tiller; so far, he had managed to
keep the craft before the wind. . . . He continued
to keep her before it throughout the night, running
eastward in open water along the China coast. That
is to say, he must have kept her before it—because
we came through the night, alive and still afloat.
But how, I cannot tell.

"For hours I was alone with the elements, surrounded by pitch blackness and the storm. I clung
to a stanchion, hardly changing my position during
the night, drenched by rain and spray, seeing
nothing, hearing no word of my companions. The
gale roared above us with that peculiar tearing
sound that accompanies the body of a typhoon—a
sound suggestive of unearthly anger and violence,
as if elemental forces were ripping up the envelope
of the universe—a sound that carries its own message of latent power, of savage impulse, of unloosed
destruction. The wind gained steadily in volume; it
picked up the sea in steep ridges of solid water that
flung us like a chip from crest to crest, or caught us,
burst above us, and swallowed us whole, as if we
had suddenly sunk down a deep well. From these
plunges the sampan would emerge after a long interval, like a whale coming up to blow. It seemed impossible that she could be kept running; to come into
the wind, however, would have been certain disaster. Every moment I expected would be our last.
Yet, as time wore on, I felt through the boat's frantic floundering, a touch of mastery. Lee Fu steered
—she still was under his control.

"So we came through, and saw the dawn. A pale, watery light little by little crept across the east, disclosing a scene of terror beyond description. The face of the sea was livid with flying yellow foam; the torn sky hung closely over it like the fringe of a mighty waterfall. In the midst of this churning cauldron our little craft seemed momentarily on the point of disappearing, about to be engulfed by the sheer wrath of the elements. It was a scene to compel the eye, while the heart whined in fear for the return of darkness or the swift downfall of oblivion.

"In a lull of the storm my glance encountered Wilbur; for a long while I'd forgotten him entirely. He hung to the rail a little farther forward, gazing across the maelstrom with a fixed exhausted expression. His face was haggard; the strain of the night had marked him with a ruthless hand. As I watched him, his eyes turned slowly in my direction; he gave me an anxious look, then crawled along the rail to a place by my side.

" 'Nichols, we're lost!' I heard him cry in my ear. The voice was uneven, plaintive; it made me angry, and revived a few sparks of my own courage.

" 'What of it?' I cried harshly. 'Turner was lost, too.'

" 'You believe that? . . .'

"I looked at him point-blank; his eyes suddenly shifted, he couldn't face me now.

" 'Why don't you own up, before it's too late?' I shouted at him.

"Without answering he moved away hastily, like innocence offended. But the strong man was gone, the air of perfect confidence had disappeared; he

was shattered and spent, but not yet broken. Pride
is a more tenacious quality than courage; men with
hearts of water, with their knees knocking together,
will continue to function through self-esteem. Besides, what would have been the use now, as he saw
it, to make confession? Nothing, apparently, could
save us; there was no shelter, no hope in sight. . . .

"Looking above his head, where the sky and the
sea met in a blanket of flying spume, I caught sight
for an instant of something that resembled the vague
form of a headland. Watching closely, I saw it
again—unmistakably the shadow of land, broad on
the port bow. . . . Land! That meant that the
wind had shifted to southward, that we were being
blown against the shore. And that, in turn, meant
that the center of the typhoon had passed inland,
behind Hong Kong, and would issue into the China
Sea somewhere down the coast.

"I worked my way cautiously aft, where Lee Fu
stood like a man of iron at the tiller, lashed to a
heavy cross-rail that must have been constructed for
such occasions. He saw me coming, leaned slightly
toward me.

" 'Land!' I shouted, pointing on the port bow.

"He nodded vigorously, disclosing that he'd
already seen it. '. . . recognize . . .' The rest
of his answer was blown away by the storm.

"By pantomime, I called his attention to the shift
of wind. Again he nodded—then ducked his
head in Wilbur's direction, shouting something
that I couldn't quite follow. '. . . Change our
tactics . . .' was what I understood him to say.

"What did he mean by that? My mind refused

to function, save in channels of fantastic conjecture.
I'd gained the impression that he was disappointed
at the present turn of affairs. Had he depended on
the center of the typhoon for his climax? Good
God, had he wanted it to catch us? As matters
stood, it was only by the extreme grace of providence that we remained alive. Now, it seems, something had miscarried, we must change our tactics . . . find some new horror to take the place of
the one that had passed us by.

"He beckoned me to come closer; grasping the
cross-rail, I swung down beside him.

" 'I know our position,' he cried in my ear. 'Have
no alarm, my friend. There are two large islands,
and a third behind them, small like a button. Watch
closely the button, while I steer. When it touches
the high headland of the second larger island, give
me the news instantly.'

"He had hauled the junk a trifle to port as he
spoke, and now with every opportunity began edg-
ing toward the land. Perilous business, in that tremendous seaway; but he executed the maneuver with
infinite patience and caution, with consummate skill.
Wilbur, now, had seen the land, had straightened his
figure and leaned forward, watching it intently. Distances were veiled and distorted in that murky
atmosphere; we were nearer to the headland than I
had at first supposed. For perhaps twenty minutes
we ran on, a tense new excitement tugging at our
hearts. Then, as we raced before the gale, I felt the
sea begin to grow calmer; glancing to windward, I
saw on the horizon a fringe of spouting reefs, and
realized that we'd entered the zone of their protec-

tion. The tall headland, which now revealed itself as the point of the second island, grew plainer with every moment; soon I made out the island like a button, and saw it closing rapidly on the land behind.

" 'Now!' I shouted to Lee Fu, holding up both my arms, when the two points of land had touched.

"He swung the sampan a couple of points to starboard, discovering close beneath our bows the tip of another reef that stretched toward the land diagonally across the path of the wind. In a moment we were abreast this point of reef; a hundred yards away its spray lashed our decks, as the low-lying black rocks caught the broken wash of the storm. Another swing of the great tiller, and we had hauled up in the lee of the reef—in quiet water at last, but with the gale still screaming overhead like a defeated demon. We reached along this weather shore in a smother of spray, until we came abruptly to the little island. This we passed with a rush, and shot forward into a relatively smooth basin that lay under the protection of the high headland on the larger island.

"It was like nothing but a return from hell. The wind held us in a solid blast; but to feel the deck grow quiet, to be able to think, to speak, to hear; to see the land close aboard. . . . By Jove, we were saved!—it seemed more incredible than the adventure itself. Heads began to bob up forward, faces drawn with terror, frantic with relief—the faces of men who had lost and found a world.

"A voice spoke gruffly beside us. 'By God, I hope you're satisfied!' We turned to see Wilbur standing at the head of the crossrail. A twitching face belied the nonchalance that he'd attempted to throw into the words. It was a new phase of the man; his former perfect poise was stripped off like a mask, revealing an inner nature without force or quality, a common empty soul. The very assumption of sang froid, a reflex of his over-powering relief, disclosed weakness instead of strength, impotence instead of authority.

" 'I don't know how we managed to come through!' he snarled. 'In the name of God, what made you try it? Nothing but luck—but now the typhoon's leaving us. We can haul up here until the blow goes down.'

" 'Is that all, Captain, that you have to say?' inquired Lee Fu, his attention still riveted on the course of the sampan.

"Wilbur clutched the rail as if he would tear it from its fastenings. 'A damned sight more, you blackguards, but I'll save that for the authorities!'

" 'You feel no thanks for your escape—and there is nothing on your mind?'

" 'We wouldn't have needed to escape, if you hadn't gone crazy. Come, let's wind up this farce and get to anchor somewhere. I'm fagged out.'

" 'No, we are going on,' said Lee Fu calmly, making no move to bring the sampan into the wind. 'No time for rest, Captain; the journey is not over.'

" 'Going on? . . .' Wilbur's glance swept the sea ahead. Until that moment, I suppose, he thought that he had won the battle; he hadn't dreamed that Lee Fu, after such a miraculous escape, would again put us all in jeopardy. He saw that, on the course we were holding, in a very brief interval we would leave the protection of the headland. What lay beyond, it was impossible to discover through the murk. He turned back fiercely; for a moment he and Lee Fu gazed deep into each other's eyes, in a grapple that gave no quarter.

" 'Yes, Captain!' said Lee Fu sharply. 'We have not yet reached the spot where the *Speedwell* met her doom. I cannot waste further time in talk. Return to your station, before I am forced to threaten you again. . . . This is merely an interlude.'

IX

"Since that experience, I've many times examined the charts of the region where we were," Nichols went on. "But they don't begin to show the whole story. Beyond the middle island, under whose headland we'd found transitory shelter, stretched a larger island, distant some five miles from the other; between them lay the most intricate, extraordinary and terrible nest of reefs ever devised by the mind of the Maker and the hand of geologic change. No wonder the surveys haven't been completed in that region; I defy any man, in the calmest and clearest of weather, to take a craft among those reefs and come out with a whole bottom. Any man, that is, but Lee Fu Chang, who isn't in the service of the Admiralty.

"The outlying fringe of reefs that had broken our first approach ended at the middle island; beyond that, to windward, lay clear water, and the nest of

reefs that I've mentioned received the full force of
the wind and sea. Five miles of water stretched in
mad confusion, a solid whiteness of spouting foam
that seemed to generate a hideous illumination, that
reflected a dingy glow into the abandoned sky. All
the cataracts of the world rolled into one couldn't
have matched the awful spectacle. We still were flying through quiet water; but just beyond the point
of the middle island the long wind-swept rollers
burst in tall columns of spray that shut off the
farther view like a curtain, where the reef of rocks
stood in an apparently unbroken wall.

"It was directly against the face of this wall that
Lee Fu was driving the sampan. The first lift of
the outside swell had begun to catch us. I held my
breath, as moment by moment we cut down the margin of safety. No use to interfere; perhaps he knew
what he was doing, perhaps he really had gone mad
under the terrific strain of the night. As he steered,
he seemed to be watching intently for landmarks;
his eyes were everywhere, but more often, I noticed,
on the shore to windward that rapidly changed its
contour as we left it on the port quarter. Was it
possible that, in this abandoned spot, he knew his
bearings . . . that there was a way through? . . .

"Wilbur, at Lee Fu's command, had left us without a word. He now stood at the rail, supporting
himself by main strength, facing the frightful line
of the approaching reef; on his back was written
the desperate struggle that went on in his soul. It
bent and twisted, sagging in sudden irresolution,
writhing with stubborn obduracy, straightening and
shaking itself at times as a wave of firmness and

confidence passed over him, only to quail once more before the sight that met his eyes . . . He couldn't believe that Lee Fu would hold that suicidal course. Only another moment!—he kept crying to himself. Hold on a little longer! Yet the power of his will had been sapped by the long hours of night and the terrors of the dawn; and courage, which with him rested only on the sands of ostentation, had crumbled long ago.

"For my part, I was cruelly afraid. Without clear comprehension, I felt the tremendous significance of the moment, sensed that the crisis had come in the battle of the wills. One or the other of them must break now; but if it didn't happen shortly, there would be no time left in which to record the triumph. My eyes met Lee Fu's for an instant, as he swept the retreating shore. He threw some message into the glance—but I had passed beyond the range of understanding. It seemed to me that he was excited, even elated, and as calm as ever—as if he'd found those marks he had been looking for, as if he knew his ground.

"The deafening roar of the breakers filled our ears, smothering the voice of the storm like an outburst of heavy artillery. I turned away, overcome by a sickening sensation. I couldn't bear to look any longer. Instead, I found myself watching Lee Fu. He waited tensely, peering ahead and to windward with lightning glances. A wave caught us, flung us forward. Suddenly I heard him cry out at my side in exultation, as he bore down on the tiller. The cry was echoed from forward by a loud scream that shot like an arrow through the thun-

der, where Wilbur had sunk beside the rail. The
sampan fell off, still carried high on the crest of
the wave. . . .

"Then, in a moment like the coming of death, we
plunged into the reef. I have no knowledge of what
took place; there are no words to tell the story.
Solid water swamped us; the thunder of the surf
crushed the mind. . . . But we didn't strike, there
was a way through, we had crossed the outer margin
of the reef. The sampan emerged from the
breakers, remained afloat, slowly became manage-
able. The wind caught us again. Ahead stretched
the suggestion of a channel. Ten minutes passed,
ten minutes that seemed like as many ages, while we
ran the terrible gauntlet of the reef, surrounded by
towering breakers, last in the appalling steady roar
of the elements. Suddenly, without warning, we
were flung between a pair of jagged ledges and
launched forward bodily on the surface of an open
lagoon.

"A low rocky island lay in the center of the nest
of reefs, a stretch of open water to leeward of it, all
completely hidden from view until that moment.
The open water ran for perhaps a couple of miles;
beyond that, again, the surf began in another unbroken line. It would take us ten minutes to cross
this lagoon . . . another interlude.

" 'Bring Captain Wilbur,' said Lee Fu in my ear.

"I crept forward, where Wilbur lay beside the
rail, his arm around a stanchion. He was moaning
to himself like an injured man. I kicked him
roughly; he lifted an ashen face.

" 'Come aft—you're wanted,' I cried.

"He followed like a whipped cur. Lee Fu, at the tiller, beckoned us to stand beside him. I pulled Wilbur up by the slack of the coat, and pinned him against the cross-rail.

" 'This is the end,' said Lee Fu, speaking in loud jerks, as he steered across the lagoon. 'From this haven there is no way out, except by the way we came. That way is closed by the gale. To windward is shelter, ahead is destruction. I will seek the shelter if you will speak. If not, I shall go on. By this time, Captain, you know me to be a man of my word.'

" 'You yellow devil! . . .'

" 'Waste no time in recriminations. Beyond these reefs, Captain, lies the wreck of your ship, the *Speedwell.* I have brought you to see the scene. There my friend met death at your hands. You have had full time to consider. Will you join him beneath the waves, or will you return to Hong Kong? A word will save you. Remember, the moments pass very swiftly.'

" 'What about yourself and Nichols?' blustered Wilbur.

" 'We go, too . . . or stay . . . it makes little difference. This is a matter that you cannot understand. We do not care.'

"At this juncture, I was fated to under-estimate Wilbur after all. I thought him broken; but a last flicker of obstinate pride remained, to prop his extraordinary ego. He pulled himself together again, and whirled on us.

" 'I didn't do it!' he snarled. 'It's a damned, scoundrelly lie!'

" 'Very well, Captain. Go forward once more, and reserve your final explanation for the gods.'

"The flicker of pride persisted; Wilbur staggered off, holding by the rail. I waited beside Lee Fu. Thus we stood, like wooden images, watching the approach of the lagoon's leeward margin. Had Lee Fu spoken truthfully—was there no way out, in that direction? I couldn't be certain. All I knew was that the wall of spouting surf was at our bows, that the jaws of death were opening again.

"Suddenly Wilbur's head snapped back; he flung up his arms in a gesture of finality, shaking clenched fists into the sky. With a thrill that tingled to my finger-tips, I realized that he was at the point of surrender. The torture had reached his vitals. He turned and floundered aft, holding his hands before his face like a man stricken blind.

" 'What is it I must say?' he cried hoarsely, in a voice that by its very abasement had taken on a certain dignity.

" 'You know. The truth, or nothing!'

"His face was shocking in its self-revelation; a strong man breaking isn't a pleasant object. I saw how awful had been this struggle of the wills. He came to his final decision as we watched, lost his last grip. . . .

" 'I did it—as you said—you must know all about it. I suppose I sunk her—I had no intention . . . You madman! For God's sake, haul up, before you're in the breakers!'

" 'Show me your insurance money,' said Lee Fu inexorably.

"Wilbur dug frantically in an inside pocket, produced a packet of bank notes, and held them out in a hand that trembled violently as the gale fluttered the crisp leaves.

" 'Throw them overboard.'

"For the fraction of a second he hesitated; then all resolution went out in his eyes like a dying flame. He extended his arm rigidly, and loosed the notes. They were gone down the wind almost before our eyes could follow them.

"In the same instant, Lee Fu flung down the great tiller. The sampan came into the wind with a shock that threw us all to the deck. Close under our lee quarter lay the breakers, less than a couple of hundred yards away. Lee Fu made frantic signals forward, where the crew were watching us in a state of utter terror. I felt the centerboard drop; a patch of sail rose slowly on the mainmast. The boat answered, gathered headway, drove forward. . . .

"It was just in time. We had run past the low island, and couldn't hope to regain its shelter in such a blow; but a pile of tumbled rocks lay off its leeward end, carving out a small sub-zone of protection. This spot we might be able to fetch, if we managed to escape the clutch of the breakers. Escape them we did, after a hair-raising five minutes, and threw out our anchors in the most precarious berth ever afforded, with our stern brushing the very fringe of the breakers. But the anchors held; and there we rode until the storm was over.

"Wilbur lay as he had fallen after the sampan's frantic plunge. He made no move; and we, on our part, left him where he was.

X

"Two nights later, under a clear starry sky, we slipped through Lymoon Pass on the tail of the land breeze. Before we reached Wanchi, it fell flat calm. We shipped the long sweeps and began rowing; the chattering crew, who'd never expected to see Hong Kong again, fell to work willingly. The lights of the city twinkled against the Peak, the sleeping fleet swung at anchor in the land-locked harbor; all was silence and tranquillity . . . as we see it now. But that night, let me tell you, the familiar scene was invested with a poignant charm. At length we reached the bulkhead, from which we'd taken our maniac departure three days before, and settled in our berth as comfortably as if we'd just returned from a pleasure trip down the bay.

"No words were said as we came in. I sat against the bulwarks, almost afraid to move, like a man awakening to consciousness after a long siege of fever. A little forward of my position, Wilbur rose to his feet. He hadn't spoken or touched food since that tragic hour under the reefs two nights before; had spent most of his time below decks, locked in a tiny stateroom, and had come out only in the last few minutes, as if in response to the nearing sounds of the land. He stood at the rail, a figure wrapped in silence and immobility, watching them berth the sampan. Then, without a glance in our direction, he walked to the gangway and stepped ashore. On the bulkhead he paused for a moment irresolute, turning and gazing across the harbor. His form stood out plainly against a bright light up the street.

It had lost those lines of vigor and alertness; it was the figure of a different and older man. A broken figure, that could never be the same. . . .

"A moment later he had lurched away, vanishing suddenly in the darkness of a side street. Three days afterward, we heard that he had taken the boat for Singapore. He hasn't been seen or heard of in this part of the world since that day.

"When he had gone, that night at the bulkhead, Lee Fu approached me; we crossed the deck of the sampan, and stood for a long while silent at the harbor rail.

" 'Thank you, Captain,' he said at last. 'As I foresaw, it has been supremely interesting. For your part, I hope that you feel repaid?'

" 'It's quite enough to be alive, just now,' I confessed without shame. 'I want to see a chart of that locality, Lee Fu. I want to find out what you did.'

" 'Oh, that? It was not much. The gods always were with us, as you must have observed. As for the rest of it, I know that region pretty well.'

" 'Evidently. . . . Did the *Speedwell* fetch up among those same reefs, or to leeward of them?'

" 'The *Speedwell?* Captain, you did not believe my little pleasantry? We were nowhere near the wreck of the *Speedwell,* at any time—as Captain Wilbur should have known, had he retained his mental perspective.'

"I smiled feebly. 'Well, I didn't know it. Tell me another thing, Lee Fu. Were you bluffing, there at the last, or was there really no passage through the reef?'

" 'So far as I am aware, Captain, there was no passage. I believe we were heading for solid rock when we came into the wind.'

"The answer surprised me. 'Would you have piled us up,' I asked, 'if Wilbur hadn't given in?'

" 'That is a hypothetical question. I knew perfectly well that I would not be forced to do it. I was only afraid lest, in the final anguish, Captain Wilbur might lose his seaman's judgment, and so might wait too long. That, I confess, would have been unfortunate. Otherwise, there was no especial doubt or danger.'

" 'I'm glad to hear it!' I exclaimed, with a shudder of recollection. 'It wasn't apparent at the time.'

" 'No, perhaps not. Time was swift, just then. I will tell you now, Captain Nichols, that I myself had begun to grow alarmed. He waited very long. He was more wilful than I had fully anticipated; a strong, determined man, and an arch-criminal. But, as it chanced, this made it the more interesting.'

"I didn't care to argue such a subtle point. 'What did you have in mind, Lee Fu,' I asked, 'before the typhoon shifted? Did you expect the center of it to catch us?'

"The question seemed to amuse him. 'Captain, I had no plan,' he explained in a puzzled tone. 'It is dangerous to make plans, or to live according to a fixed design. There was a task to be begun; the determination of its direction and result lay with the gods. It was plain to me that I had been called upon to act; beyond that I neither saw nor cared to see. Action once begun, I seized events as they came my way. . . . How characteristic that you ask me for my plan! Would you have the temerity to inquire into the divine control of events? Or do you think that a man really may shape his destiny?'

"I could believe his statement only because I'd witnessed his incredible calm.

"He waved a hand toward the city. 'Come, my friend, let us sleep,' he said. 'We have earned our rest—and that is something not always won from life. But beware of over-confidence, and never plan. It is by straining to see the future that men exhaust themselves for present usefulness. It is by daring to make plans that men bring down on their heads the wrath of heaven. We are the instruments of the gods; through us, they put their own plans in operation. The only failure in life is not to hear when the gods command. In this case, however, there could have been no question; the design was too apparent. From the first, I was sure and happy. There constantly were too many propitious signs.' "

OUTWARD BOUND

Windlass Chanty

Oh, soon she'll bite the swell—the breeze is singing;
Sandy Hook is dropping fast astern!
Come, walk her up, my boys—the pawls are ringing;
And the long low coast goes down.
Then it's good-bye, and a year we'll be a-sailing;
Sandy Hook is dropping fast astern!
So sheet your topsails home—the dawn is paling;
And the long low coast goes down.

Losing the Land

The sea seemed very blue and wide
After the muddy harbor tide;
The slender masts looked strange and high,
Towering with canvas to the sky;
The deck became the scene of tales
Under the shadow of the sails.
A new life entered in the ship;
We watched the main-truck wheel and dip,
And felt her lift beneath our feet
With able lunge and motion sweet.
She slipped along with scarce a sound;
The broad horizon hemmed us round;
Over the ocean's floor appeared
The lonely spirit never feared;

To us who knew and loved the sea,
It seemed like home—and we were free.

TRADE WINDS

Northeast trade winds bore us south,
   Southeast drew us on;
We met the ships from every port
   For Good Hope or the Horn.

Seas so quiet, skies so blue,
   Little squalls of rain;
The winds that blew about the world
   Filled our hearts again.

FERNANDO DE NORONHA

We lay becalmed; the white-hot sun
   Beat down above an even swell;
And, clear upon our starboard bow
   Stood out your spar-like Pinnacle.

THE WESTERLIES

Cold winds, dead aft, and heavy running seas
That swung us onward faster than the breeze;
Bleak days, and lurid sunsets, and wild skies,
And lonesomeness that broods as the day dies.
Abandoned course, below the happy world;
A staggering ship, with upper canvas furled,
Flooded by crashing seas, day after day,
In the Roaring Forties, where the wind has its way.

Christmas Island

One day we raised your lonely hills
Like clouds against the sky,
And proved our course, and kept our faith,
And passed you by.

Java Head

Ships of all nations and all venturing times
Have passed and left you on the starboard lee,
Dark headland, guardian of strange Eastern climes,
Above the shimmering purple Indian sea.

The North Watcher

What poet named you, setting your beacon there
On a lone island, lighting all the miles
Of dangers, pointing for ships your channel fair,
North Watcher, heading the Thousand Isles?

Gaspar Straits

We passed the Watcher late at night,
And dawn put out its sinking light;
All day we held the fair monsoon,
All night we ran beneath the moon;
And in the early morning hours
We smelled the near land and the flowers,
And saw, abeam, the hillsides on
The southwest point of Billiton.
A little lighthouse, white as snow,
Looked out upon the strait below;
Each garden was a tiny square,
Terraced and blooming everywhere;

Toy cows were grazing on the grass,
Toy men ran down to see us pass;
It must have been a pleasant place,
To wear that glad and smiling face;
But we held such a steady breeze,
The village soon was lost in trees.

THE FISHING FLEET

Brown sails of fishing boats
    On a sea of jade,
Startled at early dawn,
    Fleeing afraid.

Far as the eye can see
    Into the sun,
Count we their endless fleet
    One by one.

Dim foreign hills in sight
    There on the beam;
Voices, now close aboard—
    Like ghosts they seem.

Brown sails of fishing boats
    On a sea of jade,
Leaving on either hand
    The wake we made.

Yellow foam of breaking waves
    On a jade-green sea;
Brown junks with brown sails
    Windward and lee.

Hong Kong

In Lymoon Pass we felt the land
Grow near and high on either hand;
Strange voices shouted through the night,
Strange junks flashed out a signal light;
And soon we reached the land-locked bay
Where all the quiet vessels lay,
And felt the touch of life again,
And smelled the fresh land after rain;
While out from ships and hill and shore
There stole a voice we knew before.

THE UNCHARTED ISLE

I

"THEY say the man is mad," I whispered, nodding across the room. "Pendleton pointed him out to me on Wellington Street this morning."

Nichols gave his twisted smile. "Yes, mad, or inspired, or something very wonderful. Who is competent to judge? But I haven't seen him up this way for a long while. Another expedition must be on foot in search of the Uncharted Isle."

"What's that? You know him, then?"

"Perhaps I am the only man in the East who does know him, in the proper sense of the word. Every one else listens, laughs, and passes on. But I believe. Yes, in spite of ridicule and life's disaster, I continue to believe . . . well, not so much in the fact itself, as in the man. By Jove, he's faithful—and that, you must admit, is marvel enough. And his madness isn't entirely impossible; it can be explained. Yet it strikes the world as being funny—and that's his crowning misfortune. A man in search of a lost and apparently non-existent island can't help being a little ridiculous, I suppose, until he becomes a thundering bore. For no one else, of course, is looking for such a thing, or wants to find one. We keep safely within the charted area. . . .
But let me tell you the story, and you can form

your own opinion. Don't attract his attention; he won't notice us here in the shadow.''

There used to be a certain tea-house in Hong Kong, the name of which was jealously guarded from touring vandals. It opened on the face of an enchanted terrace high above the harbor and the town; from the parapet the eye travelled inland over the low peninsula of Kowloon, as far as the foothills of China, the fringe of a mighty land veiled in mystery. Romance came to that terrace, filtering through lacy bamboo leaves, borne on the night breeze along with the fragrance of flowers and the music of hidden voices. The place wasn't a temple of the conventional. It isn't running now; the songs are still, the little cups no longer tinkle in the half-darkness, and no sweet, startled faces peep out at visitors from behind the dragon-screens.

Nichols and I had been sitting there some time that evening, when the man came in. Of course Nichols knew him; who with any pretentions to a history wasn't catalogued in his omnivorous files? While I waited, I listened to a rapid conversation in Chinese somewhere in the back of the establishment. Dusk had swallowed the white houses and green slopes below us; the riding lights on the harbor had begun to prick out the berths of ships; with the coming of night, voices seemed hushed among the yellow lanterns.

"What is madness? Who will lay down the line between madness and sanity?" demanded Nichols suddenly. "They are like right and wrong, or good and evil . . . much as you want to believe. If we dared for a moment to face the logic of exist-

ence, I think we would find that we're all a little
mad, each in his own way. An entirely sane man
would sort of puff out, like a candle. It's our madness that keeps us going, feeds the flame. The
world's an illusion, anyway, of course; ergo, why
aren't the maddest people the sanest? Certainly,
the maddest man of all would be he who tried to
define the states of the human mind.

"For that's beyond our province. They say, for
instance, that Devereaux is mad: what they mean is
that they can't fathom him. His life, likewise,
hasn't been charted. Well, what's the difficulty?
All the lives and islands haven't been discovered
yet. And there are certain bald facts, written in
black-and-white records, which seem to support his
claim. . . ."

A waxy Chinaman changed our tea. Nichols
gazed thoughtfully into the soft darkness beyond the
terrace, getting his story under way.

"Devereaux is no longer a young man, as you
see," he began slowly. "I'd say he was about our
own age. He was born and reared, I believe, in
distant New England, though I've never heard the
name of his home town. I presume he had parents
there once, brothers and sisters, maybe a sweetheart.
The Devereauxs, you know, are a fine family, with
strains of originality cropping out here and there,
which might once in a while have mounted to genius
in a free atmosphere. They're a high-strung breed.
I'd be willing to affirm that, even before the episode
of the island, this particular Devereaux was a serious and romantic soul. Look at his face, hanging
in the glow of that lantern. Temperament, sensi-

bility, melancholy. . . . But what he was, and what
he might have been, are both sunk in the tremendous
distances of a lifetime, obscured by the apparition
of an island, the wraith of a tragic destiny.

"He went to sea, in the wake of his generation.
At the age of twenty-one, he had worked up from
the forecastle to a room on the port side of the
forward cabin; in due time he became first mate
of the ship *Evening Star*. I forget who was captain
of her, or what was the name of the second mate
who managed to reach Callao in the whaleboat.
Those who survived the disaster have vanished
along with those who never returned, and Devereaux alone has perpetuated the event in nautical
history because of a madness that descended on him
out of the sky.

"They sailed from New York for San Francisco
in a year which likewise is immaterial, and had a
long and tedious passage around the Horn. It was
one of those unlucky and exasperating voyages, you
know—calms, and uneven trade winds, and unseason-
able storms; so that when they finally got headed
north in the Pacific, they were a disheartened ship's
company. The southeast trades in the Pacific failed
them completely; whatever wind they found, from
20° south up to the line, came from the east and
north; and with the best course they could make,
the ship was crowded over far to the westward of
the regular track. Then, approaching the line, the
northeast trades settled down in earnest, and nothing for it but to hold her on a N.N.W. course, as
close to the wind as possible on the starboard tack.
They managed to weather the fringe of the South

Sea Islands by a few hundred miles, and drifted across the line somewhere in the neighborhood of 135° west longitude. Provisions and water were holding out well, though one hundred and seventy-five days had passed since they'd lost sight of Sandy Hook.

"One evening in the early dog-watch, they noticed a few land birds flying about the ship. Devereaux told me that they were quite excited over the incident for an hour or two, with the quick sympathy of sailors for an unusual manifestation of life-forces. The nearest land at that time was the Marquesas, five hundred miles away to the southward. Some of the men tried to entice the birds to alight on deck or in the rigging, but they didn't seem at all weary, and scorned the blandishments of food.

" 'Wonderful creatures—birds,' said the captain, as they were discussing the occurrence on the quarter-deck. 'Five hundred miles isn't a drop in the bucket to them. All the bob-o'-links at home go to Brazil and back every winter.'

" 'They've probably run over from the Marque sas since supper,' chimed in the second mate. 'Half an hour from now they'll be back there, perching on some tree above an island beauty. God, I'd like to be a bird!'

"But Devereaux demurred at their conclusion— he knew something of the habits of birds. 'That's all right in the migrating season, but these birds don't migrate,' he said. 'You can see that they aren't bound anywhere in particular. And land birds don't fly five hundred miles to sea for the fun of going back again. They do get tuckered, too. I think it's mighty strange.'

"He had the first watch. It was one of those typical Pacific nights—a velvet sky, a smooth sea, the air somehow expressing the character of an ocean illimitable and magnificent, an ocean that spreads like the floor of the universe. After the captain had gone below for the night, Devereaux cast his imagination adrift to follow those birds, to see the land again. What could their visit have meant? Was there any land nearer than the Marquesas—perhaps an uninhabited island? He promised himself a careful survey of the chart when he went below at midnight. . . . He'd been thinking in this desultory fashion some time, lost in the dreams of night watches, when a sharp cry from forward struck him like a knife flying through the darkness.

"You know those single cries on shipboard, in the dead of night—cries of warning, of apprehension, of impending danger. The heart stops for a moment at the sound. Then a thousand possibilities crowd into the mind at once, a thousand processes of thought leap into action. There can be no indecision; moments are priceless. And there must be no mistake.

"The cry met him a second time as he passed the mizzen rigging, running forward. *'Breakers ahead!'* Instinctively, he shouted the order over his shoulder as he ran.

"'Put the helm down! *Hard down! Hard down!'*"

"But it was too late to save her. He told me that he paused at the break of the poop, listening, and in a sudden hush that went over the ship, heard distinctly a low sucking sound under the bows—the horrible gasping of water over rocks awash. He clung to the rail, cowed by the only fear a sailor knows. At that moment, she struck heavily, and stood still. She had been making about five knots, enough to give her plenty of momentum. The shock was terrific: some of the top-hamper crashed to the deck, and the voices of men suddenly broke out in screams of terror. The ship rose a little by the head, seemed to draw back, and surged forward again with a dull, rending, sickening plunge.

"But what's the need of rehearsing the details of that oldest tragedy of the sea? There was time enough for them to get out the boats, time enough, even, fully to provision them—and that's more than some have been allowed. But the ship was dead and done for. Her whole bow must have been stove in under water. Five minutes after they pushed clear of her, she slumped like a rock, and they lost her in the darkness. A whirlpool of foam showed for a while on the surface of the black water. Then that, too, faded; the wide, open Pacific received them in their three boats as frail as cockle-shells, and the velvet night covered it all.

"The captain commanded the longboat, the second mate and Devereaux had a whaleboat apiece. Devereaux's was the smallest; his crew consisted of six men besides himself. The boats drew together on the quiet water for a consultation. A deep stillness invested the place, the stillness of a lofty cavern, of an empty world; and somewhere off in the gloom that awful sucking sound went on, now loud,

now dying out to a faint echo, like a demon chuck-
ling over human disaster.

"All night they played hide-and-seek with that
demon in the darkness. The breeze fell off, and
after a while it grew flat calm. At times the voice
of the reef was hoarse and low and languid; at times
it purred and bubbled energetically; at times it
would be silent so long that they'd lean over the
gunwale to listen, thinking they had lost it—when
unexpectedly it would snarl out again, close at hand.
In the middle of the night they did really seem to be
losing the sound, and were afraid they'd drifted
from the vicinity; they bent to the oars rather aim-
lessly, for no one could judge the exact direction,
and before they knew it were almost running afoul
of the hideous thing. Some of the men swore that
the sound moved on the water; this seemed plaus-
ible, for it was to be supposed that the reef extended
a considerable distance, yet the notion nevertheless
gave rise to a vague superstitious fear. Either it
moved, or they were surrounded by a nest of reefs
—one was about as bad as the other. Devereaux
said it was a night to drive a nervous man crazy,
a night that they began to think would never end.

"When dawn came at last, they looked about them
and saw nothing at all—nothing but an unbroken
horizon, a boundless ocean, a few spars floating idly
in the midst of a great calm, and a little dark dot
like a pimple on the face of the waters, just in front
of the rising sun.

"They rowed toward this pimple on the surface.
It opened and closed with the sucking motion of a
loose mouth, and between the monstrous flickering

lips of water a point of rock protruded, black and swollen like the tongue of a drowned man. It seemed impossible that this solitary rock had made all the commotion of the night, had invested them as if with an army of breakers; yet there was absolutely nothing else in sight—the rest had been imagination.

"They rowed across the south face of the rock, where the ship had struck, and found the water there deep past all knowing. The rock wasn't coral, and no coral formation surrounded it. In the clear blue water beneath them huge banners of kelp waved and winnowed like lifeless hands. Not a vestige of the *Evening Star* remained; she had disappeared in the unfathomable gulfs of the Pacific. It was a mere crag that had caught her, a needle-point piercing the floor of an otherwise unobstructed ocean, the topmost spire of some mighty mountain sunk in the bowels of the world. It may never before have been seen by mortal man; it certainly wasn't indicated on the best charts of that day. She would have had to seek a thousand years to touch it. A ship's length either side would have cleared her. . . .

"They waited beside the rock till noon, to get an observation. Then they rowed away to the north-ward, bound for the Sandwich Islands. The dark spot on the water dwindled and disappeared in their wake. Devereaux told me that, quite unaccountably, he felt his heart sinking as they lost sight of it; after all, it was their only link with a remote and perhaps unattainable world.

"The first night after the disaster, a heavy squall separated the boats. They couldn't find each other, and never came together again. The second mate

reached Callao after a terrible journey, the first to
report the loss of the *Evening Star*. He had been
nearly swamped in that first squall. For two days
he had hunted frantically for the other boats. Then,
not being a good navigator, and having a very im-
perfect chart of the Pacific Islands, he had changed
his course and steered due east, knowing that he
would strike the American continent if he could keep
on going. The fact of his arrival in Callao, its
date, and his reported date of the disaster, are
beyond dispute; for my own satisfaction, I have
looked these matters up in the official records.

"The captain, in the longboat, was never heard
from again. Him and his crew the Pacific took for
toll.

"Devereaux was picked up at sea, alive, well, and
alone in the *Evening Star's* small whaleboat, *exactly
one year and three months after the ship went
down.*"

"Easy, Nichols!" I remonstrated. "Say that
again, please. You can't expect me to swallow it
whole at the first try."

"Those are the facts, I tell you," said Nichols
calmly. "I also have verified this latter statement,
through correspondence with the captain who picked
him up. It really happened—and the dates were as
I said. He was picked up just north of the equator
in the Pacific Ocean by the ship *Vanguard,* and
brought in to San Francisco. I was informed by
the captain of the *Vanguard* that he had been driven
out of his course by meeting the northeast trade
winds too far south, and had sighted Devereaux
adrift one morning in about 135° west and 2° north.

The man was nearly dead from thirst, and was quite mad when they took him aboard; raved about an island nearby, said he'd been blown away from it, and begged them to cruise in search of it before they left the ground. There was no island in that vicinity, of course, nearer than the Marquesas. 'I was sorry for the poor fellow,' the captain of the *Vanguard* wrote me, 'but we couldn't waste time in indulging his fancy. He quieted down after a day or two, and seemed to settle into a sort of dull melancholy.'

"This castaway, giving his name as Devereaux, claimed to have been mate of the *Evening Star,* lost in that same quarter of the Pacific the year before. The people on the *Vanguard* had heard nothing of this disaster; in fact, the first report of it, brought in by the second mate, had just reached San Francisco from Callao when they got in. To corroborate the story, however, the whaleboat in which Devereaux had been picked up had presented a battered and weather-beaten appearance, her paint peeling off and her bottom badly scarred, as if she'd been used a good while on the beach; and on her stern they had been able to decipher the letters—ENI-G —AR. Devereaux claimed that his ship had touched a needle of rock and had sunk immediately; but no danger of that nature was laid down on the *Vanguard's* chart. A year later, as a result of these conflicting and sensational tales, the United States Government sent a gunboat to look for the rock, perhaps with secret instructions to keep a weather eye open for Devereaux's island; but nothing was to be found. Devereaux couldn't remember the *Evening*

Star's exact latitude and longitude on the day before
the disaster; his records and instruments had vanished along with his crew in the heart of a deep
mystery. And the second mate, who alone came in
in regular order, was a poor navigator, you'll
remember, and may easily have made an error as to
the location of his departure. At any rate, nothing
was to be found. On the charts of the Hydrographic
Office today you'll see, in that position, a dotted
circle, marked Evening Star Rock, with an inter-
rogation point after the name.

"Devereaux's story was a nine days' wonder in
San Francisco, confirmed in substance as it was by
the recent authentic report from Callao. The newspapers made good copy of it. Many believed him
outrightly; a man doesn't float about in the Pacific
for over a year and emerge from the experience in
robust health, without there being some simple and
practical explanation. Yet sensational publicity
quickly prejudiced the case, as it invariably does.
After the first flush of pleasurable excitement, public
interest began to put him down either as a hoax or
a madman, and then promptly forgot him. One of
the papers tried to start a subscription for a
schooner, so that he might search for his island, but
it met with little response. The return wave of
prosaic life rolled over him, left him submerged and
helpless. For a while he went about seeking sympathy and assistance, but his melancholy tale soon
came to be a nuisance, doors were shut in his face,
and men avoided him.

"At length he had the good sense to go away. He
wandered to the East, moved about from place to

place. The story followed him, distorted in the passage of time. And so we meet him here, a man with a strange hallucination—an interesting case, and romantic, but unquestionably mad.''

II

Nichols leaned toward me, his eyes kindling. ''Let me take you back to the morning after the squall that separated the boats,'' he said. ''The sun rose in a clear sky; the quick tropic storm had entirely disappeared. Devereaux looked about him, and saw no sign of the others. One hardly realizes, until one has experienced the fact, how easy it is for boats to become separated in the night, especially under severe conditions of weather, or how rapidly a dozen miles may spring up between them. And a dozen might as well be as many hundreds, for all chances of their coming together again. The wind had die¹ to a baffling breeze that seemed to be trying to blow from all directions at once. Devereaux had no chronometer—nothing but a pocket watch, a sextant, a compass, and an old general chart of. the Pacific. After an hour's study of his situation, he came to a quick decision. The chart and the pocket watch couldn't be trusted to get him to the Sandwich Islands; like the second mate, somewhere within a radius of twenty-five miles from him at that moment, he changed the boat's course and steered due east in search of a continent.

''While they were getting up the sail to catch a wandering air that seemed to have settled in the west, a man forward shouted in tones of horror that the water cask was empty. A frantic investigation verified the fact. An oar carelessly thrown down had loosened the plug in the head of the cask, and their precious supply of water was washing around in the bottom of the boat. They tasted it, but found it too salt too drink; the boat, fresh from the top of the forward house, was leaking quite a little.

"Then began the nightmare of heat and thirst. The sun that day was pitiless. They had no luck with the wind, which soon fell flat calm; the exertion of rowing added to the misery. Not a drop of rain fell. By noon, the horror of the first day's thirst had begun to grip them; by nightfall it had them cowed and broken, whining for water. It's that first day which always is the worst, you know— until the end. Devereaux still hoped that he might pick up one of the other boats, and all hands kept a sharp lookout; but the hope died as the hours wore on. The sheer loneliness of the vast Pacific under a brilliant sun oppressed them like a foretaste of death, like a vista of eternity. They made little progress that day.

"A night passed, between sleeping and waking; dawn once more showed them a deserted sea. After a couple of hours' rowing, they threw down the oars in despair. What was the use of making little dabs with a wooden blade at an ocean beyond span or circumference? Devereaux says that he, too, was completely disheartened. They rested all that forenoon, waiting for a breeze. By this time the thirst had eaten into their vitals. Spots were dancing before their eyes, and frequently one of the men would insist that he saw a boat on the horizon; but after a while they learned to accept the cruelty of this delusion.

"Some time a little after noon, Devereaux was in the stern sheets steering; he had persuaded the men to take up the oars again. He was gazing off on the port quarter, in an aimless state of misery, when all at once he thought that his mind must be breaking with the thirst. A vision swam before him—a vision of a peaceful island, fringed with palm trees, crowned by a low green hill, all shimmering with heat and inverted in the sky. He says that he gazed at it a long time without daring to speak; he was afraid the others wouldn't be able to see it, afraid that it wasn't real. Finally he could stand the suspense no longer.

" 'Look!' he cried, pointing. 'Is anything there?'

"And they saw it, too. For it was nothing but the mirage of an actual island, an indeterminate distance away. It hung in the sky like a mysterious apparition. They regarded it fixedly, with glances almost hostile, as if questioning its integrity; but the vision persisted. Then they turned the boat, and rowed like madmen throughout the afternoon. The mirage had faded in the course of an hour; but Devereaux urged them on by arguments and promises, explaining the nature of the phenomenon and enlarging on their chances of deliverance. Hadn't they all seen it? It couldn't be far off; it must lie somewhere along the line of the compass bearing which he had taken.

"That night they rowed by watches, Devereaux himself taking stroke oar with either crew. And

when morning dawned, the real island lay right side
up a couple of miles ahead, fair and alluring on the
steel-blue rim of the sea. You can imagine the
hoarse shout that went up from parched throats!
Weak and wild, they struggled painfully at the oars;
and shortly after sunrise the boat entered a little
cove that split the front of the island, where the
ground swell at once dropped off under the shelter
of a curving point of land. A few strokes more,
and the surf caught them. A long roller flung them
high up the beach—a lucky thing, for God knows
they wouldn't have had the strength to save themselves. The roller went out, leaving them planted
upright on a white coral strand; in the silence
before the coming of another wave, they heard the
drip of a little stream running down the hillside at
the head of the cove. Water! They left the boat as
she was, the oars cock-billed in the rowlocks, the
sail, which they'd hoisted just before dawn and had
been too weak or excited to take in, flapping loose
across the gunwale, and ran with the last strength
in their bodies toward the sound. The rivulet had
cut a shallow channel in the coral, from the jungle
to the water's edge; they threw themselves face
downward, buried their mouths in the stream, and
drank like animals.

"For some time afterward they lay as they had
fallen, saturated like so many sponges, feeling the
water sink into their blood. Then Devereaux, who
had exercised his will power and drunk as sparingly
as possible, got to his feet and turned toward the
jungle. A second time he thought that his eyes were
deceiving him. A woman stood there in the half-

shadow, still grasping the branches which she had parted as she stepped out on the beach. She didn't appear frightened, but gazed at him frankly in wonder and admiration. He thought she was the most beautiful creature he had ever seen. His heart went out to her in that astonishing moment of their meeting, went out freely, without restraint or volition . . . and she's held it ever since, and always will. One hardly can imagine, to see him sitting over there so dejectedly, that off on the floor of the Pacific, years ago, and utterly unseen of the world of men, he lived such a transcendent moment, that such a romance came to him under the sun we all know. It takes one back to the days of Sinbad and Urashima and Oisin.

"He advanced toward her, making signs of friendliness—of affection, it's to be supposed. Their hearts were free as the air, and they went naturally, like God's children, into each other's arms. She remained unafraid . . . so he discovered that she loved him, too. Their meeting at the head of the beach had been unobserved; they melted together into the jungle like creatures of the light, and the boughs that she'd parted as if opening the door of life silently closed behind them.

"A little later he returned to the beach and aroused his crew; the men had fallen into a sort of stupor as they lay in the hot sun. The girl led them inland to the main village of her people, where they were received like gods dropped from the sky."

Nichols leaned back in his chair, smiling crookedly. "The story of the advance of civilization," he said grimly, "is the story of how savages have had

to learn that white men aren't gods. It's an old
story now—old and threadbare. It's been pretty
nearly completely learned. . . . These people
among whom Devereaux and his party had fallen,
had never seen a white man before. The story was
all new and fresh to them. But owing to the wholly
exceptional circumstances, its ending didn't run
according to the usual distressful formula. In fact,
it resulted in a real victory.

"The white men were very few, to begin with;
and they couldn't call on their governments, at the
head of the organized world, to support and further
with mechanical engines of destruction their various
lusts and designs. Happily, three of them died
within a week after they had landed, from the effects
of that first drink of water and the intemperate eating that followed. The other three, however, rapidly recovered strength and peccancy, and began
casting their eyes on the women of the village. You
know the ripe, luxuriant beauty of the Marquesan
women: these people were of the same root stock.
It wasn't many days before a number of violent out-
rages had been committed, which rang around the
island—a couple of husbands murdered, maidens
violated, and wives put to shame.

"Now, these people were moral, of course, after
the wise and simple code of nature; and the chief of
the village was a man of character and decision. He
didn't waste time in parley; when the crimes were
brought home beyond peradventure, and it was seen
that the gods had turned to clay, he had the offending sailors taken into custody, and himself dis-
patched all three of them with the same club. Later

their best parts were eaten at a feast of fairly legitimate rejoicing. Devereaux was spared because he had behaved himself, and because of the love of the girl, who, it appears, was the chief's daughter.

"We've all dreamed of a life of truth and freedom; but few of us have won it and lost it both, in the brief span of a year. You should see Devereaux's eyes kindle, while he tells you of it, while he's trying to convince you that he isn't mad. The people of this island had no traditions of their origin, no legends of visits from the outside world. It happened, through the fact of prevailing winds in the Pacific, that no sailing ship route passed near this region; steamers, also, gave it a wide berth, for it didn't lie between anywhere and anywhere. It was a place apart, visited by human agency only on the remotest chance. It may well be that during a period of many years the only two vessels to wander down those particular miles of waters were the ship that left Devereaux floating on the ocean and the ship that picked him up in the same spot over a year later. Thus it was that the island had remained undiscovered, peopled by a race without knowledge of the world. They were honest and lovable children—much as God intended all of us to be, I reckon, much as we might have been if we hadn't found a way temporarily to surmount our destiny.

"The island itself was an emerald anchored in a field of cobalt, a jewel floating on the broad bosom of the sea. The rustling palm trees waved day and night before the steady trade winds; the air hung cool in the shadows, the white surf broke on the reefs in constant thunder, and the tropic sunlight surrounded the gem with a halo of misty gold. Devereaux lived there a year, and the love that came to him partook of the nature of the place—fresh, divine, alluring, rich with color and meaning, pure as the light, true as the unchanging wind. A son was born to them. Nothing crossed their lives of sorrow or evil. They had forgotten time and its desperate occasions. The new day was but a repetition of the old.

"But I can't begin to show you half the peace and beauty of that year. Ask me what the heart of man desires, and I'll answer that every element of it existed there on the island—conquest, honor, joy, creative impulse, love—enough for a dreamer or a doer, the wise design of nature with her uneasy and aspiring offsprings. Devereaux grew to love the people; and because he seemed so different, yet conformed naturally to the island proprieties, they exalted him. And, marvellous to relate, he knew the worth of what he had found; he fulfilled the opportunity, he appreciated the honor, he was worthy of the romantic choice."

Nichols struck the table sharply with his fist. "Beware of too much happiness!" he growled. "That's another lesson of a jaundiced civilization. It isn't expedient to embrace truth too hard. . . . Who could have conceived an existence safer than Devereaux's, or one more likely to last? The broadest ocean in the world guarded him; the place of his retreat had never been discovered. The people adored him, the arms of a great love enfolded him; and he was glad to stay. What better ramparts could life have built for his defense? But fate,

the old destroyer, willed it otherwise; and he was
sent back to us, to an unbelieving world—to point
some obscure moral, I suppose, perhaps in another
attempt to show the hollowness and unreality . . .
if we had eyes to see.

"They had saved the whaleboat, of course; Devereaux used to cruise about the island in her, catching wonderful fish, for he was a sailor at heart, and
couldn't keep off the water. One day something led
him far off shore—a speck on the horizon, which he'd
no sooner seen than he wished to investigate. It
looked like a piece of wreckage, or a boat; he became
suddenly excited to think of finding traces of his
fellow-men. Thus the devil with a memory lured
him to destruction. The object was farther away
than he had at first realized; it continued for a long
while to look like a boat with a man's figure propped
up in one end. But when he finally came up to it,
he found nothing more interesting than a tree floating half submerged with a huge root that indeed
resembled, even at close range, the fancy his mind
had created.

"About this time it fell flat calm; he noticed a
heavy squall gathering on the eastern horizon. He
took down the sail, and started to row with two short
oars which he carried for an emergency. But four
or five miles lay between him and the island; before
he'd covered a third of the distance, the squall met
him head on.

"It was one of those savage arch-squalls that
occur on the fringe of the trade winds once or twice
in the course of a year. The island lay to windward of him; he didn't set the sail, of course, for

he would have been unable to do anything but run before it. In fact, there was nothing left but to try to keep her head in the wind with the two short oars. The squall became more violent; a short choppy sea sprang up as if by magic, and spray flew from the wave-tops in blinding sheets. At last he had to give it up. He managed to save the oars; with one of them in his hand he scrambled aft. The boat flew around like a chip as his weight settled in the stern. Then she gathered headway, and he began to steer, running away from the island. Darkness was falling; he couldn't see how fast he was dropping the land. But his sailor's instinct told him all about it. As night closed in, he realized the worst; he and the whaleboat were being blown to sea.

"It seemed as if the squall would never end. The gale rushed at him for hours, a veritable hurricane of wind, accompanied by a deluge of warm rain. He was badly frightened, not so much for his physical safety as on account of his imagination. He says that during those long hours of tumult and darkness, a premonition of doom became as real to his fancy as if an actual spirit, an embodiment of disaster, had settled down out of the night to keep him company. He didn't feel alone—fate sailed with him.

"In the morning, the island of course had disappeared. The squall had at length passed over; the sea grew calm, and the hot sun burned down on the water. It remained calm all day, so that he couldn't use the sail. He rowed the heavy boat until his hands could barely touch the oars, steering as best he knew how by the sun. He had no compass, and his idea of the direction of the island was vague; the squall, he thought, had struck him from about E. S. E., but he couldn't be certain. It might have veered a point or two in the night, blowing him off at a new angle. And what did it matter?—for he couldn't pick out the points of the compass with the wind gone and the sun directly overhead. A horrible fear oppressed him that with all his frantic pulling he was shaping a course past the island. But which side—which side? As the day wore on, with no land appearing, this fear became a certainty.

"The second night was terrible; he had begun to comprehend the immensity of the ocean. He was lost on the Pacific. Nothing but a miracle of miracles would lead him back to the island. In his mind's eyes he saw a chart of the region; a dot marked the island, a smaller dot his present position—the rest was a waste of waters. Thousands of lines radiated from the smaller dot; these were the possible directions which he might steer. Only three or four of them approached the island; the rest led nowhere.

"He remembered that he was far from the track of vessels. Not that he wanted to return to the world, but a vessel might help him to find the island. He was too full of life to want to die. . . . Scenes of the island crossed his mind with poignant intensity. They would be searching for him in their frail dug-out canoes. The women would be wailing behind the village. Would his love believe that he had left her? No, he felt her faith, across the silence. In fancy, he saw her standing at the head

of the beach, where she first had appeared to him.
But her face now was drawn in wild sorrow, her
streaming eyes ranged the horizon as if she would
pierce the veil of death. He cried out to her; but the
vast cavern of the sky swallowed his words.

"It would have been merciful to kill him there in
the boat; hunger and thirst of the body are nothing,
are soon over with. But think of the surpassing
cruelty of saving him! Great pains were taken to
that end; winds were manipulated, a ship was
selected and driven from her course; it was as if the
elements had conspired together and the whole
machinery of the universe had paused a moment for
the consummation of the act. On a certain morning
he was sighted from the quarter-deck of the *Vanguard;* an hour later he was picked up, half dead
from thirst, and babbling of an island—as mad as a
hatter, of course, since the nearest land was the
Marquesas, five hundred miles away."

III

"I've often tried to imagine Devereaux's outlook
on life, as he begged the captain of the *Vanguard*
that morning to turn his ship about and institute a
search for an uncharted island. How the refusal
must have stunned him, with the reality still a living presence in his heart. By Jove, you know, the
smell of the land lingered in his nostrils as if he'd
just that moment left it; he could hear the voices,
could feel the touch of lips that barely were parted
from his. . . . But they were rough and practical

on board the *Vanguard;* they had to be, for weren't
they sailing in the employ of a strictly ordered
enterprise? They laughed at him, and held their
course. It was then that he began to hate a world
that wouldn't listen. He's used to it now; like the
savages, he has learned his lesson. And his inter-
pretation of it is accepted only as a further indication of his madness. He says simply that we have
lost our souls.

"On top of this, came the experience in San Francisco. To have his hopes raised so high, only to be
shattered overnight when public interest threw down
the new plaything, was the final stroke of disillu-
sionment. He went back to the sea; this was his
only means of livelihood, and in spite of the romantic hallucination he remained a good sailor. The
ship on which he sailed from San Francisco took
him south through the Pacific, along the route of
homeward bound vessels. This, of all Pacific sailing
routes, strikes nearest to the region where Devereaux had been lost and found. But it doesn't run
quite far enough to the westward actually to cross
it. Devereaux went to the captain, told him straightforwardly the inwardness of his trouble and adventure, and begged him to shift the course a little—
just to run to leeward, so that they would fetch the
longitude of the place. He didn't ask to waste any
time in searching. But the captain, who'd heard
about his mate before he shipped him, saw nothing
in this but a mild outcropping of the madness, and
of course wouldn't listen to the appeal. Running a
ship to leeward was a matter of dollars and cents.
. . . So they drew near the island, passed it a few

hundred miles away, and left it astern as they picked up the southeast trades.

"This was the first of many voyages; he remained in the San Francisco trade for several years. Half a dozen times he passed the island, always leaving it far to leeward; and the memory didn't grow cold. Rather, it burned warmer and higher under this harrowing tantalization, a flame fed by hope and clarified by love. Some time, if he waited patiently, the elements would be propitious, the right chance would come.

"But he, too, became practical about it, recognizing that until he was his own master he wouldn't be free to seize a chance if it came his way. He saved his money, and worked hard to advance his reputation. In due time he was rewarded with the command of a little bark. For a number of voyages his owners sent him to the China Sea; it was at this time that I first met him, to fall under the spell of his romantic destiny. At last, however, he arrived in Singapore one voyage to learn that he'd been chartered to carry coals from Newcastle, New South Wales, to San Francisco. He felt a wonderful elation at the news. It looked like his long-awaited opportunity.

"In the natural order of things, you know, on the passage from Newcastle to California, he would cross the Pacific in the westerlies below the southeast trades, strike north through the trade winds close hauled on the starboard tack, fetch within a reasonable distance of the coast of Mexico, pick up the northeast trades there, and take a weatherly departure for the last leg of the journey. By cross-

ing the equator in 135° west longitude he would be
thrown to leeward heavily on that last leg. But he
must chance it; no one would know, and he could
make his easting in the North Pacific, above the
trades. Chance it?—he couldn't have failed to
accept the opening, his whole life was centered on
the play. God knows, he'd waited long enough,
devotedly enough, for deliverance from this pro-
tracted anguish, for the resumption of happiness,
for another glimpse of the form of love and beauty,
for a sight of the island that more and more
appeared to him in the nature of a vivid dream.

"And, by Jove, when he got there, he couldn't find
it! It didn't seem to be in existence any longer; at
least, it wasn't to be discovered in the region where
he had expected to come across it. He couldn't
remember the exact latitude and longitude, you'll
remember, although he had an approximate position
which ought to have served the purpose. He cruised
in the locality for over a week, back and forth,
around and around, combing every square mile of
its waters; but he saw no sign of land. He had a
terrible feeling that he might have passed it under
cover of the darkness, that if the night could have
been turned to day he might have caught a glimpse
of it on the distant horizon. It was at night, he
says, that the sense of its nearness was most acute,
an ethereal presence lying all about him in the soft,
impenetrable obscurity. At times he could almost
smell the land. He felt that she, too, had remembered, and had remained faithful to him; that the
pain and longing in her heart hung in mysterious
vibrations about the island, to guide him to her if

ever he came that way. But, as of old, he couldn't
tell the direction; it always was his bitter fate to
lack a compass at the crises of life. He didn't find
either the island or the rock which had split the
Evening Star; and in the end he had to go away.

"He tried again, some years later, but with the
same unsuccess. I have an idea that his latitude and
longitude were away off; yet the location where he
had been picked up was exact enough. Or perhaps. . . . But what's the use of speculating on a
hypothesis without tangible grounds? He couldn't
find the island. *He* is the story—as you see him
over there.

"By this time a hopeless melancholy had settled
on him; yet he persisted in what he conceived to be
the main business of life. His faith, indeed, was
unquestioning; he apparently couldn't have done
otherwise, and all his days and designs arranged
themselves around this central purpose as naturally
as mists rise to the sun. He quit the sea, and went
into the pearl fishing enterprise down on the north
coast of Australia. He wanted to make money—and
he made it. As soon as he possessed the means, he
bought a schooner, fitted her up for a year's cruise,
and disappeared over the eastern rim of the Pacific.
It was well over a year, in fact, before he turned
up again.

"I happened to be in Singapore when he arrived
from that first cruise. Going down the Jetty late
one afternoon to take my sampan, I met him wandering in the opposite direction. One look at his
face told me that he'd failed again. He had come in
at noon, wasn't going anywhere, didn't know what

he wanted to do. I took him aboard with me to
supper, and we had a long evening on deck under the
awning.

" 'Devereaux, has it ever occurred to you that the
island may have sunk in a volcanic disturbance?' I
suggested, after he'd gone over the affair for the
twentieth time.

"The idea gave him comfort, strange as it may
seem; he could contemplate the entire destruction
of his beloved as an event of minor importance. It
offered something to fall back on, in his mental
agony; a practical explanation to dull the edge of
the frantic feeling that all the while the island
existed, if he could only find it. When I noted how
he devoured the suggestion, I enlarged on its possi-
bility.

"You see, you haven't been able to find the rock,
either," I pointed out. 'And I remember you told
me there wasn't any coral formation in the neighborhood of that rock. A sure sign of recent volcanic
activity. I'd be willing to bet that it hadn't been on
the surface very long; it had been poked up recently
for your especial benefit. And where volcanic action
is busy poking things up, it's just as liable to sink
them down again.'

" 'But the island had been there a long while,' he
objected. 'It had a coral reef all the way around;
our boat crossed it by a miracle that morning. And
the people, Nichols—people don't rise full grown
from the sea, or drop down out of the air.'

"I wondered if they didn't, in this case. 'Never
mind, this was the way of it,' I said. 'The rock was
an indication of volcanic action that hadn't yet

extended to the island. But the whole area was in danger, and the next outbreak, which happened to be one of depression, dragged down the island, too.'

"We left the question pending, and went our various ways. Now and then I'd run into him, wandering about the world, as the years went by. He's never wholly given up the search. The singular thing about it is that material fortune fairly has pursued him. He's made a lot of money, and sunk it all in fruitless expeditions. Too bad he couldn't have possessed a scientific bent; he knows all there is to know of the Pacific islands on their practical side— that is, on the side that isn't worth knowing."

Nichols struck the table again. "Well, what do you think of it?" he demanded. "There he goes, now—alone, always alone. Why was he sent back to us? What's his obscure moral? Is there any clue?"

"Nichols, do you yourself believe in the reality of this island?" I asked.

He glanced at me keenly. "Isn't that wholly beside the point?" he said. "I don't believe the island exists today, if that is what you mean. But there's a year in an open boat, back at the beginning of the record, to be explained. The point is that he believes in the island. By Jove, he remembers it— do you understand? See that droop in his back, as he stands absently looking out the door? He's growing old, and the woman would be past middle age today, and the boy would be a man; but they have a trick of remaining young in his memory. Oh, he faces the fact, of course, in his practical moments; wonders what they have come to, if the

boy ever matured, if the woman waited, or gave him
up for lost and married another man. He can speak
about these things, because he's quite determined
to believe that the island is sunk under the ocean,
that they're all dead. But when the moon's out, and
he gets to dreaming, they come back to him just as
he left them, a young and beautiful woman with a
child at her breast, both of them perfectly alive.
How can you ask me . . . if I believe in the
island?"

IV

The day following this conversation, Nichols intro-
duced me to Devereaux; I met and talked with him
several times before I left Hong Kong. If he was
mad, the circumstance didn't affect his daily inter-
course. He was a man of charming personality; a
man who held something back, of course, but this
merely added interest to the charm. Only his eyes
were strange; as he talked, they invariably wandered upward, and were recalled to the scene in
intermittent sharp flashes.

Then I left Hong Kong, and forgot all about him
for a couple of years. At the end of that time I
found myself in Batavia on business, when who
should arrive but Nichols in the bark *Omega*. I left
a message for him at his broker's, and that evening
he called on me at the hotel. Already, I had determined to ask him for a passage north.

"But it'll take me a couple of months to reach
Hong Kong," he told me. "I'm going from here to
Macasser, then on up the straits to Cebu and Iloilo."

"Time is no object to me," I answered.

"Good," he said. "I'll be glad enough of your company. I have one passenger already, but he's hardly exhilarating. It's Devereaux—you remember him. The fellow who lost an island in the Pacific."

"Yes, indeed. How is he now?"

"He's in bad shape," said Nichols, tapping his head significantly. "I've had him aboard the round trip, for his health, but it hasn't seemed to help him. I'm afraid he really is breaking up, this time."

So it was arranged that I accompany Nichols northward. I went off on board with him that night, to enjoy the fresh sea-breeze in the outer roads. There I renewed my acquaintance with Devereaux under more intimate circumstances.

The change in him was decidedly noticeable. His manner was odder, more distrait; throughout the evening he sat with his chair pulled close to the side, speaking only when spoken to, gazing off into the night and drumming constantly on the rail with his hand. We sailed from Batavia in a couple of days. Quite abruptly, the morning of our departure, Devereaux approached me with a new manner, as if anxious to enter into confidences. The anchor had just fetched away, the ship had begun to turn on her heel. Something had moved him to the depths, some gleam of color, some distant view of the palm-covered islands in the offing. He stopped me in the weather alley-way, his delicate features working with a powerful emotion.

"I've tried . . ." he began; then broke off for

an instant, and drew nearer. "You know, I hardly
said good-bye," he told me impressively. "I went
off in a great hurry that morning." He gazed at me
profoundly, like a man looking at his own image in a
mirror. "Do you know the Pacific?" he suddenly
demanded.

"Not very well," I answered. "I've been to
Honolulu, and New Caledonia. Nothing in between."

"Oh . . ." he murmured. "Then I must tell
you." Without warning, he plunged into a relation
of his own tale. I listened politely, then curiously,
then with growing excitement. The tale transported
him, inspired him. It was poetic drama, tragic and
magnificent, that I heard; scene after scene unfolded
itself before me as he talked, made real by his unconscious perfection of detail, and invested with
truth by his air of fervor and simplicity. I saw the
island in bold outline, in vivid coloring; I felt the
hunger and thirst, and tasted the water that they
found there on the beach; I looked up with him to
behold the woman of his dreams. His dreams, or his
memories—which was it? Had there ever been an
island? The question seemed never so baffling as
at that moment, when his present madness stood so
openly revealed.

After this experience he retained me in his confidence—didn't want to talk about anything else but
the vision that he saw and the sorrow that lay on his
heart. It was very distressing. One morning as I
came up the companion-way after breakfast, he
plucked me nervously by the sleeve.

"Look here," he said, leading me to windward.

"Nichols knows the location of that island. He's trying to pass it . . ."

"Nonsense, Devereaux!" I exclaimed. "You mustn't credit such a thought. Nichols knows less about it than we do."

"He's always poring over the chart," said Devereaux darkly. "He tries to keep our position from me. Oh, I can see it in his eye!"

"But we aren't in that part of the world," I argued, like a man wrestling with the wind.

He passed a hand wearily across his eye. "It looks the same," he said. Suddenly he shot at me a piercing glance. "I don't know whether to believe you or not!" he snarled. "You're all against me, every damned one of you!"

He quickly dropped the mood of suspicion, however, for that evening we had another long talk about the island. The next forenoon he took a notion to go aloft; spent a number of hours perched on the main royal yard. There we could see him steadily searching the horizon. We seized the opportunity to talk over his case at length in the cabin, but could come to no decision beyond that of letting affairs run their course.

"Good Lord, Nichols, suppose he really sights an island, up there!" I suddenly exclaimed. We bent over the chart, pricking off our position that morning; and breathed a sigh of relief to discover that, as we were going, we wouldn't sight any land till the following day.

It was in Macassar that we saw the first evidence of violent aberration in Devereaux. The three of us had gone ashore for the day; after an early dinner, we were taking a short drive in the cool of the evening through a region of small rice and coffee plantations. Somewhere beyond the outskirts of the town, a native woman stepped from the road in front of us to make way for our horses. She drew back against a fringe of bamboo trees alongside the roadside, stretched out her arms to part the branches behind her, and stood there motionless, in sharp relief against the sunset, watching us pass by. Beside us, Devereaux uttered a wild cry, some unintelligible name, and leaped from the moving vehicle.

We found him prostrate at the feet of the woman, babbling in a musical, strange tongue. The light on his face was the very madness of joy. The woman shrieked, drawing back among the bamboo stems. Nichols reassured her in the Bugis dialect.

"Devereaux, come away!" he commanded sharply. "You don't know her. For God's sake, come away!"

Devereaux got up slowly, gazing at us in wild alarm; then held out his arms to the woman. She struggled farther back in the bamboo thicket. Again he turned to us, drew himself together, and spoke with authority and defiance.

"She is my wife!" he said.

It was pathetic and terrible—the very devil of a scene. He fought and struggled; we had to take him to the carriage by main strength. A crowd had gathered. At last Devereaux grew quiet. Nichols explained as best he could to the woman, while half a hundred ears listened eagerly to the astonishing tale. A rapid colloquy ensued; though I couldn't understand the words, I heard the woman's voice melt with pity.

"She wants to know if your wife had a birthmark on her bosom?" Nichols interpreted, turning to the carriage.

Devereaux shook his head; he still was dazed with the struggle. The woman left cover, and came close to the carriage without fear. The upper part of her sarong slipped down, disclosing a broad red blotch on the dusky skin above her right breast. Leaning forward, she spoke a few words in a soothing voice.

"She says that you must be mistaken," repeated Nichols. "She says she is sorry—but now you have seen that it cannot be."

Devereaux stiffened in his seat, and the light suddenly went out of his eyes. He gazed at her a moment like a rudely awakened somnabulist. Then he slumped in the corner, as if felled by a sharp invisible blow. The woman nodded to us, and we drove rapidly away.

He was ill for several days after that, keeping close to his room. When he was able to come on deck again, we had reached well across the Celebes Sea, and were about to make Sibutu Passage on the coast of Borneo. We watched him anxiously that forenoon for signs of a return of the malady. But he'd evidently forgotten the incident in Macassar; he talked with us all day in a normal manner, without reference to his affairs. It seemed as if the worse of the attack was over.

A long, narrow island lies on the west side of Sibutu Passage, clear of the mainland and hiding several smaller islands behind it. This was sighted

while we were at dinner that noon; when we came up
for our cigars, it stood in plain view on the lee bow.
Being an island against the main, with land rising
behind it as we came on, we didn't think of it as a
possible new source of excitement. As the afternoon passed, however, Nichols called my attention
to Devereaux, who was acting strangely again. For
a while he would lean against the lee rail, talking
rapidly to himself; suddenly he would leave that off
and take to pacing the deck in short, quick turns,
rubbing his hands together. His eyes, it was to be
noticed, kept watching the island, now less than four
miles away. His face worked with nervous energy.
His whole air was one of suppressed excitement,
mingled with a certain quiet elation.

"He's using that Polynesian dialect!" Nichols
exclaimed in a worried whisper. "What can we do
with him? We must pass the island."

"Can't you stop there long enough to set him
ashore—convince him that it isn't his island?" I
suggested.

Nichols considered soberly, then shook his head.
"It wouldn't work," he said. "First place, the currents are bad, there's no harbor or village, and no
anchorage, so far as I'm aware. Second place,
would anything convince him? Even if there once
was a real island, mightn't this one, in his present
condition, look as good as the next to him? Suppose he were to insist on a hunt for the inhabitants?
We'd have to bring him away in the end—and that
might only prolong the agony."

"I guess you're right, Nichols; but what's the
alternative?"

"Tack ship, and stand away till night," he answered without hesitation. "Slip through the passage under cover of darkness. Trust to luck that he'll change the mood again tomorrow, and forget what he saw this afternoon. We can get him to sleep some way—drug him if necessary."

"But he'll make a row at once, when you tack ship."

"I suppose so. We'll have to play him at his own game."

It seemed the better plan, and Nichols acted on it immediately. Devereaux, lost in his own sphere of unreality, didn't discover that the ship was coming about until the island began to change its position along the rail. He watched it a moment, looked up to see the sails flat aback, then turned in alarm and ran towards the stern.

"What are you doing?" he cried. "You can make the anchorage on this tack. The cove lies just around the first point."

"I know," said Nichols easily. "But it's getting late, and I am afraid of the reefs. The channel is narrow, the wind's dying, the currents can't be trusted around the entrance. I'm going to stand off and on all night, and wait for the morning."

"Nonsense!" urged Devereaux. "We could easily make it! Why, Nichols, I know that channel like a book. There's plenty of daylight left. . . ."

"Sorry, old fellow, but I just don't dare to try it," said Nichols decisively, throwing into the words all the power of his normality. "You must remember that I have the ship on my hands."

Devereaux regarded him sourly, in a sort of hostile dejection. His case throughout was marked by a singular docility, as if all things assumed an illogical aspect to him, and were to be met by circumlocutory methods. "Well, I suppose your word is law," he allowed. "But it's damned hard on me. I've waited a good many years, Nichols, for this night." Without deigning to discuss the matter further, he went off down the companion like a sulky child. Following him a few moments later to reconnoitre, I found the door of his stateroom tightly closed.

He didn't appear at the supper table; as the evening passed it seemed evident that he wasn't coming out again. We began to have hopes of getting through the night without another painful scene. When I looked into his room after supper and found him sound asleep in the bunk, it seemed too good to be true. Nichols at once tacked ship again, and we stood back toward Sibutu Passage.

Our plan for slipping through under cover of the darkness, however, had failed to reckon with the moonlight; that both of us had forgotten it, is a good indication of our state of mind. For the night, when it settled down, was positively radiant. A great soft moon hung high in the heavens, flooding the sea with a subdued glare, and revealing every detail of the land as we came abreast the point of the island shortly after midnight. Sleep was out of the question. Nichols, of course, had to navigate the ship through the intricate passage. Thus it became my duty to run below every little while, keeping a watch on Devereaux's door. But no sound or movement came from the closed room.

We already had forged past the main point of the island, which lay abaft the lee beam, less than a half mile distant, when I started on this errand for the last time. Going down the companion, I was struck by an uneasy feeling, and found myself hurrying through the entry. When I reached the cabin, Devereaux's door stood open, a black hole in the dim light of the swinging lamp above the chart table. A glance into the room showed me that he no longer was in the bunk. I ran to the forward cabin door, but seeing no one out there, turned and jumped up the after companion on the dead run.

"Have you seen Mr. Devereaux come on deck?" I cried to the helmsman.

"No, sir."

Nichols, at the stern rail, had heard my question, and ran forward to meet me. "Isn't he in his room?" he asked.

"No. I can't find him anywhere in the cabin. Must have gone up the forward companion."

Together we hurried forward along the weather alley. Reaching the corner of the house, where the main deck opened before us, we made out two men standing to leeward of the mainmast, apparently in earnest conversation. One seemed eager, excited; the other evidently was on the defensive. Devereaux and the mate, we saw the next instant. It crossed my mind that the mate was ignorant of the intimate details of Devereaux's malady; he wasn't the sort of fellow to take into confidential relations.

We heard his voice, now, sharply raised, as if in a final attempt to quell the other's insistence.

"But we aren't going to stop here, I tell you! There's nothing to stop for, no place to call. . . . "

"*Not going to stop?* . . ." Devereaux repeated wildly. He turned toward the rail, holding his arms stiffly outstretched in a gesture of utter distraction. Who can imagine the thoughts that leaped through his heart at that moment, or fathom the depths of the disappointment that suddenly crushed his already broken mind?

"Look out," cried Nichols at my elbow. "Don't let him get away!"

But it already was too late; Devereaux had heard the warning, too, and accepted it as a challenge. With a wild cry that seemed to tremble among the upper sails and echo back from the wooded heights of the island, he leaped forward, dodging the mate, and gained the bulwarks just abaft the fore preventor backstay. For an instant he stood there, silhouetted against the bright track of the moonlight, confronting the vision that was reality—then plunged with a magnificent abandon, and disappeared under the silvery surface of the water.

'We saw him strike out towards the island. The ship forged ahead, carrying the moon-track with her; before we could get out a boat, he had vanished in the shrouded wastes astern. We sought for a night and a day, but could find no trace of his body. In that swift current setting seaward, it was impossible that he could have reached the land.

SERVANT AND MASTER

I

"STEWARD!"

"Yes, sir, Cappen."

The little old Chinaman looked up from the brass threshold which he was polishing. Kneeling at the entrance to the forward cabin, with his back toward Captain Sheldon, he peered around his shoulder with a gnome-like movement, his hands pausing on the brass.

Captain Sheldon laid down his book. He pointed an accusing forefinger at the stateroom threshold, which the steward had just finished.

"That's dirty, Wang. You haven't half polished it. What's the matter with you lately?"

"All light, Cappen, all light. Eye gettee old."

He shifted his pan of brick-dust, scuttled across on his knees to the stateroom threshold, and attacked the brass again. With head bent low and hands flying, he worked silently. His back disclosed nothing beyond the familiar mechanical impersonality.

Captain Sheldon watched him with narrowing eyes. He realized that he was beginning to "get down on" the old steward; yet to his mind there was justice in the feeling. Wang wasn't so neat or careful as he used to be. He frowned as he noted the greasy collar of the Chinaman's tunic. A dirty steward!—he always had abhorred the notion. To his strict ideas of nautical propriety, it meant the beginning of a ship's disintegration. The time was not far distant, he saw clearly, when he would have to get rid of old Wang.

He had inherited the steward along with the ship *Retriever* when his father died. "Wang-ti, His Mark," the entry had stood voyage after voyage on the ship's articles; young John Sheldon had grown up taking the venerable Chinaman for granted. He was the "old man's" trusted servant, as much a part of the vessel as her compass or her keel. He took entire charge of the ship's provisioning, as well as of the cabin accessories. He kept the commissary accounts, with never a penny out of the way; his prudence and honesty had saved the ship many a dollar. John often used to hear his father boast that he wouldn't be able to go to sea without Wang-ti.

In his boyhood on shipboard, there had existed a natural intimacy between the captain's son and the factotum of the nautical household. John's mother was dead, he roamed the ship wild from forecastle to lazaret; and Wang had guarded his fortunes with the wise faithfulness that knows how to keep its attentions unobserved. The captain even had permitted his son to sit in the steward's room, watching him smoke a temperate pipeful of opium after the noon dishes were done; this was the measure of his trust in the old Chinaman.

Indeed, John Sheldon, had he been disposed, might have recalled a great deal that went on in Wang's narrow room on the port side of the forward cabin—incidents fraught with deep importance to boyhood. The room was a place of retreat, a zone of freedom. It made little difference whether Wang were there or not; the two understood each other, conversed only in monosyllables, and the Chinaman apparently took no interest in what the boy did. In return, the boy throughout this period never so much as made an inquiry into Wang's life; that matter, too, was taken for granted. Many an afternoon he would lie for hours on the clean, hard bed, his head buried in a book, while the steward sat beside him on a three-legged wooden stool, sewing or figuring his accounts, neither of them speaking a word or glancing at the other. The click of the stone as the Chinaman mixed his ink, the rustle of the pages, and the faint creak of the wooden finish in the cabin, would mingle with the fainter sounds aloft and along decks as the vessel slipped quietly through the water.

But this was long ago, before life had opened, before days of responsibility and authority had overlaid youthful sentiment with a hard veneer of efficiency. The door of that room had closed on John Sheldon for the last time when he had left the ship in New York, a boy of thirteen, to spend a few years at home in school; he was not to share another hour with Wang until the final hour. When next he joined the *Retriever's* company, it was in the capacity of a rousing young second mate of seventeen, broad shouldered and full of confidence, believing that his place in life depended on strength and self-assertion. He picked quarrels with the crew largely for the sake of fighting; he was aggressive and overbearing, as befitted the type of commanding officer which appealed to his imagination. In him, real ability was combined with a physical prowess beyond the ordinary; he failed to meet the reverses which teach a much-needed lesson to men of lesser combative powers, and the years conspired to develop the arbitrary side of his character. As an instance of this unfortunate tendency, he had allowed himself, after rising to the position of first mate on the *Retriever,* to quarrel with his father over some trifling matter of discipline; so that at the end of the voyage he had quit the deck on which he had been brought up, and had shipped away in another vessel.

It was on the voyage immediately following this incident that his father had died suddenly at sea, half way across the Indian Ocean on the passage home. John Sheldon had arrived in New York from the West Coast almost in company with the *Retriever,* brought in by the mate who had taken his place. The first news he heard was that his father had been buried at sea. The ship was owned in the family; it seemed natural, in view of this stroke of destiny, that he should have her as his first command. The officers left, he took possession of the cabin and the quarterdeck that had been his father's province for so many years; and Wang continued his duties in the forward cabin as if nothing had happened. The Chinaman had nursed Captain Sheldon when he took to his bed, had found him dying

the next morning, had heard his last words, and had
laid out his body for burial.

Six years had passed since then. John Sheldon
was a dashing young shipmaster of twenty-seven;
and now Wang was failing. No doubt about it. The
dishes weren't clean any longer; a greasy knife
annoyed Captain Sheldon almost as much as an
insult. Lately, he had begun to notice a heavy,
musty smell as he passed by the pantry door. A
dirty steward!—it wasn't to be supported, not on
his ship, at any rate.

The Chinaman finished polishing the brasses,
gathered up his pan and rags, and started for the
forward cabin. Captain Sheldon laid down his book
again.

"Steward, have you got a home?"

"Oh, yes, Cappen. My got two piecee house, Hong
Kong side."

Wang paused in the doorway, turning half around
and steadying himself as the ship lurched. His
fingers left a smudge on the white paint. As if
sensing rather than seeing it, he wiped the place fur-
tively with the corner of his cotton tunic, only
spreading the smudge. Captain Sheldon, watching
the maneuver, sniffed in disgust, and continued the
inquiry.

"Have you got a wife?"

"She dead, seven, eight year."

"Any children?"

"Oh, my got some piecee children, maybe three,
four."

"For God's sake, don't you know how many children you've got?"

"Yes, sir, Cappen. Four piecee, all go 'way. Maybe some dead. My no hear."

"Hm-m." The captain knit his brows ponderously, a habit he had acquired in the last few years, and fixed a severe glance on the old Chinaman. "Don't you ever want to go home?"

"Oh, no, Cappen. Why fo' go home? My b'long ship side."

After waiting a moment in silence for further questions, Wang realized that the conversation was not to be concluded this time. He turned slowly and shuffled off through the forward cabin, head bent and eyes peering hard at the floor. Captain Sheldon did not see him stumble heavily against the corner of the settee.

In the protection of the pantry, Wang put down the pan of brick-dust and stood for a long time motionless, holding the dirty rags in the other hand, facing the window above the dresser. He could see the small square of light plainly, but the rest of the room was vague. His tiny, inanimate figure, in the midst of the dim clutter of the room, expressed a weary relaxation; he stood like a man lost in vacant thought.

No one would have suspected the feelings behind the wizened face; Wang's countenance, as he gazed steadfastly at the square of light, was an expressionless blank. He seemed scarcely to breathe; the spark of life semed to have sunk low within him, to have retreated in fear or impotence. The hand holding the rags paused rigidly, as if petrified in the act of putting down its grimy burden. Had Captain Sheldon come upon him at that moment, he

would have ordered him shortly to get busy, begin
doing something.

All his thoughts, there in the silence of the pantry,
were of loyalty. That uncommunicative intimacy of
the past had been fruitful to one, at least, of the
parties to the contract. "Young Cappen," who as
a boy had been Wang's pride and charge, was his
pride and charge still. Had not "Old Cappen," on
his deathbed, whispered the final order: "Keep an
eye on the boy, Wang. He's stepping high now—
but the time may come when he will need you." But
of these words, his father's last utterance, "Young
Cappen" of course knew nothing. They remained
a profound secret between Wang and the dead.

If it were true, Wang recognized in that unwavering gaze, that his days of usefulness were over, he
would be no longer able to discharge the obligation.
Not that his strength was less; his withered, cord-
like sinews ached to scrub and polish, to keep his
domain in its old efficient order. But this voyage
he hadn't been able to see what needed to be done.
He had hardly dared to allow his mind to formu-
late the explanation. Now he must face it. He was
going blind.

He comprehended fully the meaning of the recent
conversation in the after cabin. The pain that held
him inert and motionless was half of love and half
of fear. Perhaps, he tried to tell himself, "Young
Cappen" was safely launched on the sea of life now;
perhaps he no longer had need of an old man's service. Yet, in the same moment of thought, Wang
knew that this was not the fact. The knowledge
filled him with a desperate tenacity; until fate

actually laid him low, he could not submit to the
turn of fortune. Old and wise in life, he realized
that "Young Cappen's" hardest lessons still lay
ahead of him. He must serve as long as he was able.

That night over the supper table, Captain Sheldon
opened a biscuit; there was a dead cockroach in it.
His knife had cut it in halves. He threw the biscuit
down in disgust. Wang always made the cabin
bread. . . . Well, why didn't the old fool take it
away? He must have seen the incident. Captain
Sheldon knew that he was standing a few feet away
in the pantry door. Taking up his plate, he snapped
over his shoulder:

"Steward!"

Wang was at his elbow in an instant. The captain
thrust the biscuit into his trembling hand.

"Look at that! Take them all away, and bring
some bread."

"Yes, sir, Cappen." The Chinaman mumbled incoherently, trying to cover his confusion. His innate
sense of the etiquette of human relations, which
even after fifty years of service had not accommo-
dated itself to the brusque callousness of European
manners, felt bitterly outraged; no way had been
left him to save face. Yet other and stronger emotions quickly submerged the insult. The biscuit
plate rattled like a castanet as he set it down on
the pantry dresser. As he cut into a new loaf of
bread, he shook his head slowly from side to side,
like an animal in pain, stopping in the midst of the
operation to bend above the offending biscuit and
examine it closely. He loosened the cockroach with
the point of the bread knife; it fell to the plate, a

dark spot on the white china. Under his breath he gave a staccato sigh: "Ah-ah-ah-ah-ah."

Captain Sheldon found himself unable to forget this trivial incident; he kept brooding over it all the evening. At breakfast next morning it came to his mind again, and followed him intermittently throughout the day—a day of petty mishaps and annoyances, one of those days when everything aboard the vessel seemed to be going wrong, when even the best efforts of officers and men to please him resulted in misfortune, and the simplest words rubbed the wrong way. Captain Sheldon was nearing the end of a long and tedious passage, with nerves and temper badly frayed.

Coming below an hour after dinner, in hopes of finding a little peace, he met the heavy odor of opium smoke floating through the cabin. The door into the forward cabin had been left open. He strode out angrily; the steward's door was open, too. Glancing into the stateroom, he saw the old Chinaman stretched on the bed, staring with glassy eyes at the ceiling, the pipe slipping from his fingers. Thin wisps of opium smoke curled up from the bowl and drifted out into the cabin.

Captain Sheldon's patience snapped suddenly. By God, this was too much! First, bugs in the bread; and now . . . the lazy old swine, lying there in an opium dream, too indolent even to close the door! The ship's discipline was going plumb to hell. His authority was becoming a joke. A dirty steward! By God, he wouldn't stand it any longer.

"Steward! Steward! Wake up, there!"

"What, Cappen?"

By a violent effort, Wang pulled himself out of the delicious stupor and sat up on the edge of the bunk. The drug had not fully overcome him; in a long lifetime, he never had exceeded the moderate daily pipeful that would put him to sleep for only half an hour.

"Steward, I can't permit this any longer. You've left your door open, and stunk up the whole cabin with the damned stuff."

"My s'pose close him, Cappen. Maybe wind swing him open."

"You didn't close it! You don't finish anything, now-a-days. It's got to stop, I tell you. I can see what the trouble is. This devilish opium is getting the best of you. It's got to stop—and the best way to stop, is to begin now. . . . Give me all the opium you've got."

"Yes, sir, Cappen."

The import of the captain's words brought the old Chinaman to his senses with a rush. He got up unsteadily, went to his chest, and began fumbling in the lower corner. Soon he brought out a number of small square packages done up in Chinese paper.

"Cappen, what fashion you do?"

Captain Sheldon snatched the packages from the steward's hand.

"I'm going to throw it all overboard! If you've got any more of the stuff hidden away, you're not to smoke it—do you understand? I won't have such a mess in my cabin."

"Cappen, no can do!"

Wang was panting; a shrill note of anguish came

in his voice. He reached out a trembling hand
toward the precious drug.

"Yes, you can, and you will. It's nothing but a
nasty, degenerate habit. You're too old for such
things. It's making you dirty and careless. Brace
up, now—show that you're good for something.
You used to be the best steward in the fleet. I'm
only trying to help you out. If things were to go on
like this much longer, I'd have to find a new steward in Hong Kong."

Captain Sheldon, struggling to regain control of
himself after the outburst of temper, stamped off
through the after cabin. Wang heard him go up the
companion. He sat down again on the edge of the
bunk, a crumpled heap, inert and silent, his eyes
dulled by a fear beyond any he had yet known. For
fifty years he had smoked daily that tiny pipeful of
opium. With all that life had brought him, could he
summon strength for this new and terrible ordeal?

II

Fire, like the rain, falls on the just and the unjust
alike, and eats up a tall ship at sea as readily as it
guts a splendid castle. They were half way across
from Luzon to the China coast, only a few hundred
miles from Hong Kong and the end of the passage,
when the blaze was discovered in the fore hold,
already well under way. Quickly it became unmanageable. Through a day and a night of frantic
effort the whole ship's company fought the flames,
retreating aft inch by inch while destruction followed

them relentlessly under decks. In the gleam of a
dawn striking across a smooth sea and lighting up
the pale faces gathered on top of the after house, it
became apparent that the ship was doomed.

Daylight found them in the boats, standing off to
watch the last lurid scene. The ship burned fiercely
throughout the forenoon. At midday, under a blis-
tering sun, her bows seemed suddenly to crumple
and dissolve; surrounded by a cloud of steam, she
settled forward with a loud hissing noise, and slowly
vanished under the waters of the China Sea.

Captain Sheldon, sitting upright in the stern of
the long-boat, watched the scene with set jaw and
snapping eyes. It was his first disaster, the first
time he had met destiny coming the other way. A
fierce anger, like the fire he had just been fighting,
ran in his blood. He was beside himself. It seemed
inconceivable that there was no way to bring his ship
back out of the deep; that the very means of authority had vanished, that he was powerless, that the
event was sealed for all time. He wanted to strike
out blindly, hit something, crush something.

Well he knew that if any blame attached to the
matter, it rested on him alone. For some occult
reason, as it now seemed, the mate a few days before
had broached the subject of fire, in conversation at
the supper table. Not that fire was to be expected;
no one ever had heard of it with such a cargo. Why
had the mate chosen that day, of all others, when
the captain had lost his patience with old Wang, to
talk about fire throughout the supper period, to follow him on deck with the subject in the evening?
The talk had aroused the perversity of his own

opposition. The mate, waxing eloquent and imaginative, had at length succeeded in frightening himself; had wanted to take off the fore hatch in the
dog watch, just to look into the hold. Had he done
so then, the fire probably would have been discovered in season for it to be overcome. But Captain
Sheldon, sarcastic and bristling with arbitrariness,
had commanded him flatly to leave the fore hatch
alone.

Well, no use in crying over spilt milk. The ship
was gone.

"Give way!" he shouted across the water to the
mate's boat. "Keep along with me. We'll strike
in for the coast, and follow it down."

All afternoon they rowed silently in the broiling
heat and mirror-like calm. The coast of China came
in sight, a range of high blue-gray mountains far
inland. Nearer at hand, a group of outlying islands
appeared on the horizon. Captain Sheldon swung
his course to the westward, heading directly into the
blinding sun that by this time had sunk low in the
western sky.

In the extreme bow of the longboat sat the old
steward, gazing straight ahead with unseeing eyes.
His head was uncovered; the sun beat down on him
without effect. He made no move, uttered no sound.
Alone and helpless, he suffered the throes of the
most desperate struggle that human consciousness
affords—the struggle of the will against the call of a
body habituated to opium.

In the latter part of the afternoon they sighted a
big Chinese junk, close inshore against the islands.
A little breeze had begun to ruffle the water. On

the impulse of the moment, Captain Sheldon decided to board the junk and have himself carried to Hong Kong under sail. The idea caught and suited his fancy; he couldn't bear to think of arriving in port in open boats. Instructions were shouted to the mate's boat, the head of the long-boat was again swung around, and a course was laid to intercept the brown-sailed native craft under the lee of the land.

All this passed unnoticed by the silent figure in the bow, wandering blindly through a grim vale of endeavor. As time went on, however, Wang seemed to realize that a change had taken place in the plan of their progress. The sun no longer shone full in his face. He glanced up dully, caught a vague sight of the junk, now close aboard and standing, to his veiled eyes, like a dark blot on the clear rim of the horizon; then pulled himself hastily together and made a low inquiry of the man at the bow oar. The answer seemed to galvanize his tortured body into action. He began to scramble aft under the moving oars.

"Here, what's the trouble forward?" Captain Sheldon tried to make out the cause of the commotion.

"Wang wants to come aft, sir."

"What for? Shove him into the bottom of the boat."

"He says he must see you, sir."

"Oh, the devil. . . . Well, let him come. He needn't hold up the boat for that."

Many hands helped the old Chinaman aft. Muttering rapidly to himself, he sank into a place beside the captain.

"What's that you say?" demanded Captain Sheldon. "What are you trying to hatch up now?"

Wang made a vague beckoning gesture in the captain's face. Behind all that floated wildly through his mind, stood the fixed thought that he must not shame "Young Cappen" by openly imparting information.

"Are you sick or crazy?" demanded Captain Sheldon again, bending above the maundering old man.

"Cappen, junk he no good!" whispered Wang feverishly. "No can do, Cappen! Must go 'way, chop-chop. Night come soon. Maybe no see."

Captain Sheldon gave a loud laugh. He spoke for all to hear.

"What damned nonsense have you got into your head now?"

"No, sir, Cappen. Look-see!" Wang grasped the other's arm with frantic strength, pulling him down. "You no savvy he, Cappen. Killee quick, no good! You no wanchee he. Go Hong Kong side, chop-chop. Night come, maybe can do. Cappen, my savvy plenty what for!"

"Oh, shut up, you raving old idiot!" cried Captain Sheldon, roughly.

At this inopportune moment the mate, ranging alongside in his boat, offered a suggestion. They were closing in with the junk now; a row of yellow faces peered over the side toward them, watching with narrow bright eyes every movement of the approaching boats.

"Captain Sheldon, I don't like the looks of that

crowd,'' said the mate nervously. "Hadn't we better sheer off, sir?"

"No, certainly not!" shouted the angry captain. "I suppose I'm still in charge here, even if the ship is gone. Do you think I haven't any judgment? By God, between a timid mate and a crazy steward. . . . Give way, boys, there's nothing to be afraid of!"

The breeze by this time had died away, the junk was scarcely moving. A moment later their oars rattled against the side. Captain Sheldon scrambled aboard. He gave a rapid glance along the low maindeck, but saw nothing to arouse his suspicion. A man, evidently the captain of the craft, was advancing toward him; the crew were crowding around to overhear the conversation. But all this was only natural. An ordinary trading junk, of course; heaven alone knew what all these native craft really did. After a moment's scrutiny, he dismissed from his mind any thought that may secretly have been aroused by Wang's warning and the mate's unfortunate remark.

"You makee lose ship—ha?" The captain of the junk accosted him in good pidgin English.

"Yes—she burned this morning. I want you to take me to Hong Kong."

Within half an hour the bargain had been struck, and they were comfortably established on the new deck. The breeze had freshened, the junk's head had been put about, the two ship's boats trailed astern in single file at the end of a long line. The *Retriever's* company had partaken of a Chinese supper; many of them were spending the last hour of daylight in examining the queer craft, passing remarks on her strange nautical points, while the native crew watched their movements with furtive gaze.

Captain Sheldon paced to and fro on the high poop deck, chewing the end of a cigar and ruminating on the unaccountable turns of fortune. The adventure of boarding the junk had for a time broken the savage current of his thoughts; but now, with the affair settled and night closing in, the mood of anger and bitterness claimed him again with redoubled intensity.

The mate ranged up beside him with a friendly air. He felt the need of a reconciliation.

"You'll be interested to hear, Captain, that old Wang has found a pipeful of opium."

"The devil you say! I wondered where the old rascal had disappeared to. How do you know?"

"He's been hanging around the Chinese crew, sir, ever since we came aboard. I went through their quarters down below forward a while ago, and there he lay in one of their bunks, dead to the world, with the pipe across his chest."

"The useless old sot!" exclaimed Captain Sheldon. "I had made up my mind to get rid of him this time, anyway. You know he has been in the family, so to speak. But I don't like the idea of his going off with this native gang. Combined with the opium business, it looks suspicious. You'd better keep an eye on him. He's got a grudge against me, you know, since I took away his stuff."

"I guess they'll all bear watching, sir."

"Oh, nonsense! There isn't the slightest cause for alarm. It's perfectly evident that this craft is a peaceful trader, and we could handle the whole crew of 'em if they commenced to make trouble. They won't, though, never fear; a Chinaman is too big a coward. This captain seems to be quite an intelligent fellow; I've just been having a yarn with him. He has given up his room to me; well, not much of a room, nothing but a bunk and a door, but such as it is, it's all he has. Funny quarters they have down below, like a labyrinth of passages, all leading nowhere.

The mate laughed. "Funny enough forward, too; a damned stinking hole, if you ask me, sir."

While they were talking on the poop, Wang appeared on deck forward, went to the weather rail, and sniffed a deep breath of the land breeze. He had had an hour's opium sleep—an hour of heaven, an hour of life again. Now he could command his faculties. Blindness was no hindrance to work in the dark; was even an advantage, since for many months he had been accustomed to feeling and sensing his way. Fate had been good to him, at the last. Now he possessed the strength to do what he would have to do.

The familiar voices of the mate and the captain came to his ears, but he did not glance in their direction. The least move on his part to give information would have been his last. He had heard enough already to know that the death of the whole ship's company that night was being actively planned, for the sake of the boats and the mysterious tin box that Captain Sheldon carried.

III

In spite of physical exhaustion, it was nearly midnight before Captain Sheldon left the deck and crawled into the narrow den under the poop-deck that had been given up to him by the Chinese captain. He could not get to sleep for a long while. He was taking his loss very hard; that inflexible, proud disposition would almost have met death sooner than admit an error. At length, however, he fell into a light and uneasy slumber.

He was awakened some time later by a faint touch on the arm—a touch that started him from sleep without alarming him into action. A voice whispered softly in his ear:

"Cappen! Cappen! This b'long Wang. No makee speak." A firm hand was laid over his mouth.

In the pitchy darkness of the close room, Captain Sheldon could see absolutely nothing. Listening intently, he heard stealthy movements outside the door. On deck there was utter silence. He became aware instinctively that the junk no longer was moving, that the wind had gone.

He lay perfectly still. The suddenness of the occasion had brought an unaccountable conflict of impulses and emotions. He felt that an alarming crisis was in the air. Along with this feeling came another, strange enough at such a time—a sense of confidence in the old steward. He immediately had recognized the voice in his ear. Why hadn't he jumped out of bed? Why wasn't he lying there in momentary expectation of a knife in the ribs—why didn't he throw himself aside to avoid it? He could not understand his own immobility; yet he remained quiet. Something in the old Chinaman's whisper held him in its command. Pride had succumbed to intrinsic authority.

The rapid whisper began again, panting and insistent.

"Cappen, you come now. Mus' come quick. My savvy how can do. Maybe got time. S'pose stay here, finishee chop-chop." The hand was removed from his mouth, as if conscious that discretion had sufficiently been imposed.

"What has happened, Wang?" whispered the agitated captain.

"Makee kill, all same I know."

"Where's the mate? Where's the crew?"

"All go, Cappen." Again the hand came over his mouth. "You come quick. Bym'by, no can do."

Captain Sheldon flung the steward's arm aside and sat up wildly. "Good God, let me go, Wang! I must go out. . . . "

"Cappen, makee no bobbery."

"Where's my revolver?" The captain was hunting distractedly through the bed.

"He go, too." The whisper took on a despairing tone. "Cappen, s'pose you gotee match?"

"Yes."

"Makee one light."

Captain Sheldon found the box and struck a match. The tiny illumination filled the narrow cabin. As the flame brightened, Wang rolled over on the floor, disclosing one hand held against his left breast, a hand holding a bloody wad of tunic against a hidden wound. A sop of blood on the floor marked the spot where he had been lying.

The match burned out. Again came the painful whisper.

"Maybe can do now. Bym'by, no can do."

"My God, Wang! You're wounded! How can we get out? I'll carry you."

"No, sir, Cappen. My savvy way. You feelee here, Cappen."

The steward already was fumbling with his free hand at a ringbolt in the floor. He guided the captain's arm to it. Captain Sheldon grasped the ringbolt, pulled up a trap-door that seemed to lead into the hold. Letting himself over the edge, his feet found a deck not far below. He stood upright in the opening, and lifted Wang bodily to the lower level. The old Chinaman struggled to be put down.

"Wang, keep still—let me carry you."

"No, sir, Cappen. Walkee-walkee, can do. You no savvy way."

Stooping and keeping an arm half around him, Captain Sheldon followed Wang through a shallow lazaret. It led forward into the open hold. They passed beneath a hatch, where Wang drew aside in the deeper shadow, listening. Not a sound came from overhead. Again they stole forward. The wounded man held on indomitably, bearing his pain in a silence that seemed almost supernatural, as if unknown to the other he had been rendered invulnerable by a magic spell. Beyond the hatch they entered a narrow passage-way, and came out suddenly into the junk's forecastle, the quarters of the

Chinese crew. A ladder led to another open hatch in the deck above.

As they reached the foot of the ladder, a fearful yelling suddenly broke out toward the stern, a sound of savage anger. Naked feet pattered on the deck overhead, going aft. Wang grasped the captain's arm.

"S'pose breakee in door, no findee. One minute have got! Boat stand off, waitee! Go quick, Cappen, jump overboard!"

Captain Sheldon heard him with a shock of incredulity. "The boats are standing off? The crew haven't been killed?

"No, sir, Cappen. All hand savee! You go now."

He felt the old man sag in his arms.

"Wang, I can't leave you here!"

"Why for, Cappen? Wang no good. Quick! Makee jump!"

The voice broke; the frail body crumpled and slipped to the floor.

Gathering all his strength, Captain Sheldon slung the old steward's unconscious form over his shoulder and swarmed up the ladder. As he gained the deck, a tall figure dashed between him and the rail; other figures were racing through the waist of the junk. An angry chatter broke out at the foot of the ladder up which he had just come.

Holding Wang to one side, he struck out heavily at the man who blocked his path, felling him to the deck. Darkness and surprise saved the day for him; their quarry had appeared like a whirlwind in their very midst. The next instant Captain Sheldon had gained the rail, and jumped clear of the junk's side.

The two bodies made a loud splash that echoed through the calmness of the night. As he came to the surface, desperately striking away from the junk and trying to keep Wang's head above water, he heard a shout a little distance off in the darkness, and the rattle of oars as the boats sprang into action.

IV

The longboat was the first to reach him. They pulled him in with his burden still in his arms. The mate, appearing beside them in the other boat, gave vent to his anxiety.

"Good God, Captain Sheldon, I thought you were done for! Why didn't you come, sir? Wang gave me your orders; we hauled up the boats very quietly as you said, and got into them, while he kept the Chinamen busy forward with talk. He said you would come, but we were discovered, and I had to sheer off. I was afraid they'd sink the boats, before we could do anything. I didn't know what weapons they had. I was just planning an attack, sir. Then I thought I saw them stab old Wang. . . ."

"I've got Wang," said Captain Sheldon solemnly. "They did stab him. Those weren't my orders— they were his. And he's the only one to pay the price!" The young captain was beginning to face a harder lesson than the mere loss of a vessel.

"I don't understand, sir. Wasn't it the right thing to do?" The mate was completely puzzled by this new development.

"Yes, yes, it was the right thing to do!" cried

Captain Sheldon impatiently. "He was right, and I was wrong. Now leave me alone."

He bent above the shrunken form of the old steward. Wang's eyelids fluttered; he was slowly regaining consciousness.

"Wang, why didn't you come and tell me, in time to save all this?"

The Chinaman's eyes regarded him with a stare of mingled surprise and affection, a stare that somehow suggested a wise and quiet amusement.

"My tellee you, Cappen. You no savvy. S'pose no savvy, no can do. Mus' wait, makee savvy."

It was a terrible condemnation. Captain Sheldon ground his teeth at the bitter truth of it. His own obstinacy, his own evil! Nothing that Wang could have said, before the thing had happened, would possibly have changed his mind. He had committed himself to error. The old servant had been forced to save them single-handed, to retrieve his master's failure with his own life.

Wang was muttering, as he neared the end. He was about to join "Old Cappen," with a good report and a clean record. No one could have known the depth of the calm that had come to that aged heart. Even the awful pain of the wound had stopped, under the shock of the cool water. He seemed to be drifting off into an eternal opium dream.

"What is it, Wang? Can I do anything for you?"

"No, sir, Cappen. Bym'by, finishee."

He lay quiet for a moment, then plucked at the other's sleeve.

"Old Cappen say, boy step high. Look out!
Maybe more-better stop, look-see."

Captain Sheldon buried his face in his hands. Had
the words come with lesser force, they would have
infuriated him; had the advice been given as advice,
it would have defeated its own ends. But now it
came with the authority of death, sealed with the
final service. It came with the meaning of life, and
could not be denied.

RESCUE AT SEA

WHEN an Arctic blizzard strikes the Atlantic Coast without warning, the coal laden schooner that puts to sea trusting in an uncertain Providence catches it off to the northward of Cape Cod or down along the Jersey shore; and you read in your morning paper how some steamer reached her in the nick of time, and rescued her frozen crew as she was on the point of going down.

But this was not always the way of it; a mechanical age has completely forgotten the day when steam was an innovation on the sea, when sailing ships were the accepted mode of travel and transportation, and when the details of rescue breathed a more romantic story. It was not so many years ago that steamers themselves were heavily rigged, relying to a large extent on their canvas when the wind was favorable. Then the lanes of the sea were crowded with handsome square-rigged sailing vessels; and your morning paper reported more often how sail had lent a hand to steam, than steam to sail.

But let me tell it in the captain's own words.

* * * * * * *

I was coming home that time from Liverpool to New York in the ship *Pactolus,* a medium clipper of the early '70s. A regular run, it was; voyage after voyage I'd been the rounds from New York with general cargo to San Francisco, from San Francisco with wheat to Liverpool, thence home in ballast, less than a year for the complete circuit. A famous course, the course that had called into being the extreme clipper ship, and the one on which her best and most astonishing records had been made.

So we were flying light, in a great hurry to swing across the Western Ocean; for my owners had cabled that the cargo was ready and the ship badly needed. A spell of dirty weather had followed us ever since leaving Liverpool; it had kept me on deck night and day, but I wasn't complaining so long as the wind hung on our tail. At length, however, the easterly spell seemed to have blown itself out, and a change of weather was imminent. Nightfall of the day that brought us abreast the Banks of Newfoundland closed in with threatening signs. I kept the deck till midnight, saw the wind shift into the south'ard, but at last decided that we weren't to catch a blow that night. It was early autumn, a season when storms in the Atlantic aren't always dependable. Soon after the watch was changed I went below, leaving word to be called in case things took a turn.

At four o'clock in the morning, when they changed the watch again, the mate stepped below and rapped at the cabin door. I came out of my bunk all-standing, thinking at once of a shift of weather and trying to feel it in the angle of the deck.

"What's up, Mr. Ridley?" I called. "Is it breezing on from the southeast?"

"No, sir," he answered through the door. "But

there's a strange light on the weather bow, sir, a long way off. I wish you'd come up and have a look at it. I think it must be a ship afire.''

I dressed immediately, and went on deck. Off about three points on the weather bow a big glow lit up the heavens, like an island burning somewhere below the horizon. It was impossible to estimate the distance it was away; but only one thing could cause it, there on the broad Atlantic with no land nearer than five hundred miles. That thing was fire. For it distinctly wasn't a natural phenomenon; all those hard violet rays that characterize electrical disturbances were lacking, and in their place were the warm tones of smoke and flame, reflected brightly in the low-hanging sky.

I hauled the ship up as close to the wind as possible, trimmed the yards carefully, and found that I could just fetch the light of the conflagration by jamming her hard. Before this, we had been running free, with the wind a couple of points abaft the beam. Almost as soon as we brought her to the wind, it began to breeze on in little gusts; the delayed southeaster, I realized, was at last rapping at the door. The skysails were already furled, and under ordinary conditions I would now have taken in the royals; but I kept them set and let her go. She was a smart vessel on the wind; the more sail she carried, up to a certain point, the better she liked it and the higher she would point. She heeled a little harder as she felt the squalls, gave a lift and a lunge, then found her pace and settled to it, heading directly for the lurid glow in the western sky.

Within an hour we were able to make out the tops

of flames above the horizon, and saw that there must
be a big vessel afire. The flames flickered, appearing and vanishing behind the rim of the ocean, as
if the world had caught ablaze and was trying to
touch off the sky. A wild sight, almost supernatural; it sent a chill through our hearts, and the
whole ship's company were terribly excited. I
thought of trying to set the skysails, but my better
judgment prevailed. It wouldn't do to carry away
anything aloft at such a time. In the freshening
breeze the *Pactolus* had all the canvas she wanted,
and was making an excellent run of it, as if she
realized that time might be a matter of life and
death.

The burning ship, when the mate first called me,
must have been about thirty-five miles away. At
half past six we had her well in view. She looked
like an enormous torch dropped on a black and
angry ocean; solid flames mounted hundreds of feet
in air, illuminating a wide arc of the western horizon. Long before we reached her, the fire lighted
our own decks with a wild glare and painted our
sails a hideous red.

At seven o'clock, just as dawn was beginning to
break, we passed a hundred yards to windward of
her, took up a favorable position a short distance
beyond, and swung our main yard. She was a large
three-masted bark-rigged steamer, a passenger
vessel, I saw with increasing alarm. Her main and
mizzen masts already had been burned away, the
middle section of her hull was red-hot like a stove,
and the sheet of solid flame that we'd been watching
for hours rose above her with a steady appalling

roar, as if a great bellows were blowing under her keel.

It had been apparent to us from the first that nobody could be left aboard—nobody left alive, that is. I felt certain, however, that if they had managed to get away in the boats, they'd be clinging to the vicinity of the disaster, in the knowledge that she would attract everything afloat through a radius of fifty miles or more. Almost immediately, this notion was confirmed; we sighted a bright light on the water just astern of the steamer, then another, and in a few minutes three flare-ups were burning in as many boats and as many directions. Nothing for us to do but keep our mainyard aback and let them row to us. Thus fifteen or twenty minutes passed, while I was on tenterhooks over the ship's situation.

At length, after a desperate struggle, they dragged one by one under our lee. The mate had charge of getting the people aboard. Men in the main channels passed a bow and stern line to each boat, others fended them off with boat-hooks, still others helped the castaways over the rail. It was a lucky chance that we reached them when we did; the three boats were badly overloaded, half full of water, the wind by this time was breezing on sharply, and the sea making up minute by minute. They wouldn't have been able to keep themselves afloat another hour.

The captain's boat was the first to come alongside. I saw them pass up a woman with a year-old baby, then an invalid man. Next came another woman, who proved to be the stewardess of the steamer; she was carrying a heavy parcel done up in a tablecloth, that rattled and jangled like a bag

of doubloons. In an overloaded boat, in half a gale
of wind, she had salvaged the ship's tableware!
The rest of the crowd were indiscriminate; except
for the women, of whom there weren't many, I
couldn't tell passengers from crew. As I stood
watching at the break of the poop, a man with a
long beard and a blanket wrapped around him came
up to me. He seemed half dazed; he was carrying
in his hand a small hatchet, the blade stained with
blood.

"What the devil are you doing with that thing?"
I demanded.

"I killed the ox, sir," he answered wildly—it
came over me in a flash that he must be the cook.
"I couldn't leave him there to burn."

The captain was the last man from that boat to
come over the side. I shook his hand, but had no
time just then for conversation; a fact which he
recognized at a glance, drawing a little way aft along
the weather alley and leaving me alone. For everything had to be done at once, you know; these people saved, and my own ship looked after. We were
in a ticklish position. With main yard aback, and
every squall heavier than the last, we might easily
get stern-way on—and that would never do. I felt
pretty confident of my gear aloft, but if anything
carried away to hinder the handling of the sails, we
would find ourselves in a pretty kettle of fish.
Above all, I kept a sharp eye on the relative position of the burning steamer. Aback as we were,
with so much canvas spread, we must, I thought, be
drifting steadily down toward her; and it would be
the end of us to run afoul of that inferno, or even

to fall to leeward of her. Watching closely, I soon
made out that we held our distance from the craft,
or rather, that she held her distance from us; incredible as it seemed, she was drifting as fast as we were.
I turned to her captain, calling his attention to this
mystery.

"Yes, I noticed it," he said. "It seems to me that
the sheet of flame must in some way be acting like
an enormous sail. I can think of no other explanation."

Neither could I—and I believe that he was right.
She had been bark-rigged, as I said, and the fore-
mast with its heavy yards, still standing, kept her
head three or four points off the wind, so that she
lay in the position of running free; her sides, too,
were high, caught a lot of wind, and gave her headway. But the sheet of flame must have helped her
progress. For here we were with a ship flying light,
and sufficient canvas spread to drive us to leeward
at a rate of three or four knots an hour, even with
the main yard holding her dead.

Too much canvas, in fact; the wind had begun to
come with a new weight and no time afforded for
proper seamanship. No time. We had taken in the
royals before we reached the steamer; had clewed
them up, but been obliged to leave them hanging,
we'd ranged past her so rapidly. As we backed the
main yard, we had let all three of the topgallant
yards run down, and hauled down the flying jib. All
these light sails were threshing and pounding aloft,
while the men who should have furled them were
busy saving life in the lee channels; the jib was slatting itself to pieces on the end of the jibboom. At

that very moment, under ordinary conditions, we would have been housed down under reefed upper topsails.

The captain of the steamer had been waiting for me to find a free moment. Now he pulled up beside me.

"My name is Potter, Captain Clark," he said. "I just heard your mate call you by name. It's needless to say anything, sir, about what you are doing for us."

"Yes," I answered, "save that for the coffee. We haven't got through the soup yet."

He gave a short laugh. "Speaking of grub, Captain, how about fresh water? We haven't much in the boats, and we're adding a good many to your ship's company."

"I've water enough to last a hundred men for a month," I told him. "Water enough for washing, and all purposes." The iron tank below the main-deck, five thousand gallons, had just been filled in Liverpool.

He looked at me a little incredulously. "Thank God!" he said. "I've been worrying about that ever since I came aboard. Your American ships go well provided for."

The third boat had then come alongside. "Is this your whole outfit, Captain Potter?" I asked.

"Good God, no!" he cried. "There's another boat somewhere—if it hasn't gone down."

"We sighted only three. But we'll find it for you, all in due time," I reassured him.

"It's the second mate's boat," he said. "The poor fellow was half blind from fighting the fire, but he insisted that he could take charge of a boat. He couldn't have lost her—he was no more heavily loaded than we were. I expect he's been left somewhere to windward, Captain; we have drifted away from him. You'd hardly believe it, but we had tough work, rowing our strongest, to keep up with the drift of the vessel. My orders were to keep her in company as long as she burned."

"Well, if your second mate is to windward, we may have difficulty in reaching him," I pointed out. "You see how it is, sir; this will be a living gale inside of an hour. But we will do everything possible. Wait till it grows a little lighter. In the meantime, what about these boats of yours?"

"I'm done with them, Captain," he answered. "You can do what you like."

There were two big steel lifeboats, and a smaller Whitehall boat. "I'll swing the lifeboats aboard, then, and let the other go," I said. "We may have a fire of our own before we reach New York; and my boats would barely accommodate my own ship's company. Mr. Ridley, rig a preventor lift on the lee main yard-arm, and hoist those two big boats aboard."

My mate, I'm sorry to say, had lost his head in the excitement and confusion. A fine old man, an excellent seaman, came from down Deer Island way; but he had outlived his usefulness, as many of us do. He was running fore and aft the ship, accomplishing nothing, and chiefly whining about his sails being slat to pieces.

Just as I gave the order to hoist in the boats, the third group of castaways, in charge of the steamer's boatswain, were coming over the rail. These men were mostly from the forecastle; for she had been heavily sparred, crossed a couple of royal yards, and carried fourteen men before the mast to handle her sails. The boatswain was an impudent little Londoner, every inch a sailor, and one of your old-fashioned chanty-men. He caught my eye from the maindeck, and whipped out his whistle.

"Shall I tyke the order, Captain?" he roared through the dim.

"Go ahead!" I told him, waving my hand. Old Ridley hadn't heard me, anyway.

"Aloft there, men!" cried the boatswain with a swagger, giving a long blow on his whistle. "Here's a bloomin' deck under yer feet again, an' Di-vy Jones'll wyt a while longer. D'ye hear the Old Man's orders? Preventor lifts on the lee main yard-arm, there, and hoist in the bloomin' boats. Lively now, lend a hand, my lads, an' show 'em what ye knows."

They sprang up the ratlines like monkeys; heaven knows, a tarry rope must have felt good in their hands again! In a jiffy they had rigged the lift, and got a sling under the first boat. A few moments later, as the boat rose slowly across the rail, I heard the little Cockney's voice aloft, raised in a hauling chanty:

> "Oh, Bony was a war-ri-or,
>   A-*way!* Ay-*yah!*
> A war-ri-or, a ter-ri-or,
>   Jean Fran-*swar!*"

His men came in loudly on the chorus; their voices

gave me a turn, to think of the vicissitudes of fortune. For they had been snatched from certain
death, and they knew it well. As it happened,
that tall fire in mid-ocean was not reported by anyone else; we were the only ship in all those waters
to sight and come up with it. And in less than an
hour after we had taken the last man aboard, we
were stripped to three lower topsails, hove-to in a
howling gale.

Full daylight had come while they were hoisting
in the boats. We still lay with the main yard aback,
to windward of the burning steamer; forty minutes,
perhaps, had passed since we'd come into the wind.
In a few minutes more we would be ready to get
under way—and no sign yet of the fourth boat with
her load of frightened humanity.

I caught a young scamp running by, a boy from
home that I'd had for the round voyage. "Here,
you young rascal, jump aloft and see if you can pick
up another boat anywhere," I said. "She's likely
to be to windward. Hustle, now! You've been
nothing but trouble all the voyage; now earn your
salt." I knew that he had the sharpest pair of
eyes aboard.

He was up the mainmast in a flash, slipped past
the slatting topgallant-sail, and reached the skysail
yard. In a few minutes he sang out:

"I see a boat to leeward, sir!"

"Where away?"

"Just abeam, beyond the steamer."

I feared that his imagination had run away with
him, so sent the second mate into the mizzen cross-
trees with a pair of binoculars. He reported a boat

sure enough to leeward—a boat with a tiny sail set.

"That accounts for it!" exclaimed Captain Potter. "I forgot that leg-o'-mutton sail in the second mate's boat. But why has he used it, to run away from the steamer, when I ordered him to stand by her?"

"I'm afraid it means that he is hard pressed," I answered. "He's had to run for it, in order to keep afloat. We must fill away at once. I hope we can manage to reach him in time."

While we were swinging the main yard, Captain Potter stood on the after house, alone beside the mizzen mast, watching his burning vessel. She was a splendid steamer, only a few years old. He watched her soberly. I left him to himself. After we had got the *Pactolus* off before the wind, with things around decks a little under control, he said good-bye to his command, as it were, turned aft, and took his place beside me on the quarter-deck.

"Can you make out the boat yet from the deck?" he asked.

"She's dead ahead. They have seen her from the forecastle."

We looked aloft. Yards were groaning, gear was cracking; under full upper-topsails the ship swept down the wind like a racehorse, fairly leaping through the water. She must have been a splendid sight to those poor fellows in the second mate's boat, waiting for her at the door of death.

"You have a fine ship, sir," said Captain Potter. "I've never seen a ship handled so smartly, in such a breeze and under so much sail. You must avail yourself of any help that my crew can give you. My officers are thorough seamen, brought up under sail."

"Thank you, sir—I see that they are," I answered. "But after we have things straightened around once more, I think we won't need any assistance." My pride was up, you know, now that the affair was beginning to turn out so well. She was a British steamer, and these officers, fine young Englishmen of the best breed, ambitious and well-trained in the school of sailing ships, were watching me and my vessel with a critical eye. I'd show them what it meant to be picked up by a Yankee clipper.

"I make this passage every year, Captain," I went on, "and always carry extra men for it. After leaving my wheat in Liverpool, I have to get back to New York in the quickest possible time, to load again for California. It's much like your steamer with her schedule. With extra men I'm able to carry on sail a little longer, handle her in ordinary weather with one watch, and save the wear and tear on the crew. The wear and tear come mostly on me. I'll have your crew to fall back on now, and will be able to hold my sail still longer. A sort of reserve force, you know, ready to jump in an emergency."

He glanced over the stern-rail, where the steamer lay blazing in our wake. In falling off we had swung a wide circle around her, to escape the path of the sparks as they whirled down the wind; and now had left her a couple of miles astern.

"She burns well, Captain," I observed. "That's the hottest fire I ever felt, or ever want to feel."

He gave a bitter laugh. "They loaded her especially for it," he said. "Cotton goods, and butter, and bacon, and hams.'' As if not caring to look at her any longer, he turned forward, mounted the steps to the top of the house, and took up his old position by the mizzen mast.

In twenty minutes after filling away, we had reached the second mate's boat. A look through the binoculars showed me that things indeed were in a bad way with them; there wasn't a moment to lose. The boat seemed momentarily on the point of filling, while half a dozen men along her sides bailed frantically with buckets and other utensils. A man in the stern sheets was waving wildly at us, as if to communicate some information. I had a notion what it was; they were trying to tell us that they wouldn't be able to bring the boat into the wind. I saw that plainly. Captain Potter, coming hurriedly to the after end of the house, evidently saw it, too.

''How will you pick them up, Captain?'' he asked nervously.

''I think we can do it without difficulty,'' I answered, as if such measures were a matter of course. In point of fact, I had never executed the maneuver that seemed necessary in this pass, and had never heard of its being tried by anyone else. As we approached the boat, I hauled the ship well out on their starboard quarter, passed them several hundred yards to port and left them a quarter of a mile astern; then swung the ship across their course, came up to leeward of them with a shock and a crash, backed the main yard, lost headway, and stopped in exactly the right position for them to fetch our stern as they ran before the wind. In other words, I cut a half circle around them and placed myself athwart their hawse, in the way of an old-fashioned naval maneuver.

We looked down on them from the quarter-deck as they raced toward us. Several men seemed disabled, water was washing nearly up to her thwarts, but a few oars were poised in readiness, showing intelligence and discipline somewhere aboard. In a moment she was on the point of our weather quarter, sweeping past our stern.

"Round the stern!" shouted Captain Potter and I together. "Get under the lee, and jump for the main channels!"

But they already had seized their last and only opportunity. A smooth patch on the water favored them; they made the turn nicely, let go their sail, and succeeded in paddling up under our quarter.

"Jump while it's smooth!" I cried. "Let the boat go."

My crew by this time had become expert channelsmen. One of them caught the painter, others used their boathooks; and the last load of castaways from the steamer tumbled over the side, more dead than alive, but alive enough to know that they'd been saved. The painter was cast off, the boat drifted clear of the quarter, filled, overturned, and was whirled away on top of a breaking sea. Safely on our decks, watching this symbol of elemental destruction, stood every soul of the steamer's company.

"I must congratulate you again!" said Captain Potter heartily. "That was a feat of seamanship, sir. You seem to be able to put your ship through the eye of a needle."

"She handles nicely, doesn't she?" I agreed. As

a matter of fact, I felt like congratulating myself; I won't deny that I had a feeling of pride, as well as a prayer of thankfulness for our universal good luck. Things had gone without a hitch, at a time when a hitch might easily have called for payment in human life.

So here we were, with sixty people landed suddenly on our decks; with whole topsails set, and a gale of wind turned loose upon us. I'd been obliged to abandon the upper sails, while we were saving the first three boatloads; they had slat themselves to shreds before we could find time to furl them. The chief thing now was to get the upper topsails in. I made up my mind that we would shorten sail with our own crew. The crowd from the steamer were completely fagged out; they had been fighting fire and the Atlantic for twenty-four hours. I told them to go below, in the after cabin or the forward house, anywhere, have a smoke, and rest wherever they could find a chance to lie down; and instructed my steward to pass around a supply of dry tobacco.

When they had faded away and the decks were cleared for action, Captain Potter approached me again. "I hardly dare to ask about provisions," he began. "I'm sorry to tell you that we brought very little. The fire cleaned out our galley and storerooms first of all, and we were barely able to save a meal or two of biscuits and canned grub."

I thought a minute, making a rough estimate. "We can furnish provisions to go with the water, Captain," I told him.

"What!—without allowance?" he cried.

"Without allowance," I said. "I never liked the idea of putting people on an allowance; it's too much like starving yourself by degrees. I can guarantee you provisions to last us for a month or six weeks, three good meals a day; and we can't in common fortune be out that long. The best of provisions, I think you'll find."

"How does it happen, sir?" he demanded.

"It doesn't happen. We're always prepared for just such an emergency. More than once I've met a ship short of provisions, and furnished him with a boatload or two. You can't anticipate what is liable to turn up; but a lazaret full of beef and flour and potatoes fills in almost anywhere."

He shook his head in amazement. "I've often heard it said that American ships were remarkably well-found," he observed. "But I wouldn't have believed a yarn like this from my best friend. Let's see, we've brought you three times your ordinary ship's company; and you have provisions and water for all hands to last longer than twice your usual run to New York. Are you positive, sir?"

"Positive. Give yourself no further worry on that score."

"Back there in the boats," said Captain Potter, "I was thinking that, if God was good to us, we might be picked up by some Slavonian bark, with only macaroni enough aboard to take him to the Banks of Newfoundland, where he'd depend on catching a few codfish, and water or not according as it rained. Then it would have been a case of Halifax or St. Johns, or else a transfer in open boats to another vessel, with more danger to my passengers and crew. This, Captain, seems like a pleasant dream.''

There was no necessity for telling him how it really did happen. In the line for which I was sailing, a captain had the fitting out of his own vessel, and was given practically a free hand. I'd found that there were many things which I could buy cheaper and better in Liverpool; and I always laid in a supply of these for the round trip. Things like hams, and bacon, and tobacco; yes, tobacco, the best American plug at a shilling a pound, the same article that I would have had to pay fifty cents for in New York. At Liverpool, too, we could get the finest French and Irish potatoes; though they wouldn't keep for the round trip, I used to lay in enough to last me to New York and down to the Line on the outward passage. We had a ton and a half of potatoes on board that trip, when we sailed from Liverpool; we reached New York with half a ton of them left, so you can judge how short of provisions we were. Then there were certain things, especially flour, and canned fruits, vegetables and preserves of all kinds, which I could buy cheapest and best in San Francisco; I'd supplied the ship there with these articles for the round trip, and a good half of the stock still remained. Butter—we had barrels of it. In fact, we actually could have fed all hands of them for two or three months without allowance; but I didn't want to spoil the effect by overdoing it. I let them continue to think that this was the accepted fashion on board of an American ship crossing the Western Ocean.

That afternoon, when the *Pactolus* was at last

shortened down, the empty bolt-ropes unbent from the upper yards, and the decks cleared for heavy weather, the question of accommodations had to be disposed of. We started with the after cabin; the woman with her baby had one spare stateroom, the invalid man another. To Captain Potter I assigned a third spare stateroom, so that he could be by himself. My own room, with double bunk, sofa, and mattresses on the floor, I gave up to the rest of the women passengers; the stewardess slept on the sofa in the after cabin, and generally looked after the ladies' quarters.

This accounted for all the spare staterooms we had. For myself, I took the upper bunk in the mate's room, at the same time moving the second mate to this room, where he and the mate, having alternate watches, could share the same bunk. This left the second mate's room free for the accommodation of the steamer's three deck officers, with two single bunks and a knock-down of pillows and blankets on the floor. In the steward's room there also were two berths; my steward kept the lower, the first steward of the steamer had the upper, and her second steward another knock-down on the floor.

In the forward house there were the galley, carpenter's shop, and sail room, all narrow rooms running from side to side of the house, each with two doors and two windows; forward of the sail room were the two forecastles, separated from each other by a fore-and-aft partition in the middle of the house, and opening forward on either side of the fore hatch. I moved all of my crew into one forecastle, since only one watch would be sleeping at a

time; and put the steamer's crew into the vacated
one, where bunks and bed clothes were ready for
them to use. The engine room crowd were assigned
to the carpenter's shop; the rest of the men-
folk, a miscellaneous lot, first, second, and third
class passengers all together, were given the sail
room.

We had on board quantities of second-hand bur-
lap and old sails, rolls and rolls of them, to be put
down under the cargo of wheat, enough to line the
whole inside of the ship when she was loaded; these
were rolled up in the 'tween-decks after we discharged at Liverpool, to be overhauled and repaired
on the passage across to New York, before being
stowed away for use again in San Francisco. They
were just what we needed for beds and coverings.
In the two narrow rooms in the forward house,
spread plenty thick on the floors, they made the finest possible knock-downs; although they were packed
in pretty tight, the men couldn't have been more
comfortable in their own berths.

Captain Potter wanted me to put them below the
hatches. We were ballasted with salt in the lower
hold, but the 'tween-decks were clean and empty;
she was in splendid trim for sailing, dry as a bone
in heavy weather. Undoubtedly, the 'tween-decks
would have made a comfortable place for the men,
with plenty of room all around. But my objection
was a perfectly practical one. Every one of these
men had saved his pipe; in many cases it seemed
to be about all that he had saved. Pipes had been
going in every mouth since they'd come aboard.
And the sight of that burning steamer was seared

into my brain. It gave me the shivers merely to think
of sending all those pipes to sit on a bed of sail-
cloth below hatches. Some kind of a fire was
only to be expected; but a fire in the forward house
would be the lesser of two evils.

With all my care, I made a serious mistake in
these arrangements; a mistake due to my ignorance
of steamship etiquette. I assigned the chief engineer to a place forward with the engine-room crowd,
and paid him no further attention. The status of
engineers wasn't in my category; I thought of them,
when I thought of them at all, as belonging to some
indefinite lower region, and lumped them all together. But I was careful to make the proper dis-
tinction with the deck officers, for this was a matter
within my own province.

Captain Potter gave me a broad hint that afternoon. "My chief engineer is a fine man, sir," he
said. "There never has been friction between us.
He is highly thought of by the office."

I received the news as something in the way of
conversation; wasn't much interested just then in
the affairs of his vessel. What did I know of steamers? I'd been brought up under sail; and a steamer
to me was nothing but a new-fangled usurper of the
ocean, a thing to be sneered at, and to be outsailed
when possible. It wasn't till some years afterward,
I remember, that I learned by accident that the
chief engineer of a steamer was next in position to
her master, over all the deck officers. The knowledge was a shock to me; I recalled Captain Potter's
remark, realized what I'd done, and saw how nice
they had been about it. Even today, it annoys me

to think of the error, and of the comment it must have caused.

We lived like kings; I gave free access to the provisions, fore and aft. The first steward of the steamer said: "I'll wait on the table." Our forward cabin table, hauled out to its full length, would seat fourteen people; he had to set it up three times for each meal, for all the passengers ate aft. The second steward said: "I'll wash dishes." So he stood all day in the pantry, digging away at an endless job; for of course there weren't dishes enough to go around three whacks. The cook joined my cook and steward in the galley forward; amongst them they kept us fed. Made up a barrel of flour into bread every day, for one item. By chance, I overheard the steamer's first officer say one evening after supper, that her fare at its best hadn't equalled ours.

They were frank in admiration of the ship; of her equipment, her sailing qualities, her cleverness, dryness, and general seaworthiness; I could see that they were a little envious, too, of the way we handled her. We had a crew of Liverpool toughs, hard men, but experienced sailors, bred to American ships and their ways. They had caught the spirit of the game, filled the steamer's crew full of tall yarns in the dog-watch, and performed feats of seamanship for them on deck whenever the opportunity offered. Once the excitement of that first day was over, old Ridley's superb knowledge of his position emerged again. My second officer was one of your tall, fiery down-east youths, twenty-one years old, smart as a steel trap and able as a whirlwind.

We put the *Pactolus* through her paces, I can
assure you; carried sail till all was blue. Luck sent
us strong and favorable winds. In the dead of night
I often would see the steamer's officers, dressed and
wandering around the decks, or gathered in a group
and holding low conversation; the ship would be
scuppers under, the deck at a dangerous angle, masts
and yards buckling and groaning, a spread of motionless canvas rising aloft as hard as a board; the
whole hull humming like a top, as she raced through
the water at a fourteen-knot clip. It made them
nervous; they wanted to give me their advice, but
being young and proud, they wouldn't do it. I suppose they called me a reckless Yankee. But I knew
my ship and trusted in my gear, knew exactly what
I could do with them; and didn't carry away so
much as a rope-yarn throughout the passage.

Only once did I have to call on our visitors for
help. Closing in with Nantucket, we had run full-
tilt into another southerly blow. It wasn't more
than half a gale, and I had kept her running under
a heavy press of canvas. After twelve hours had
gone by, I knew that soon the wind would jump into
the westward in a flurry, as all southeasters do in
the end. Feeling secure, with extra men to draw
on in case I got caught aback, I held my sail and
course till the last gun was fired. We were running
with the wind on the port beam, under three whole
topsails, whole mainsail and foresail, spanker, mizzen, main and foretopmast staysails, and inner jib.

And before I knew it, I really had got caught.
The wind jumped without warning, jumped quick
and hard; one minute it was our old half-gale from

the southward, the next minute it was a howling
westerly squall. Before we possibly could pay off
to the northward, the ship was flat aback. Then it
was, "All hands on deck to shorten sail!" with a
vengeance, the vessel lying down to port, the masts
cracking, the shrouds slackening with an ominous
sag, and things in general looking badly for a while.
The officers of the steamer ran on deck feather
white, feeling the ship go over to windward; her
first mate ranged up close beside me, and kept glancing back and forth from my face to the masts, as
if he expected them to go over the side any minute
and wanted to watch me when they fell.

As soon as I'd seen that we were caught aback,
I had let the three upper topsails come down with
a run. My crew were aloft now on fore, main and
mizzen, furling these sails, which I couldn't afford
to lose. Neither could I afford to lose the mainsail
or to break the main yard; but at that moment there
were no men to spare from the topsails, where the
second mate was working like a demon; while old
Ridley had all that he could do on deck, letting go
gear and attending to the three topsail yards. With
every fresh puff of westerly wind, I saw the main
yard bending like a bow; it was a big spar, over
ninety feet long. The mainsail was a new piece of
canvas, and probably would hold; but the tack or
the weather brace might carry away under the un-
equal strain, and then the yard was gone.

"You can blow your whistle, sir," I said to the
young officer who had been watching me so closely—
they all carried whistles in their pockets, to call
their men with. "Take charge of that mainsail, if

you please, and get it off her as quickly as you can.''

He needed no second invitation; was off in a flash, blowing a loud toot as he ran forward. I heard the call answered by another whistle in the waist; that little Cockney boatswain had been getting anxious, too. Out came the steamer's crew with a rush from their side of the forward house, where they'd fallen into the habit of loafing regardless of what went on outside. Clew-garnets and buntlines were manned with seamanlike precision, the tack was started, the sheet was eased away, and in a remarkably short time they had smothered the big sail and hauled it up to the yard.

But they didn't intend to leave the job half finished. "Aloft, boys, and out on the yard!" cried the mate. A moment later he sprang up the ratlines himself, to superintend the job; the little Cockney took the weather yardarm, piping a song as he perched above the water; they furled the sail smartly, reaching the deck along with our own men from the topsail yard.

Captain Potter, who had come on deck in the interval, was watching his men with manifest pride. I was glad that it happened so, and took especial pains to compliment the chief officer before all hands. He blushed like a school girl, now that the emergency was over. The little Cockney, however, couldn't resist a stroke of impudence.

"We thanks ye, Captain," he sung out loudly. "That's the w'y we does it aboard of a bloomin' lime-juicer."

The sally brought a roar from the whole main-deck, in which I'd have been a stick if I hadn't joined.

"What do you do with such saucy rascals?" I called to Captain Potter. "Shall I keel-haul him, or serve him an extra pint of grog?"

"Myke it a pint o' grog all around, Ol' Bo-ri-i," giggled the boatswain, dodging around the mast.

"I would if I could, my men," I laughed. "But as you know, we have no grog or lime-juice in a Yankee ship. Beef and biscuit, work and wages, is what we sail on. You need no grog, if that's a sample of the way you feel." And I pointed aloft to the neatly furled mainsail.

With stern way on, we had by this time hauled out to port, braced the yards sharp up, and caught the wind in the foresail and three lower topsails. Our visitors perhaps had saved us from a serious accident; at any rate, they'd demonstrated their ability. It gave them something to brag about on their own account; while the effect on my crew was only to intensify the spirit of rivalry. In fact, the incident brought a great improvement to the tone of the ship; for I had noticed during the last couple of days a growing animosity between the steamer's forecastle and ours, due to the forced inactivity of the former.

On the following day the westerly breeze blew itself out; in the early afternoon a steamer overhauled us, bound in for New York, passing about four miles to windward. We then were off to the southward of Nantucket, having come about on the starboard tack during the night. I set a string of signals: "Come closer. Have important news to communicate." The steamer made them out, changed her course, and ran down within hailing distance. She was a German vessel, one of the first oil-tankers to cross the Atlantic, they told me in New York; her name was the *Energie*. Her captain couldn't speak English fluently; but he had picked up a New York pilot somewhere on the Banks, a man who'd been carried to sea by another vessel in a storm. He was the fellow who talked to me from the bridge, although I didn't know it at the time.

"Steamer ahoy!" I hailed. "The British steamer *Santiago* has burned at sea. I have on board her entire ship's company, and am taking them to New York. No one was lost, either passengers or crew. Please report us all well."

They held a consultation over this news on the bridge of the *Energie*. Soon I was hailed in a familiar South Street twang.

"Captain, don't you want to be relieved of your guests? You must be short of provisions."

I heard Captain Potter chuckle behind me.

"There's your chance to get to New York ahead of us," I said, turning to him. It was a smooth day on the water, with little prospect of wind.

"Do you want to be rid of us, Captain?" he asked.

"No, sir," I said emphatically.

"Then we'll stay aboard, if you don't mind, and reach New York when you do."

I hailed the steamer again. "We need no assistance, thank you. Please report us all well, and inform the steamship company."

The *Energie* went on about her business, and soon passed out of sight ahead. Late in the afternoon a

fresh breeze sprang up unexpectedly from a little to
the eastward of north; a breeze that was destined
to carry us all the way to harbor. We braced the
yards around to starboard, set every rag of sail, and
laid a course for Sandy Hook with the wind a couple
of points free on the starboard quarter.

Throughout the next day we were running along
the southern shore of Long Island, in smooth water,
the breeze still fresh and steady, every stitch of
canvas drawing, and the ship at her best point for
sailing, logging some fifteen knots an hour. The
days of the extreme clipper ship had long since gone
by, at the time I'm telling of; but many a medium
clipper of the later years, with fuller cargo-carrying
capacity, but retaining many of the fine lines of the
greyhound of the seas, and embodying all the best of
their experience, could reel off a day's run that
might astonish the nautical historian. I'll never
forget that wonderful reach in the *Pactolus* under
the lee of the Long Island shore. She was a trim
and lofty vessel, lean and graceful on the water; a
cloud of canvas aloft, she heeled at a constant angle,
as if moving through a picture, while the long curl
of a wave rolled out steadily from her lee quarter,
as she swept like a bird over the smooth sea.

At three in the afternoon, a steamer was reported
dead ahead, some ten or a dozen miles away. Within
a half hour, it was apparent that we were crawling
up on her; and in an hour's time, we could estimate
that we had overhauled her by something like five
miles. I had a strong suspicion that she was our
old friend, the *Energie,* but said nothing about it
just then. Every one aboard was excited over the

race, the *Santiago's* company no less so than my
own. In fact, the young British officers could hardly
contain themselves, wouldn't for anything have seen
us fail to overtake her, kept running to me and sug-
gesting this and that, or asking if the wind would
hold.

Another hour of this terrific sailing brought us
near enough to read her name. And she was the
Energie, sure enough. I thought that handsome
young first officer of the *Santiago* was going to fling
his arms around me, when I took my eye from the
long glass and told them the news.

"Hurrah for the *Pactolus!*" he shouted, running
forward and waving both his hands. "By Gad, they
won't have the chance to report us this time! We'll
do our own reporting."

"She must be foul—although these freighters
don't pretend to any speed," observed Captain Potter, a little concerned, I thought, for the reputation
of steam.

"She's making about ten knots," I said. "And
we are logging fifteen steady, and sixteen by spurts,
when the breeze puffs a little."

"You don't tell me!" he exclaimed, glancing over
the side. Then he looked up at the clumsy old
steamer, plowing along a quarter of a mile to leeward. "By Jove, Captain, we're passing her as if
she were standing still!"

Indeed, we were; the spectacle, from a romantic
point of view, was an inspiring one, although it must
have been a jealous sight for the German captain.
But now we were drawing in toward the approaches
of New York harbor; our race had been with day-

light as well as with steam. For I'd promised myself that, by hook or crook, we would arrive that
night. I scanned the horizon anxiously for a pilot
boat—in those days the New York pilot boats
were small but exceptionally sea-worthy two-masted
schooners; and at seven o'clock in the evening,
with half an hour of daylight still remaining,
caught sight of one standing toward us on the
weather bow. We came together rapidly. By
this time we had left the *Energie* a couple of miles
astern.

When the pilot boat was within a mile of us, I
called Mr. Ridley and the mate of the *Santiago,* and
had a private conference with them; gave them instructions to place all hands in position for certain
maneuvers, but to keep the men out of sight behind
the bulwarks. Stepping to the after companion-
way, I sung out below: "Captain Potter, ask the
ladies to come on deck and see us take the pilot on
board." They hurried up in a flutter of excitement,
the captain in their wake. A glance along the main-
deck told him that something unusual was about to
transpire, but he held his own counsel. It's hard to
educate a taciturn Britisher to new ways, yet the
constant surprise of the experience through which
Captain Potter was passing had begun to make an
impression.

The pilot boat now was running down to us on the
opposite tack, about four points on our weather bow.
She expected us, of course, to heave-to and wait for
her. We kept on, however, at a racing clip, making
not the slightest move to check our terrific progress.
To add zest to the game, the wind puffed substan-

tially at that moment, sending us through the water with a rush really magnificent.

I could see that, on board the pilot boat, they didn't know what to make of it. As we drew up on them, changing the angle of their bearing, they shifted their course little by little, letting their craft fall off before the wind and following us with her nose. In another moment she stood directly abeam of us, less than three hundred yards away. With a gesture of dismissal, as it were, they hauled the schooner up again on the port tack, prepared to stand away to sea and leave us to our own devices.

At that instant, I waved my hand, and gave a sharp order to the helmsman. The men jumped from their concealment under the bulwarks; up went the courses like a piece of magic, down went the helm, and ship and main yard swung together, as if both controlled by a single turn of the wheel. The *Pactolus* came into the wind with a bird-like swoop, felt the main yard aback, checked her pace, and stopped dead in her tracks; there she lay, nodding sweetly to the slight swell, the last rays of the setting sun striking through her sails.

A shout went up from the pilot boat. They fell off immediately, jibed to the port tack, crossed our stern waving their hands, and dropped their skiff overboard. In a few moments the pilot nosed up under our lee quarter.

"Good Lord, Captain!" he cried, as he came over the rail. "What are you running here, a packet ship? I haven't seen a trick like that turned since the days of the Black Ball Line."

"I'm in a hurry to get in," I answered, "and I

don't want to waste time over it. I have a double crew aboard to help me. This is Captain Potter, pilot, of the British steamship *Santiago,* burned at sea.''

Later that evening we took a towboat off the lightship, and clewed up our sails. I thought I'd be extravagant and have a second tug, since I saw another coming toward us; the wind had suddenly shifted into the northwest, dead ahead, and every one was anxious to get in. A hard enough tow it turned out, even with two boats ahead, for the wind soon settled down in earnest for an old-fashioned off-shore gale. I told our passengers to go to bed as usual; that all was safe now, and they would wake up next morning to find the ship at anchor.

At three o'clock in the morning we came to off the Statue of Liberty, and dropped a hook into the bottom. They had passed us through quarantine under extraordinary dispensation, meanwhile sending word of the disaster and its happy outcome up the bay ahead of us. At daylight, the *Santiago's* company hurried their biggest tugboat alongside, stocked with emergency provision, if you please, for they expected us to be half starved. Captain Potter met the representative of his company at the rail; when they had talked for a while in private, I broke in on them.

''Captain,'' I said, ''it would give us the greatest pleasure if you and your ship's company would stay on board and have a last breakfast with us. Permit me to extend the invitation to this gentleman. Tell your tug to wait for you alongside until we're through.''

"Thank you, sir—we'll do it," he answered heartily. "Mr. Folsom, this is my good friend Captain Clark. He has treated us to a reception aboard the *Pactolus* unique in the annals of the Atlantic, as you'll be able to see for yourself when you go below. I'll promise you as good a breakfast as you would find ashore."

So the tugboat with her emergency provisions waited, while we enjoyed a hearty breakfast. I finished as soon as possible, however, and said goodbye to my guests; for a tugboat from my owners had come alongside in the meanwhile, and I was in a hurry to get ashore. Reaching the deck with my papers, I found the German tanker *Energie* churning past us, bound somewhere up the East River. She already had been discovered from our forecastle; all hands lined the bulwarks forward, laughing and jeering, waving their caps at her.

At my appearance on the quarter-deck, a group of three men, led by the Cockney boatswain of the *Santiago*, detached themselves from the others forward and met me at the break of the poop.

"Committee from the crew o' the *Santiago*, sir," announced the boatswain. "We has to inform you, sir, that we votes your ship is a beauty, your officers is gentlemen, and yourself is a man we'd like to sail with whenever you're looking for a crew. You've treated us like kings, sir—and we're the boys as knows when we're well treated. We thanks ye, sir, from the bottom of our hearts."

I was taken aback for a minute, not being a ready speechmaker. "Well, boys," I said at last, blinking back a tear of emotion, "it's been a pleasure to me to be able to make you comfortable. I can only answer you in the same words, in a way we all understand: if I needed a crew, I'd rather have you in the forecastle than any crowd I ever saw. You have handled yourselves like seamen under trying circumstances. And . . . well, I'm damned glad that I came along!"

I jumped aboard the tug, then, to forestall any further demonstration. But as I drew away from the ship's side, Captain Potter, with Folsom beside him, mounted the after-house.

"Now, my lads!" he cried. "Three cheers for Captain Clark! And give them with a will!"

They gave them.

"Three cheers, now, for the good ship *Pactolus!* And when we're cast adrift again, pray God she picks us up!"

You could hear the cheer all over the upper harbor. The Staten Island ferryboat, on her way from the Battery to St. George, changed her course and passed close beside us, to see what the excitement was.

GOOD-BYE, CAPE HORN!

CHANTY FOR THE OPENING OF THE PANAMA CANAL

I

Fifty sail o' noble ships, threshing 'round the Horn,
　　Lean and handsome clipper ships, lifting by the
　　　fore,
Swooping like the albatross, riding like the swan;
　　Well, you won't see them no more.

Oh, you won't see them no more, a-swinging south,
　　With a white surge underneath the bow,
Racing through the gale, cracking on the sail,
　　For to get there, never mind how.

*Then it's good-bye, oh, Cape Horn! (We loved you,
　　too.)*
　　With a hey-yah! And a good-bye!
*For the times are changed, and the courses laid
　　anew.*
　　Oh! Good-bye, Cape Horn!

II

They've gone and dug the Isthmus through, peaks o'
　　Darien,
　　For cargo boat, man o' war, brutes o' heavy beam;
They'll lock 'em up on one side, and lock 'em down
　　again,
　　To the glory o' the days o' steam.

168

Yes, glory o' the days o' steam.   (Our sails are
    furled.)
    Jungle-jangle!   Full speed ahead!
Dirt and grime and grease, wallowing the seas,
    In the lanes where the galleons led.

So, it's good-bye, oh, Cape Horn!   (And sailor's
    pride.)
    With a hey-yah!   And a good-bye!
But once we owned our souls upon the tide.
    Oh! Good-bye, Cape Horn!

III

And how the time'll stretch along, years beyond
    discern,
    With you a-sitting lonesome above the southern
    floe,
Silent, bleak, forsaken, guarding of the turn
    Where the white ships used to go.

Where the white ships used to pass, and pay their
    toll,
    Pounding through the wind and the rain;
Where the birds that made their home on our wakes
    o' flashing foam,
    Will scour the seas in vain.

Singing, good-bye, oh, Cape Horn, my Stormy Boy!
    With a hey-yah!   And a good-bye!
For the ships have gone, and the men left the
    employ.
    Oh! Good-bye, Cape Horn!

UNDER SAIL

I

It was at the time of New England's success and prosperity on the sea that young Captain Bradley took the ship *Viking* on her maiden voyage. In those days the building and sending forth of a ship was a community enterprise. One sharp November morning, the seaport that had seen her keel laid down the previous winter, had watched her rise on the stocks through the long days of summer, and had launched her successfully in the early fall, turned out to bid the *Viking* good-bye and Godspeed. Her crew was made up of home boys; Captain Bradley himself had been born and reared in the town. He had started out before the mast at the age of fifteen; now, at twenty-four, he had set his foot on the top rung of the nautical ladder. The town was proud of him. It was proud of all its boys; but especially of one who had shown such steadiness and ability as young Frank Bradley, the old man Jabez Bradley's son.

Perhaps Captain Bradley was a little proud of his own achievement. He could look back over a clean, hard record. In his nine years of seafaring, he had not spared himself. Obey, work, learn, develop judgment and decision, be able to handle any job or meet any emergency; these principles had ruled his life, the *sine qua non* of old-fashioned seamanship. The reward had come unexpectedly. Captain Marshall, the leading shipowner of the town, whose fortune and influence lay behind the building of the *Viking*, had offered the ship to him that summer as she stood on the stocks.

"I've had my eye on you for a long time, Frank," the old man had told him. "I knew your father before you, and you're a chip off the same block. I guess you're just the man for my new ship."

But young Bradley already had received too many hard knocks, had learned too thoroughly how to discipline himself, to be unduly puffed up over success that came in the course of a deserved advancement. His real pride, from that moment, was in his ship. She was the finest square-rigger that ever had been launched in the town, a ship of eighteen hundred tons, crossing three skysail yards. Her lines were those of the medium or commercial clipper. As he looked up from the quarter-deck at her lofty spars that November morning, while they waited for the tide—at the maze of freshly tarred rigging and new manila running gear, at the brightly varnished yards, at the furled sails that stretched from yardarm to yardarm like caps of snow—a thrill of genuine sentiment coursed through his blood. His ship—and he loved her already. Soon those white sails would be set to the breeze, soon those strong, slender masts would sway against the sky, bearing aloft their press of flattened canvas, soon those new ropes would snap and sing, settling into a taut network from deck to truck and from masthead to masthead, whose every strand would have its use and meaning. Soon the ship would surge beneath him—his to control, to guide, to learn, to play upon, as an organist brings out the tone and volume of his instrument. His trust, too, and his future; at moments like this, responsibility weighed with crushing force. The greater the chance, the greater the danger; the greater the success, the greater the failure if things went wrong.

"I won't fail her!" he cried in a rush of emotion. "We're going on together, the *Viking* and I. By God, I'll sail her as long as she stays afloat. She shall be my first and last command."

Suddenly he thought of the face that would be appearing every few minutes, on this morning of his departure, at the southern window of a house in town. He could see the house plainly, a high brick mansion facing the bay. "It will be only a year," he had told her the previous evening. "Then I'll be back, dear, and we can be married, and you can go to sea with me. No more of this sailing and staying home alone; it's miserable business."

She had looked up at him bravely. "Yes, Frank, I know. But come back safely. Think what could happen in a year!" It was the cry of the sailor-woman. She had learned it from her mother—and from her father, who had been lost at sea with all hands one voyage when his family had remained at home.

An hour later, when, with all sail set, the *Viking* had gathered headway before the light land-breeze, taking her first steps into the world, Captain Bradley went to the stern-rail and gazed back at the lessening town. He stood there a long while, lost in thought. He still could make out the familiar pattern of streets and houses. Home. It seemed to him as if he always had been either leaving or returning. His short, quick boyhood already was half-forgotten, like a snatch of another existence. Five years before, his mother had died there in the town; he had received the news on his arrival in Singapore. His father had vanished in a sea tragedy long before he could remember. No home for him remained, either there or here; he would have to make one. What was this seafaring life, that he now had asked a young girl to share? Every day he heard men call it a dog's life, growl that the game wasn't worth the candle. Perhaps so—but she knew all about it. She had been born in a ship's cabin; she loved the sea. And here was the *Viking,* young, strong and beautiful—what better? A fierce determination swept over him to *make* life worth while, even the life beyond the horizon; to give her a worthy gift, a home of love and happiness, all he had. Any life could be worth while, if full enough of love.

Glancing over his shoulder, to make sure that no one observed him, for it would not do to give his men the materials of a jest, he leaned across the rail and waved his handkerchief toward the town. She would expect it—would be watching with the glasses from that southern window. Sailor women saw the last of their grief; they didn't turn away and hide.

"I'll try to make up for the waiting, Grace," he whispered; then swung forward resolutely, to face the coming years.

II

Autumn returned to the old seaport, and with it the *Viking,* back from her first China voyage. Captain Bradley was welcomed with a hearty "well done." The voyage had been prosperous; the homeward run from Hong Kong had been made in the remarkably fast time of eighty-two days. Hereafter, the *Viking* would be a favorite among Chinese shippers.

A month after his arrival, young Captain Bradley was married in the high house fronting the bay. That night he and his wife left town to join the ship, loading in New York for Yokahama.

Then began ten happy years of life. They were the last ten years of American maritime prosperity, the close of the sailing ship era. Charters were plentiful; the *Viking* made money. Captain Bradley found himself a man of means. Without question, he invested his earnings in ship-property; most of the transactions passed through Captain Marshall's hands. Why not put his money into ships? Ships had been his life and the life of five generations before him, had made him a good living, had taught him all he knew. Most of his friends were doing the same thing. Few there were in those days among the old shipping people, who saw into the next quarter-century, who realized the nature and magnitude of the coming change.

One year, five thousand dollars went to build a new house in the home town. Every captain built a new house, whether he used it or not. Captain Bradley's house was occupied for the length of one China voyage, while Mrs. Bradley remained ashore and gave birth to a son, their only child. Except for this voyage, she accompanied her husband constantly on the sea. She had been reared to the life of wind and wave. In the *Viking's* spacious and comfortable cabin, they made their home from year to year. Their son passed his boyhood on shipboard. He was the apple of his father's eye. Captain Bradley invariably spoke of him as "my Frankie," with a note of pride and affection in his voice. Sturdy and manly, the little boy filled the ship with the interest and activity of childhood.

On a quiet evening in the trade winds, when Frankie had placed his mother's deck-chair near the weather rail and crouched beside her, perhaps weaving for her amusement one of the strange fancies of which his head was full, it seemed to Captain Bradley that life had brought him all that a man could desire. A happy wife, a beautiful son, a splendid ship—good times, comfortable circumstances, a pleasant prospect: in youth he had dared to hope for such things, but had not expected to see the hope come true. Now life had given him confidence. He would sit on the weather bitts beside them, dreaming of the future, of the day when their son would be grown up, when he and his wife would retire from the sea.

But the future, in those years, after all seemed unsubstantial; Captain Bradley believed in enjoying the present reality. A large share of the money that he earned he spent. He spent it extravagantly, spent it with a flush hand. In the China ports where all of his charters led him, there always were a dozen or twenty American vessels lying in the roads. Lavish entertainment went the rounds of the fleet. "What's a little money, more or less?" Captain Bradley was fond of saying. "Times are good, aren't they? More will come." He was forever buying pieces of cloisonne and rare porcelains for his empty house at home, silks and embroideries for his wife; things to be packed away in camphor wood chests after she was dead. The habit of extravagance grew upon him; he spent more money than he realized.

In fact, from a selfish standpoint, Captain Bradley was a poor business man. Seamanship was his vocation; he understood few of the ins and outs of a financial order founded on usury. Its sentiment and psychology he understood not at all; these were considerations entirely alien to him. To his mind, money, to be clean, had straightforwardly to be earned. The plain transactions of a ship's business were all he needed to know. A certain sum of money put into a ship would, if she were properly handled, yield certain dividends; a charter at so much the lump sum, would pay so much on the voyage. Thus it always had been; thus, if he ever gave the matter a thought, he supposed it always would be.

As the flush years went by, he developed into a typical sea captain of the old school; a man of honor, of ideals, of simple dignity and original thought,

careless, buoyant, at times a little reckless, a stern
disciplinarian, a wise judge of human nature, a senti-
mentalist at heart, a believer in the inherent right-
eousness of things, a man of sincerity and individ-
uality. Dishonesty, laziness, hypocrisy, he hated as
he hated crime. Inefficient men found him a hard
taskmaster. By nature and training he was arro-
gant and imperious; the instinct of command ran
strongly in his blood. He spoke his mind at all
times; he was equally ready to defend his position.
His pride in his wife, in his boy, in his ship, in
everything he loved, was enormous. In short, he was
a man singularly adapted to the high and responsible calling of master mariner—singularly ill-fitted
for his coming encounter with the world.

III

The first stroke fell out of a clear sky. Captain
Marshall died suddenly, leaving his business affairs
in a bad way. For three months, the town was in
turmoil. At the end of that time, it became apparent that the old shipowner had involved all of his
own property, as well as that of many others, in a
series of disastrous speculations. No one hinted at
dishonesty, but the hard fact remained. Ship property had greatly fallen off in value in the last few
years; this, it would seem, had been the immediate
cause of Captain Marshall's financial stringency.
He, too, had banked heavily on the old times.

Captain Bradley arrived that year from Hong
Kong, to find himself poorer by more than half of

his modest fortune. All of his ready money was gone in the wreck; what remained was a bundle of pieces of vessels, quarters and sixteenths and thirty-seconds. Worst of all, the *Viking,* the one ship that Captain Marshall had owned outright, with the exception of the eighth share standing in Captain Bradley's name, would have to be sold at auction to satisfy the creditors.

In this crisis, Captain Bradley's idealism overcame all other considerations. "By God, I'll buy her myself!" he cried. His friends told him that he was a fool; but this only heightened his determination. He called the creditors together, and made them an offer. By great exertions, he managed to negotiate on his various ship holdings, disposing of some at figures below their value, mortgaging others, selling the house, and finally raising sufficient money to carry out his word. It took all he had; but he was glad that he possessed enough property to do it. When he sailed from New York on the next voyage, he was the sole owner of the vessel. His confidence, momentarily shaken by the failure of one of the pillars of his world, had begun to return. He realized that times were not what they had been; but it seemed impossible that the demand for sailing ships ever would wholly go by.

The next few years, however, seriously undermined his assurance. Freights were falling rapidly, were even becoming hard to get. One time he had laid her up in Hong Kong for six months, resolving to wait for a better figure than had been offered, and had at length been obliged to accept a charter that barely paid the ship's way. Steam was to blame for it all. He began to hate steamers with a bitter and unreasoning hatred. They were driving the fine old sailing ships off the sea.

Then, as suddenly as the financial crash, came the blow from which he never fully recovered. On the homeward passage, shortly after rounding the Cape of Good Hope, his wife sickened and died. She had been ailing ever since they left Anjer, but he had not realized the seriousness of her condition. They already had caught the trades in the South Atlantic; it was hopeless to think of putting back to Capetown. He urged the ship with every rag of sail, trying to reach St. Helena in time; but the trades held light, the elements were against him. For three days of nearly flat calm he paced the deck in agony, or sat beside his wife's bunk while she talked to him in a low voice, telling him of her love, of what to do when she was gone; trying to make it easy for him, for she knew that she was dying. On the third day, she died in his arms. That night his hair turned from black to white. He came on deck the next morning an old and broken man. The wind continued light and uncertain, there was no chance of reaching St. Helena in season for the last rites; and he buried her there in the deep sea.

That voyage, they had left their son at home in school. Alone now in the empty cabin, Captain Bradley's thoughts were much of his boy. He himself could stand it, must stand it. But how could he tell Frankie, his Frankie? Night after night he paced the narrow floor below, going back over life, living in the past from which he now definitely had been cut adrift. Perhaps he was not quite sane for the remainder of the passage; he never could remember clearly those weeks before his arrival. But always, behind every conscious thought, lay the dread of what he would have to tell Frankie. This he remembered; it seemed to have been beaten into his brain.

Then a wonderful thing happened. He arrived home to find that the boy they had left behind had grown into a young man, had developed a strong and resolute character of his own. He came to meet his father at the train; the news had reached him already. "I did all that I could, Frankie," were Captain Bradley's first words, as they faced each other on the gloomy platform. His son looked at him steadily, fighting back the tears. "I know you did, sir." It was the son who put his arms around the father's shoulders; Captain Bradley had felt a strange hesitation, almost akin to shame or fear. But now his heart rose for the first time since his wife had gone. This was the stuff that men were made of. His son.

They entered the house together—the old Bradley house, where Frankie lived with his aunt when he was at home. Captain Bradley greeted his sister, took off his hat, and sat down heavily. Suddenly the boy cried out and fell at his father's feet, holding him by the knees, his whole body shaking.

"My God, father, your hair is white!"

"Yes, yes, Frankie. That doesn't matter. Poor mother, poor mother!" He leaned forward to hold the heaving shoulders. For a long while they cried in each other's arms.

As the days went by, Captain Bradley found himself depending more and more on the new young strength. The two were inseparable; they seemed to meet on common ground. Captain Bradley was one of those men who never lose their youthful outlook; while the boy in reality was older than his years.

When the time came to sail on another voyage, Frankie insisted on leaving school and going away with his father. For the next eighteen months they lived together on the ship, at sea and in foreign ports, and their intimacy grew profound. They talked, read aloud in the evenings, studied navigation and history, discussed the mysteries of life and love; side by side they stood on the quarter-deck through storm and fair weather, and Frankie learned the lore of seamanship at the hands of a past-master. Gradually, Captain Bradley got back his grip on life. The boy had renewed his courage. He even began to dream of the future again—of marriage and a career for Frankie, no following the sea, but a safe career ashore.

Then another long voyage, alone this time, for Frankie had entered college to tackle his education in earnest. He had decided to become a civil engineer. This voyage was a hard one in many ways for Captain Bradley. Business was poor; he had a great deal of trouble with his crew, for only the outcasts of society could now be induced to enter the forecastle of a sailing ship; a succession of storms followed him, and at last he lost a foretopmast off the coast of Luzon. He had to face the fact that the *Viking* was growing old; for several years he had been acutely aware that her top-hamper needed extensive overhauling.

As for ·himself, he knew too well that he had turned the corner of life. The voyage dragged on to its close. He reached the Atlantic Coast in the dead of winter. Three weeks of threshing around outside in the teeth of northeast snowstorms and icy northwesters completed the disheartenment. But at length ship and man, icebound and weary, passed in by Sandy Hook and made a harbor once more.

The news that met Captain Bradley seemed too heavy to be borne. A month before his arrival, when the *Viking* had been somewhere off the Windward Islands, running up in the northeast trades, his son, skating on the river beside the college, had fallen through the ice and been drowned.

IV

After a while, Captain Bradley gathered up the fag-ends of his life and started out in the *Viking* on another voyage. She was all he had now. A few more years went by, years of increasing discouragement, aimless and fugitive. Times were becoming very hard. The day of China charters was over; steamers monopolized that business now. The *Viking* became a tramp ship, they picked up what freights they could get, and the old ports knew them no longer. The vessel barely paid her way; operating expenses were retrenched on every hand, there was no money left for upkeep, and Captain

Bradly literally saw her falling to pieces before his eyes. But the old hull remained sound.

He lived a blank life; but he continued to live, which was something. The old days indeed were passing, and with them the ships and the men. Sailors were not what they used to be; business ethics was not what it used to be. He began to feel as if the very fibre of mankind had changed. Nothing seemed left but memory and the remnants of an invincible pride. He could not realize that he had made what commonly would be called a mistake, in buying the *Viking* with his last dollar. His philosophy did not provide the materials of such a conception.

The day came when the old *Viking* was almost the last of her race, the only wooden full-rigged three-masted ship to sail out of Atlantic ports. All her lofty companions had passed away, or had been converted into coal barges. Her arrival in New York was an item of news. This was the one substantial reward of Captain Bradley's declining years as a ship-master; he had sailed his ship beyond her era, he had flaunted her in the face of a new generation. That compact made with the *Viking* in her maiden hour had been no idle sentiment; it had been life's supremest dedication, and he had kept the vow.

A few old friends remained to him, though he had made no new ones in the latter years. These friends kept urging him, every voyage, to sell the *Viking* for a coal barge while there was time, while even this way offered for the disposal of an outworn hull. The coal companies were beginning to build their own barges. The *Viking* still would be worth some fifteen thousand dollars as a coal barge. He could retire on the proceeds, and live in modest comfort for the rest of his days.

"Never!" he invariably answered. "Do I look like a man who needs to retire? She shall never be a coal barge while I live."

Yet it had to come to that; perhaps he had long foreseen it, perhaps the vehemence of his denial was only the face of pride set against the inevitable. On a certain voyage he had been obliged to go into debt, to fit out the vessel. The voyage netted less than nothing. When he returned to New York the ship was attached for the debt. There was no business in sight; the bottom at last had dropped out of the shipping world. He did all that was possible, but he could not raise the money; he and the *Viking* were no longer a good risk as borrowers—their credit was gone. The ship was sold at auction, in equity proceedings, and was bid in by one of the large coal companies operating along the Atlantic Coast. Captain Bradley, at sixty years of age, found himself stranded on South Street without a penny in his pocket. The proceeds of the sale had barely covered the debt. But his honor, at any rate, was clear.

"Another wreck for Snug Harbor" the word was passed, as he stalked out of the room where the transaction had been completed. But they reckoned without their host. That afternoon the *Viking* was towed to Erie Basin, to be stripped for a coal barge. At almost the same hour, Captain Bradley disappeared from South Street. The shipping world never saw him again.

V

A tramp steamer, dirty and ill-kept about decks, streaked with iron-rust alongside, came up the bay from Sandy Hook and anchored off Quarantine. She had arrived from a long and wandering voyage. When the health officer had left the vessel, the captain called the second mate to the bridge. An old man stumbled up the steps.

"Mr. Bradley, get your things together and go ashore with me. I'll pay you off at once. You old trouble-maker, you're not going to stay aboard the ship an hour longer."

The old mate gazed at his superior officer in silence. Tears of anger rose to his eyes. He turned away to hide them, walking to the end of the bridge. His cup of bitterness was running over. Frank Bradley, commander on the high seas for forty years, discharged from a second mate's billet on a tramp steamer—discharged by an incompetent captain, because his incompetency had been found out. He shut his jaws grimly, recalling the scene of two days before. Out there in the fog he had refused to obey the captain's orders; had wrested the wheel from the hands of the quartermaster, had held them both off with threats of physical violence, while he steered the ship himself; and thus had kept her from running ashore on Diamond Shoal. The captain's orders had been completely wrong. He probably had said some sharp things about them; it had been no time for mincing words. Touch and go—but he had saved the ship—saved the captain's certificate, too.

He stood at the end of the bridge, staring down at the gray water. What should he do now? While he struggled with himself, his eyes rose slowly, resting on a hulk that lay at anchor close alongside, between the steamer and the hills of Staten Island. For a moment he regarded her with a dazed and absent concern, trying to fathom the significance of half-awakened sensations. Then, with a suddenness that stopped his throat, his heart gave a great leap of recognition. Neither coal dust nor dismantlement could hide those familiar lines. The *Viking,* his old ship, lay before him.

A hoarse cry escaped him. Through the dreadful pall of the latter years, through bitterness, shame and inertia, burst in a blinding flood the memory and presence of other days. The shock passed instantaneously, and left him utterly changed. Facing his old ship, he became once more the man her master had been. Decision and authority returned to him, as they always did in a crisis; for they were intrinsic, in spite of life and destiny.

A rowboat was passing the steamer; he hailed it sharply. "Rowboat ahoy! Come alongside, and wait there for me." He crossed the bridge with strong steps, stood before the captain, gazed at him steadily, until the eyes of the other fell.

"I'll leave your dirty tramp immediately, sir. You can keep my wages—I don't want them. Take them and buy a book on seamanship. You'll need it the next time you get in shoal water."

"You insolent old devil . . . !"

"Don't touch me!" The old man's voice was level and hard; his hands swung at his sides. He

advanced threateningly. "You didn't dare to touch
me at sea; don't do it now. I . . . " Speechless-
ness overcame him. Too much: it could never be
put into words. "My God!" he murmured, turning
away, "I was master of a ship before he was born."

Ten minutes later, seated in the rowboat with all
his worldly belongings stacked around him, he
directed the boatman to row him aboard the *Viking*.
As they passed under her stern, he looked up at the
well-remembered letters. They were dim now; time
and weather had worn off the gilt. An afternoon in
Hong Kong harbor came back to him; he recalled it
vividly. He had been coming off from shore in
his sampan, full of news; the ship had been chartered for home. Grace would be delighted. Approaching the ship, he had overhauled her with a
critical eye, and found no blemish in her; then, as
they rounded the stern, had looked up at these same
letters. His Frankie had called from the rail, running forward to meet him at the gangway. Time
and weather—the awful dimming of life. He bowed
his head in his hands, and wept like a child.

VI

A stroke of luck was about to befall Captain Bradley. When he gained the *Viking's* deck, he found no
one in command of the barge. Four frightened sailors gathered around him, taking him for their new
captain. Piecing together their incoherent stories,
he learned that the captain of the barge had been
killed that morning in an accident at the loading

berth. A hopper had broken loose, and had brained
him as he stood beside the hatch. The mate, a
drunken rascal, had disappeared on shore the evening before, and the captain had not expected him to
return. The moment the scene of the accident had
been cleaned up, they had towed the barge into the
stream, in order to free the loading berth. There
she lay, waiting for a new set of officers to be sent
off from shore.

When he had learned this much, a strange idea
came to Captain Bradley. It seemed a slender
chance; but a surprising energy and hope had taken
possession of him. He got the address of the coal
company's shipping office, the place where these men
had found their jobs; left his things aboard the
Viking, gave the boatman two dollars to hurry him
ashore, and went at once to the number on West
Street where he had been told to apply. Luck followed him. He found the shipping office in a quan-
dary over the *Viking's* case; they had no waiting list
of barge officers, the tow for Boston was to be made
up that afternoon, and the barge could not be sent
to sea without someone in command. Captain Bradley told his story simply, showing papers that covered a career of nearly fifty years on the sea. His
dignified and authoritative presence bore out the
tale.

"Well, Captain Bradley," said the shipping super-
intendent kindly, "the job is yours. You must go
aboard at once."

"Thank you." Captain Bradley gave a wry smile.
"I think I can fulfill my duties. I'll try to give
satisfaction, sir."

He had not told them of his own relation to the *Viking,* fearing the injection of sentiment into a business-like application. That afternoon he joined his old command, at forty dollars a month and found.

He would not have called it a stroke of luck in the other days. How incredible, then, to look ahead, would have seemed the natural development that time had wrought. Could he have foreseen the end that he was coming to, he would have blown out his brains. But life had accomplished it easily and inexorably; failure at last had ground down the keen edge of his spirit, disappointment had rounded off the corners of his imperious nature. As he stepped across the rail of the barge *Viking,* only a great and pathetic happiness found place in his heart. His fight was finished. He had kept his pride at too terrible a cost. Now he gave it up, freely, gladly. Perhaps he would be allowed to die in peace, aboard the ship that had shared his better days.

Fine old ship—life had gone hard with her, too. The lofty masts and spreading spars had been lopped away; nothing remained above decks but the three lowermasts. The decks themselves were grimy with coal dust; the woodwork had not seen paint for years. How well Captain Bradley remembered her appearance, when, spic and span from the shipyard, the best production of her day, he had taken her on her maiden voyage. It seemed impossible that a whole era of intense human activity could so completely disappear, carrying its lore, its lessons, its origins, its very worth and meaning, into the oblivion of time. An economic empire had passed away.

Dingy, battered, neglected, yet Captain Bradley loved the old vessel—loved her all the more for the hard knocks she had seen. A sentiment that he had thought to be dead reawoke in his heart. He had not known, he had not dared to admit, how much he had missed her. He felt as if he had come home.

His duties were light. There were four men besides himself on the barge. He found time to clean her up. After every loading or discharging, he would have the decks thoroughly swept and washed down, and all the paint work scrubbed. Later, out of his own pocket (he had no use for money now), he bought paint and freshened her appearance about decks; for the coal company, knowing that she would not last much longer, would provide nothing for upkeep. The cabin, the scene of so much that was sacred to him, he scrubbed and painted with his own hands, spending many quiet hours over the task while the barge was towing up and down the coast. It was a labor of peace and love.

For a long while the matter of sails gave Captain Bradley deep concern. The barge was rigged on the three lowermasts with fore-and-aft sails, to be used in an emergency, when she had broken adrift from her tow. Often these sails would be set to assist her progress when the wind was fair. Smothered in coal dust, exposed to sun and rain, the first suit that had been given her as a barge was now worn out; the canvas would hardly hold together to be hoisted. Not that Captain Bradley cared a pin for his own safety; nothing would better have pleased him than to be lost at sea aboard the *Viking*. But the condition offended his sense of seamanship and responsibility. It was an indecency to the old ship to fail to provide her with the ordinary weapons of battle; and there were other lives than his involved.

At length, seeing that it was hopeless to expect her owners to furnish the barge with a new suit of sails, he began to save his money. In a year's time he had laid up enough to supply them at his own expense. It seemed like a touch of the old seafaring activity to be drawing up their specifications; he ordered thick duck and stout bolt-ropes, for this was to be a suit of real heavy-weather sails. When, one afternoon under the coal chute at Perth Amboy, he was able to stow away this strong white canvas in the lazaret, together with a couple of coils of first-grade Manila for reeving off new sheets and halyards, he felt that he could go to sea again with a clear conscience.

That evening he sat for a long while alone in the cabin. The interest of looking over and stowing away the sails had passed; he saw the truth now, saw how things really stood. Buying a suit of sails for a coal barge: was it for this that he had spent his hard apprenticeship, had learned and practiced the intricate lore of the sea? He could remember greater triumphs. For two hours of grim thought he sat with hands clenched on the arms of the chair, facing the world's defeat without surrender. In his heart of hearts he knew that he had not failed. He had kept respect and dignity, saved his honor, been true to himself through it all.

He sat on into the night; the storied cabin enclosed him as if with loving arms; slowly, as the mood of revolt wore away, his mind drifted back into the old days. He remembered how his wife used to sit there beside him, on evenings at sea, busy with her sewing; he remembered how little Frankie used to come running in. These things had happened so often, so naturally. But not for a long, long time. . . .

Gone with the era, gone with manhood and success, gone with the further use of life's endeavor. The old man's head fell back against the chair; tears streamed down his cheeks and sank into his beard.

"What have I done?" he cried in agony. "I cannot understand it. What have I done?"

VII

Two more years passed by, and winter came on. It was the hardest winter in a decade along the Atlantic Coast. Beginning the latter part of November, snowstorm after snowstorm struck in from sea in quick succession; one of those easterly spells that, to the mariner, seems destined to hang on forever. Early in January, the wind backed for a few days into the northwest, and the harsh weather offered a temporary respite. Seizing the opportunity, three heavily laden coal barges, in tow of a powerful seagoing tugboat, set out from Hampton Roads bound for Boston. The old *Viking* was the last barge of the string.

The weather permitted them to get well outside the Capes of the Chesapeake; then it changed.

Wisps of cloud gathered in the southern sky, a heavy bank loomed just above the horizon; the wind began to sing in the rigging with a low moaning sound. Captain Bradley, pacing his quarter-deck at the tail of the tow, plainly recognized the signs. Another spell of easterly weather was coming on.

They already were too far outside to think of turning back, and too far offshore to run for Sandy Hook. Nothing for it but to push on toward Vineyard Haven. The towboat was doing her best; a nasty head sea remained from the last storm, and this began to pick up as the wind veered to the northward and eastward. The barges strained at their hawsers, pitching and rolling incessantly. Captain Bradley never could accustom himself to this motion, so different from the motion of a ship under sail. It annoyed and distressed him to the core of his being. Together, he and the *Viking* once had roamed the sea boldly, the man striking off the course, the ship leaping forward along it, bending to the wind, sailing free under the sun and stars. Now they dragged about at the end of a hawser, engaged in a servile traffic, trailing in the wake of steam.

Minute by minute the clouds piled up from the southward; a gray gloom fell on the ocean. The wind, now settled in the northeast, rose steadily, lifting the sea before it. The air grew colder, the chill of the coming storm. The old ship wallowed and plunged, groaning in every timber. She was very low in the water; already green seas were coming over her bows. Soon the night shut in, black as a cavern—and Gay Head light not yet in sight.

At six o'clock Captain Bradley went below to put on his oilskins and drink a cup of tea. Coming on deck a little later, rigged for the storm, he paused a moment beside the binnacle, as an officer fresh from below always will. In that instant, the hawser parted. He heard no sound, he saw no sign; but he knew that the ship was free. The fact was communicated to him through the deck, through the motion of the hull. He sprang to the rail, and ran forward along the starboard alleyway. Abreast the mainmast, he stumbled against the mate in the darkness.

"Hawser's parted, sir!"

"I know it. Turn out all hands, and loose the foresail. She's falling off to the westward—the wrong way. We must wear her around on the other tack, and scratch offshore."

"They'll be back to pick us up, Captain, as soon as they miss us."

"Not if they know their duty. It would endanger the other two barges; this is going to be a bad blow. We'll have to look out for ourselves now."

"Good Lord, sir, what can we do with this old hooker?"

"Do?—everything! Do as I say. Up with that foresail, now, and be handy about it. There was a time when you wouldn't have called her an old hooker! I'll show you what she's made of."

Then it was that the labor of love which Captain Bradley had expanded on the *Viking* bore worthy fruit. Every block was in order, every rope was

clear and fast to its proper pin. Unconsciously,
under his training, the crew had acquired a measure
of seamanship. They had learned to obey orders, at
any rate; had learned, too, to respect and trust their
old wind-jammer commander.

For the first time in many years, an emergency
confronted Captain Bradley. He faced it without
hesitation, filled with a certain fierce joy, sure of
his power and ability. Almost before the ship had
lost her towing headway, he had decided on his
course. He and the *Viking* more than once had
clawed off the Jersey shore in the teeth of a north-
easter. They could do it again. Then, when the
storm had broken, he would take her to New York,
as if they were arriving from a China voyage.

Before the little foresail, the ship wore around
sweetly, came up to the wind with her nose pointed
toward the broad Atlantic, and hung there steady
and true. The old free motion had returned to her
deck, the old life ran along her keel. Immediately,
they set the spanker, mainsail and jib; this was all
the sail she had. The whole area of it hardly would
have equalled her former mainsail, dropping its
solid square of canvas from an eighty-foot mainyard; but it was enough for the purpose, and the
Viking answered to it. The gale had struck; the
ship heeled sharply, plunging forward on the port
tack at a three-knot gait. She made considerable
leeway, but headed up to east-south-east. Captain
Bradley knew that if he could drive her on this
course for the next twelve hours, they would stand
a chance of clearing the danger that lay under their
lee.

Pacing once more the quarter-deck of a ship under sail, a tempest of recollections beset the old man's mind. Past voyages, dangers, storms, past conquests of the elements, thronged upon him at the call of an awakened vocation. Adrift, now, in a long-pent flood of creative effort, other memories flashed before his eyes; scenes of love and achievement, scenes of weakness and self-indulgence, scenes of error and wrong. Life always had been hard for him to live, even at its happiest; his high spirit ever had been in arms against itself. He seemed tonight to be able to remember all of it—snatches of conversations, lights and colors, tones and meanings, touches of hands and the unspoken messages of hearts—all that had ruled his life and formed his character.

Through these recollections constantly appeared the figures of his wife and child. He thought of them deeply, tenderly, calmly. Once, when they had been at sea with him, the *Viking* had run into a cyclone off Mauritius; he recalled his going below in the midst of it, to reassure them. "How is it, Frank? Will it blow much harder?" "No, dear, the worst has passed." "Oh, Papa, aren't you afraid?" "No, my son, there is nothing to be afraid of in the world." He had said these words—he laughed, now, to remember. God had punished him well for his audacity.

He was surprised to find himself thinking of these things without pain. A change had taken place within him, a change born of the familiar exigency. In some inexplicable way, he was happy again. A task of seamanship lay before him; lives depended on his strength. He was a master mariner, in charge of his old ship—his ship, as truly as she had been that other morning, when, full of ambition and pride and courage, he had looked up at her untried sails. He felt her surge beneath the heavy cargo, rising, flanking the seas, flinging them off savagely, like a man striking out from the shoulder. He knew, he understood—that was the way he felt about it, too. A couple of old hulks, living beyond their time; but the spirit was in them still.

Unseen, surrounded by darkness, Captain Bradley stood upright against the weather rail, an indomitable figure, facing the storm. The world could crush them—never the sea and the wind. The sea was their home, the wind was their brother. This was the fight that found them armed.

VIII

The storm increased; the air was thick with snow, cold with the breath of Arctic winter. In the middle of the night, the foresail and mainsail blew out of the bolt-ropes. They bent and set the heavy new sails. Soon the spanker went, and was replaced. Captain Bradley was driving the ship without mercy; for the wind was hauling inch by inch into the east, heading them off toward the dangerous lee shore. The *Viking* stood the strain; her seaworthiness never had been put to a harder test, never had shown itself so handsomely. She had been built in a day when work and honor had gone hand in hand.

The morning dawned on a wild scene. Great waves rushed at the ship, lifted her high in air, broke above her bows, and stopped her progress as if she had run against a wall. It was high time to heave her to. They lowered the mainsail, foresail and jib, and managed somehow to get them furled. The quarter-deck was comparatively dry; they had no difficulty in double-reefing the spanker. In his specifications to the sailmaker, Captain Bradley had insisted on a double row of reef-point for this sail.

To this tiny patch of canvas the *Viking* rode hove-to for the next forty-eight hours, while the storm howled down on them from the waste of waters. The decks were piled with snow, the ropes and sails were clogged with ice; slowly, mile after mile, the ship drifted against a pitiless lee shore. Captain Bradley constantly kept the deck. There was nothing more to be done—but he had to see the business through.

When the storm broke, they were less than five miles off the Jersey shore at Atlantic City—so close had been their call. The drive through the night at the beginning of the storm had saved them; without the offing made at that time, they long since would have landed in the breakers at Barnegat. The wind jumped into the southwest, the clouds quickly rolled away. They chopped the gaskets, cleared the ice away from booms and sheets and halyards, and set all sail. The ship paid off, heading up the coast; from the frozen and snowbound shore the sweet land-smell, always a miracle to sailors nearing port in winter, came off to them. Night fell, the air grew crystalline, stars sparkled white and big in the cloudless sky. Minute by minute the easterly swell decreased, knocked down by the offshore wind, as the old barge crept northward. She sunk the lights of Atlantic City, picked up Barnegat, brought it abeam, dropped it on her port quarter. Then Captain Bradley left the deck, for almost the first time in three days.

He could not have kept on his feet any longer. The pain in his chest, that had set in the night before and grown by leaps and bounds during the last day of the storm, had now become so intense, at spasmodic intervals, that he felt unable to conceal his distress. At times it was well-nigh unbearable. His heart seemed trying to burst out of his body. Perhaps rest would ease the pain. At any rate, he wanted to sit down somewhere, alone, in an effort to face and compass this new development. He wanted to give his courage an overhauling.

They had sounded the pumps at sunset, with no result; the splendid old hull had not leaked a drop throughout the storm. But at midnight they found two feet of water in the hold. The mate, frightened half out of his wits, rushed below with the news. Captain Bradley sat like a statue in the big chair, gripping the arms, his face white and drawn. In his excitement, the mate did not notice his extraordinary pallor and rigidity.

"Captain, Captain, she's sprung a leak! There's two feet of water in the hold already!"

"Two feet of water? . . . Impossible!"

The old man heaved himself to his feet and stumbled on deck, walking slowly and carefully, holding tight to the rail. The shock of the news

had loosed the terrible pain again; at every breath
he drew, something seemed to be stabbing him with
daggers. He sounded the pumps with his own
hands, to find that the mate's discovery was only
too true.

"What can have happened, what can have happened?" he kept muttering. "The change of tack
must have done it. That's it!—the change of tack."
Now that he had found an explanation, he could
face the issue. They manned the pumps at once—
this was before the day of steam pumps aboard
coal barges. But the leak gained steadily on them,
in spite of all they could do.

It was a race with time now—for both of them.
Captain Bradley gave a bitter laugh; he and the
Viking were throwing up the sponge together.
The breeze had freshened, but the old ship was piti-
fully slow. He swore to himself as he clung to the
weather rail, watching the water drag past. He was
thinking of the speed that she would have shown
under her former canvas; twelve to fifteen knots,
she easily would have reeled off with skysails set in
this smashing breeze. While he watched, the swift
stabbing went on in his chest, as if some invisible
enemy were taking full and cruel satisfaction. Was
he not to be permitted to bring his old ship to port?
Was this final insignificant success to be denied him?

The winking eye of Navesink came in sight just
before dawn. At eight o'clock, they were abreast
the Highland lightship. The old barge was very
low in the water, but she still retained a margin of
buoyancy. With Captain Bradley, conditions for
the last hour had been a little better. He had kept

the deck since the pumps began, refusing to give up
to a physical encumbrance; and the pain had eased
away, as if temporarily succumbing to his invincible
will.

Soon after passing the lightship, a towboat
approached them, hauling up alongside.

"Barge ahoy! What barge is that?"

"*Viking.* Broke adrift from a tow—three days
ago—off Montauk Point."

"The devil you say! I'll send a hawser right
aboard."

"You'd better. Snatch us—up the bay—quick as
you can. Five feet of water—in the hold."

"Perhaps I'd better beach you somewhere inside
the Hook?"

"No—tow us in. I guess—the leak will stop—in
quiet water."

Whether it was judgment or prescience, Captain
Bradley's surmise proved correct. As they towed
up the bay, pumping continually, the water in the
hold at first remained for a while at a constant level,
then slowly began to fall, enough to show that they
were gaining on the leak.

Below the Narrows, the tugboat dropped astern,
ranging up on the *Viking's* quarter.

"Well, old man, where have you decided to go?"

Captain Bradley stood in the starboard alley-way,
one hand grasping the rail, the other the corner of
the after house. It was the only way that he could
hold himself upright. In the last half hour the pain
had returned with fresh violence. Since its return,
he had known what he would have to do. The ship
was all right now; but, for him, little time remained.

"Anchor us—at Tompkinsville—close inshore. Send word to my office. Get some men—my crew are—worn out. Bring off a doctor—for God's sake. . . ." The strained voice broke in a shrill cry.

The mate ran aft along the alley-way. "Captain!—what's the matter, sir?"

"Sick." Captain Bradley's hand flew to his breast, clutching his coat in a great handful. His face turned deathly white, his eyes closed, his mouth twisted in the intensity of the pain. For an instant he swayed; then opened his eyes again, and pulled himself upright against the rail.

"I brought her in!" he cried loudly. "My old ship . . . under sail."

The mate was just in time to catch him as he pitched forward insensible.

IX

The doctor came out of the captain's stateroom with a grave look on his face. The mate stood in the middle of the cabin floor, nervous and unstrung; he had been fond of Captain Bradley. The afternoon sun streamed through the cabin skylight. For several hours they had been watching the old man struggle for breath. The mate's gaze roved uneasily over the top of the chart table, where, according to his invariable habit, the captain that morning had spread the tablecover that he used in port, and had set out a few pictures and ornaments, to make the cabin look more homelike. He had done it between spasms of pain, while they had been towing up the

bay; had done it for something to occupy his mind.
He always tried to arrange the things as he remembered his wife used to do.

"He can't last much longer," said the doctor.
"His heart is practically gone."

The mate nodded without looking up. "Is he suffering much pain?"

"Not now. I've just given him another hypo-
dermic. That's all we can do for him."

They went together into the stateroom. Captain
Bradley lay quietly against a heap of pillows, with
his eyes half closed. He had regained consciousness
as soon as they had brought him below. As the mate
bent above him, he opened his eyes and stared dully
around the room. He was muttering to himself.
The mate leaned closer—then drew back sharply,
realizing that the words were only the product of
delirium.

"Hello, hello! . . . that you, Sargent? When
did you arrive? Let's get a couple of chairs this
afternoon, and go along Glenealy Road. I want to
see Hong Kong harbor again through the bamboo
trees. . . . Remember that day we had a picnic
on Glenealy Road? You had your wife with you
that voyage. My Frankie got tired; I had to carry
him in my arms. . . . Frankie never grew up.
No. . . . He died."

The mate shook his head violently, as if to throw
off the mortality of the scene. He turned away from
the bunk. "Why does the old man have to wander
so?" he demanded sharply.

"The opiate," said the doctor. "Don't worry—
he isn't suffering now."

Captain Bradley regarded his officer with a long and profound stare. Suddenly, recognition dawned in his eyes.

"Oh, Foster!—what do you say? How much water do the pumps give now? Any chance of the leak drying up?"

"Only a couple of feet left in her, Captain. Four men have come off from shore to relieve our crew. We'll soon have her as dry as a bone, sir."

"No use." Captain Bradley rolled his head on the pillow. "You'll find her garboard strake started —port side of the keel. She's finished. She'll have to go to the junk heap now." He lay quiet a moment, thinking. "If I had my way, she should be towed to sea, and sunk in deep water. I ought to go along with her. . . . But I suppose she's worth a few dollars as junk." Suddenly he sat up in bed, threw off the clothes, and raised his clenched hands above his head. "Oh my God!" he screamed. "I've been working all my life, and I haven't a few dollars to redeem my old ship!"

"Lie down, Captain. You must keep quiet. Lie down, sir. You'll feel better in a little while."

"Yes, yes." The paroxysm passed; the old man fell back exhausted. Again his mind wandered; he seemed to be sinking off into a doze. Like a child at the end of the day, half way between sleeping and waking, he babbled of endeavors on the playground of the world.

"After that typhoon, I rigged a jury rudder and brought her into Manila. . . . Oh, yes, they said it was. . . . You wouldn't expect an accident in the trade winds. . . . The fore-topmast went at the head of the lowermast, carrying the jibboom with it; but in a couple of weeks we had her rigged up again. . . . Pleasant weather, pleasant weather. . . . I looked up, and saw his green light almost hanging over my bow. . . . Funny, isn't it, how things come round? . . ."

Gradually he stopped muttering. The doctor took his pulse, then beckoned the mate to follow him into the cabin. "It can't be long now," he whispered. "Who was the old fellow, anyway? He seems to have a strange assortment on his mind."

"I don't know much about him. He was a fine man. . . . Say, you stand in the door, there, and tell me when he's finished. I can't bear to watch him any longer."

They had been waiting some time in silence, when a quick movement in the bunk started them running toward the stateroom. Captain Bradley was sitting up in bed again. All trace of pain had left his features. His hands lay quietly on the coverlet, his eyes were fixed on something far away. The faint shadow of a smile crossed his face, illuminating it with an expression of wisdom and serenity.

"Grace! Frankie! *Under sail!*" he cried in a loud voice—then settled slowly back among the pillows, his last voyage over.

ANJER

I

"Do you see that mass of trees in the deep shadow?" asked Nichols, pointing toward the shore. "There's a house behind them—the old consulate bungalow. Years ago, when the China trade was flourishing, all ships used to stop at Anjer for mail and orders; for this reason, I suppose, our government used to keep a consul here, though he wasn't much but a postmaster. Anjer was the first port of call after the long outward passage; every man who has sailed to the East remembers it with affection. You crossed the Indian Ocean in the "roaring forties," then swung abruptly north through the southeast trades. At length, one morning, fresh from a three months' chase of the empty horizon, you sighted Java Head, that black old foreland looming out of the water like a gigantic sperm whale; and before the day had gone, you'd entered the Straits of Sunda, with Java to starboard, close aboard, and Sumatra in the distance to port; had passed Princes Island, sighted and drawn abreast of Krakatoa, taken your cross-bearings on the Button and the Cap, turned off at Thwart-the-Way; and, toward sunset, had drifted into Anjer Roads before the last puffs of the sea-breeze.

"You had reached the land again. Reached it?—you'd plunged into its very heart. And such a heart —and such a land. The Gateway of the East, the Portal of the Dawn—a scene of love and longing, the ecstacy of life, rich with tumultuous growth, and charged with the passionate odor of blooming flowers. You had come to it from the ocean, remember; from wide expanses of waste and emptiness, from the high sky and the brooding night and the homeless wind, from the mental standpoint of one who had forgotten his measure of comparison, who had lost his grip on reality. The very strangeness of the limited and circumscribed sea, with shores on every hand, with mountains piling the whole horizon, inspired a sensation of wonder and curiosity, as if this had been your first view of the terrestrial world. But ere this sensation, the breaking of the sea-habit, the shortening of the focus, the opening of the door, had fairly possessed you, other allurements were striving for the mastery. There was the hand of the East, held out in alien greeting; there was the breath of romance in the nostrils, the call of love in the heart, the smells, the voices, the colors, the whisper of adventure, the touch of magic and mystery. All this, in the old days, was meant to you by Anjer, by that cluster of bamboo houses beyond the fringe of the banyan trees, that point, that lighthouse, those hills climbing the eastern sky, and this secluded anchorage, where we happened to drift before the tide—deserted now, as you see it, and quite forgotten, but once the toll-keeper of the sailing fleets of the world."

Nichols waved a hand.

"What about the old consulate bungalow?" someone asked.

"Oh, yes; I'll tell you." The captain of the
Omega pulled himself up abruptly. "I knew it first
as a boy before the mast. My maiden voyage was
made into the East; I came to Anjer, saw the native
dugouts gather around the ship, examined their
wares of fruit and birds and monkeys, rolls of
painted cloth and wonderful shells; I saw the consul's boat bring off the old tin post-box that visited
every ship calling at Anjer—it disgorged for my
delight, I remember, a letter from my mother, the
first home letter that I ever had received at sea; and
later in the day, I pulled bow oar in the captain's
boat when he went ashore to pay the consul a social
call. From that time onward, hardly a year passed
that I didn't see the consulate bungalow. When
I became master of a vessel, I always used
to go ashore and visit the place; it's situated
beautifully among palm trees, with an open view
of the roadstead and a winding path leading up
from the landing. Old Reardon was glad to
see a countryman; we'd have a drink or two,
chat for an hour over some month-old piece of
news that had just reached this outpost of civilization; then part for another interval, he to hold
the lodge of the Orient, I to continue an endless
pilgrimage.

"Yes, I felt that I knew the consulate bungalow
of Anjer pretty well. But, in these quick lands, a
house is a mere incident, is nothing but its inhabitants; and my familiarity with this structure in Reardon's time didn't exactly prepare me for what I

was afterward to meet between its walls. . . . And
now I'll have to begin at the beginning.''

II

He waited so long in silence that we commenced to grow impatient. A faint evening breeze
drew across the water, bringing the heavy scent
of the land. Above the Anjer hills hung a full
golden moon. In vague translucent shadow,
the shores of Java seemed sunk in an enchanted
calm.

"I was wondering if I could show you the sort
of man Bert Mackay was,'' Nichols resumed suddenly. "It's difficult enough to lay down the lines
of any human being; and Bert was a doubly complex
subject, chiefly, perhaps, because the key to his
nature was so simple. Simplicity seems the most
erratic of qualities to a world trained in suppres-
sion and negation. He was one of those startling
fellows whom people instinctively like, but daren't
approve of. He was brilliant but not entirely well
balanced, let us put it; as primitive a soul as I've
ever come in contact with. In fact, he really was
wild, like nature—didn't attempt to pause or reckon, but let life come and go; and like nature, too,
his growth was a series of instinctive processes.
A man of the open, swift-minded, magnetic, and sin-
cere, he was a tremendous vital force, stirring life
violently wherever he touched it; while a romantic
conscience, which plunged him into moods of con-
trition and despair, seemed to bring him out of

every experience with a clear eye and an innocence apparently unimpaired.

"You can imagine, with all this, that his way with women was rash, sudden, appalling, and awfully fascinating. He couldn't talk well, but had a presence and manner which spoke for him louder than words. He was tall and dark and virile, a devilishly handsome chap. In fact, he possessed that secret of power that can't be cultivated or affected, the emanation of love, a glorious and terrible inheritance. Something quite different, you know, from any trace of carnality; he wasn't a sensual man at all. He broke many hearts, I'm afraid; how, in the ordinary course of life and days, could it have been otherwise? I used to warn him to watch out; to tell him that some day, in a stroke of divine retribution, his own heart would be broken past mending.

" 'I hope so, Nichols!' he used to fling out, with that serious gayety which was one of his most charming characteristics. 'You can't imagine what a lost soul I am. Nothing else will save me.'

"I'a known Bert Mackay since college days, when for a couple of years we had roomed together and established one of the priceless understandings of life. The affection that lay between us was closer than that of brothers, close enough mutually to excuse our faults in each other's eyes. He became an electrical engineer, went to New York, and rose rapidly in his profession; while I, as you know, followed the sea. Every now and then I'd come to New York; and while in port, would move my things uptown and live with him. He was well connected, knew many groups of interesting people, and

seemed, to my eye, to be living the richest sort of
of life. Our intermittent relation was an ideal one
for two friends; our intimacy grew closer, as voyage followed voyage, and I supposed there wasn't
an adventure of his that I didn't know about. But I
might have realized, of course, that when the bolt of
divine retribution actually struck him, it would be
the last subject on which he'd give me his confidence.

"However that may be, I wasn't aware of any
trouble, hadn't anticipated disaster, and was both
shocked and alarmed, on my arrival in New York
one summer, to find a brief note from him saying
that he had gone away. He gave no address, and
told me not to hunt for him. The letter was four
or five months old. 'I am trying to do the right
thing,' he wrote. 'God knows, I've done enough
wrong things. Perhaps you'll hear from me again,
perhaps you won't. It will depend on how I feel.
I'm throwing up the whole game here. Something
pretty hard has come into my life, and I have got to
go. I must work this out alone. There isn't much
of a chance—but that doesn't matter. The price
has to be paid just the same.' Then, after a few
instructions about some of his private affairs, he
asked me to forgive him, said that I was not to
worry, and assured me of his unfailing affection.

"You can imagine how the news took hold of me.
The nature of the affair was unmistakable; a tragedy of the heart had overtaken him—that fate that
I'd often lightly predicted, and that he as often had
expressed a willingness to find. Well, he was saved
now, it would seem. I wondered. . . . Searching

the past for a clue to this untoward development, I recalled his air of mingled restraint and melancholy at the time of our last meeting, the year before. I had noticed it only to put it down to one of his many and incomprehensible moods. The night of my departure, I remembered, after we'd come in from the theatre, he had spent hours, it seemed, on the couch in the studio living-room, strumming on an old guitar and singing to himself in an incoherent form of improvisation, a habit of his when he was feeling especially blue. I'd been trying to write some letter, and the maddening mournful sounds, with the notes of the guitar picking through, at length had driven me to desperation.

" 'For God's sake, sing something!' I cried, dashing out of my room—he was a brilliant musician. 'But if you go on whining like the wind through a knothole, I can't be answerable for the consequences.'

" 'All right, Nicky, I'll quit,' he had answered with a grin. 'I'm a selfish ass, I know. But I'm not whining. . . . No, I don't feel like singing tonight.' I realized now that, even then, he must have been in the toils of the tragedy.

"So this was the end of a comradeship all too brief, as life goes. Friends are scarce enough, heaven knows, without a fellow's losing one in such vague circumstances. But the years went by, and I didn't hear a word from Bert. At first, I missed and worried about him acutely; then, little by little, he faded off into the background, as even the sharpest details of the great picture of life do if we keep moving. The perspective changes, too. I continued,

of course, to think of him now and then, wondering
what he might have lost or found. But I never felt
occasion to doubt the nature of his quest; he had
come into that heritage foreordained at the launch-
ing of his sensitive and romantic soul. Something
had called him down the wind, some note, some fragrance, some face of beauty, some revelation of
delight; and he'd gone out to find the answer and
consummation—love or death—that hearts like his
pursue.''

III

Nichols reached for a cigar. ''Ten years and
more had gone by,'' he went on slowly, ''when, one
voyage, I reached the Straits of Sunda, bound for
Hong Kong and Amoy. The southwest monsoon
was on the point of breaking; for several days we'd
been treated to baffling winds. It was in the latter
part of the afternoon that, favored by an unexpected
slant of offshore wind, I managed to fetch the anchorage here, slipped into Anjer Roads with quite a
rush, and dropped my anchor in a berth abreast the
landing. I hadn't been through Sunda for a couple
of years.

''The first boat that came off from shore—Reardon's old whaleboat—brought me disappointing
news. Reardon himself, it seemed, had been trans-
ferred to Batavia the year before, and the consulate
had been discontinued; my letters, if any had been
sent to Anjer, were being held in Batavia or Singapore. Old Sa-lee, Reardon's boatswain, was still in
charge of the boat, but seemed to be merely follow-

ing a lifelong habit in coming off to every ship that
called. He wanted to see his old friends, to gossip,
and to mourn the decline of human institutions.
While we talked, leaning across the rail, he told me
in the way of conversation that, some time after
Reardon had left Anjer, the consulate bungalow had
been occupied by a stranger. The fact wasn't of
sufficient interest to me just then to elicit an inquiry.
I just had reached the realization, with a shock of
deep regret, that Anjer the beautiful had taken its
place with the rest of the world's lost glories, that
another page in the romantic annals of seafaring
had closed.

"The air was hot and heavy that evening—one of
these nights of threatening showers that never come.
After supper, I had settled myself morosely in a
deck-chair; it seemed quite unaccountable not to be
going ashore in this familiar situation. The moon
was high and full above the hills, as it is tonight,
but clouded by a faint mist like descending veils of
dew. The ship seemed resting after the long passage; on the forecastle-head a couple of men were
singing, accompanied by an old accordion. Across
the water, as if in answer, floated the voices of
natives somewhere in the jungle, lifted in wild and
startling melodies. The same breeze fanned down
from the land—the breeze that seems always to be
blowing here in the early evening, filling the straits
with the overpowering sweetness of bloom and
decay.

"It must have been quite late—the moon had
risen overhead, and the singing had died out forward and ashore—when I first noticed lights in the

old consulate bungalow. I thought at once of the
stranger whom Sa-lee had mentioned. Who could
he be? What misanthrope had chosen that house of
solitude for his habitation? How did he manage
to pass the time? It went without saying that he
was a European; Sa-lee would not have mentioned
him otherwise. I kept my eye on the light, which
seemed to travel about, vanishing now and then as
if behind a closed door. As I watched, my interest
became more and more awakened. I began to imagine all sorts of people in that bungalow; a tremendous failure, a fellow who'd fled from the wreck of
a tragic past; an exile, for some romantic reason
or other, who had seen my ship in the offing, had
hurried home, and was making ready for a visit,
longing for the sight of a strange face and a word
from the outside world; a criminal, who feared my
presence in the roadstead, who even now was busy
concealing evidence, sweeping tables, locking
drawers.

"Suddenly it occurred to me to go ashore and
satisfy my curiosity. Why hadn't I thought of it
before? I called my mate. 'Mr. Hunter,' I said,
'send some men aft and throw the dingey overboard.
Then haul her up to the side-ladder.'

"Handling the tiller-ropes of the dingey, with two
men rowing, I directed her bow toward Reardon's
old landing. Under the hills the land loomed high.
You know that feeling of strangeness, of transmutation, which comes at the end of a voyage at sea,
when for the first time you step from the ship's deck
into a small boat, when you look across the water
from a lower level, see the shore approach, and hear

the rote of waves on a beach close at hand. There's a trace almost of apprehension mingled with it, the instinct of the sailor warning him of shallow water and dangerous proximity. I felt it, a nameless tingling excitement; besides, I had by this time worked myself to quite a pitch of fancy over Sa-lee's stranger.

"Reardon's landing was already dilapidated; I scrambled up it and picked my way to the shore, telling the men to wait there for me without fail, for I didn't want them straying to the village. Striking the path at the head of the pier, I hurried forward, keeping myself as much as possible in the deep shadow of palm trees that lined the uphill slope. I wanted to catch this fellow napping, whoever he was, wanted to observe his face in a moment of surprise. Then I would better be able to place him. The air under the trees was thick with the reek of tropic earth; sounds made themselves heard distinctly in the great silence. I advanced up the path noiseless and unseen, and in a few minutes arrived in plain sight of the bungalow.

"The little house, with its broad flanking verandahs, stood surrounded by trees and underbrush. It had a neglected appearance; even in the night, I could make out how the jungle had closed around it in the two years since Reardon's departure. The light inside the bungalow was gone; heavy shadows filled the verandahs, so that I couldn't have seen a person sitting there. I began to wonder if the tenant had turned in for the night; stepped aside from the path, and started to skirt the house, with that instinct that invariably leads a man to the rear when he's eavesdropping; and was about to strike across a patch of bright moonlight toward the side porch, when a strange sound broke the intense stillness and knocked me back into the shadow as if by a physical blow.

"Someone had commenced picking a guitar on the verandah. The next moment a voice came out on the night, soft and suppressed, a voice like an echo, that seemed to lose itself in the silken chamber of the night. Either a baritone or a very deep contralto; but I felt it to be a man's voice, without understanding why. I listened, but couldn't hear distinctly. While I listened, I was conscious of an exquisite perfection of emotion. I semed to stand at the heart of an old and visionary land, the witness of an ancient parable; the voice was the voice of Adam singing the first love song in Eden, and the veiled languorous moon was the same moon that had stirred that song through the untold nights of men.

"Suddenly the voice rose and swelled; I caught the words, the tone, the melody. . . . All at once I remembered—and knew, with a shock of recollection, who it was. The quality of the voice hadn't changed; the song itself was familiar. I'd heard it often, as he lay on the couch in the New York studio, or sat at the piano in one of his wandering musical moods. It seemed impossible. How could he be here? I choked, in the midst of uttering a low exclamation—must have made quite a fuss. He got up abruptly, breaking off the song; I heard the guitar strike the floor with a hollow clash.

" 'Who is there?' he asked softly, as if expecting a visitor from that direction.

"I pulled myself together, started across the patch of open ground, and came into the moonlight. When I'd reached a little nearer, I saw him standing at the rail of the verandah; he leaned out, showing his face—a good deal older than I remembered, but unmistakably the face of my vanished friend.

" 'Who is it?' he asked again, sharply now, for he had discovered that it was a man.

"I felt the need of making an excuse for introduction. 'Bert,' I said, 'I haven't been following your trail. It's just an amazing stroke of chance. That is my ship in the roadstead. I happened to call. . . .'

"He leaned out farther, a look of helpless bewilderment on his face. Then recognition dawned with a great rush. 'Nichols!' he cried desperately. Gazing at me wide-eyed, he repeated my name in a lower tone, in accents of simple wonder. Suddenly, as he gazed, the weight of the years seemed to strike him with crushing force; he crumpled, dropped to his knees, and buried his face on the railing. When I took his hand, he gripped me like a vise. We didn't speak for a long time.

IV

"After I'd sent my boat back aboard, with orders to come ashore for me in the morning, we sat talking on the verandah till late in the night. Ten years of life had to be reconstructed; the astonishing thing was that I had found him even then. 'Of all places on earth,' I asked, 'how did you happen to land in this God-forsaken spot?'

" 'Oh, I came up from Australia, about eight months ago,' he said. 'A friend of mine down there, a sea captain, told me about it; said the bungalow was vacant and could be had almost for the asking. It's quiet here, and yet a fellow sees ships and things—watches life go by.' He had been pacing back and forth, and now stopped in front of my chair. 'It's heaven!' he cried. 'Nothing to raise a row, nothing to fight for, nothing to live for, much. . . . Nothing to bother—that is. . . . You can't imagine how quiet and peaceful it seems.'

"His words confirmed the impression I'd always had of his disappearance; yet, even in the midst of his hopelessness I seemed to detect a note of hesitation, something concealed from me—perhaps concealed from him, for he rarely analyzed his own reactions. I led him away from his story for a while, trying to fix the status of his existence. We talked of old times; he remembered them keenly, kept citing queer details, jests that used to amuse us, chance remarks that seemed to have lodged in his mind. Almost at once, his infectious laugh came into play. The old spirit was unquenchable. By Jove, the man wasn't half so hopeless as he would have himself believe. . . . I took my eyes away from him, looked around at the jungle rising against the hills; and all at once it struck me how closely he resembled, in essential nature, the land he'd stumbled on. A land full of the instinct of beauty, the gift of love; weary, too, and wise with age, yet fired with the undying youth of quick vitality.

" 'Why don't you stay here?' I demanded. 'Why talk of going home? I have a notion that you belong here. Why don't you love, be happy? . . .'

" 'No, no!' he interrupted hurriedly. 'You don't know what you're talking about.' He stopped short gazing at me as if he were searching my mind. 'Love won't come to me again,' he said.

" 'Nonsense!' I answered. 'That's morbid, Bert. What possible reason . . .'

" 'Good God!' he burst out. 'Haven't I the right to know?' He wandered to the railing, leaned against a post there, and turned his face away. 'Long ago,' he said slowly, 'I took every ray and hope of love out of my heart, and took them in my hands—so—and crushed them, and killed them, and threw them down—as if I'd taken my heart itself and squeezed the last drop of blood out of it like a sponge. I tell you, Nichols, the thing's dead.'

" 'But you haven't told me,' I reminded him.

"He took a longer walk this time, around the corner of the verandah; when he came back, he sat down beside me like a man tired with carrying a load. 'Do you remember a little girl I used to talk about?' he asked. 'I think you met her once in New York, the year before I left. Her name was Helen Rand.'

" 'A slender girl with dark hair and brown eyes?'

" 'Yes. . . . Well, she went away. She's got the same eyes now—wide, childish. . . .'

" 'Now!' I shouted. 'You don't mean—she isn't . . .'

" 'No, no,' he said. 'I haven't seen her for these

eight months. She's down in Australia—was then
—Melbourne.'

" 'What have you been doing now? . . .' I began, but he cut me off sharply.

" 'Nothing,' he said. 'She isn't mine—never has
been.' He leaned toward me. 'But I've been near
her night and day—as near as I could get. Ready
to help, you know—anything. God, I had to be in
the same place. But perhaps you won't understand.' He hesitated, then went on doggedly. 'I
found out too late that I loved her. I found it out
just one day too late. I've been paying for that one
day. And all I've done, all I could do, wouldn't
begin to balance the account. I wonder if you see?'

" 'How could you keep it going so long?' I asked.

"He laughed harshly. 'I knew you wouldn't understand. Just because you think that love means
faith and chastity, quietness, placid days and years,
you have no eye for the love that lives in the fires
of hell. But it's the same love. Bad as she is, I
can't help loving her.'

"The story, coming brokenly, by fits and starts,
achieved by its very barrenness a certain grim intensity. The white light of his extraordinary narrative revealed a background somber and hard,
against which stood the drama of his ineffectual
warfare, a play without hope and without reward,
only saved from inanity by the tremendous fervor
of his love. She had fled from New York without
warning, it seems, flying from life, from him, from
the scene and memory, perhaps, of that one day.
He had a slight clew, but it took him half a year to
find her. When at last they met, she didn't want

him, didn't need him, wouldn't have him. This was in San Francisco, where she went on the stage again, and lived for over a year, successful, apparently happy, and growing more beautiful every day. 'People talked about her, you know,' he told me. 'She became quite the rage. Such a little girl, with serious eyes. . . . '

"She must have been clever, too, for she kept a good grip on herself. Soon she married a man of twice her years with a considerable fortune, and passed into another world. Bert had forsaken his profession, and had gone into journalism; he could have done anything passably well. One thing, however, he could not bring himself to do again, and that was to enter society. He didn't get on as a journalist—couldn't put his heart into the business of life. He told me that for a time he went shabby and hungry. Once in a great while he would see her, perhaps in passing, and they would have a few words together; but the occasions became more and more infrequent.

"Then she left her husband, in the whirlwind of a sensational scandal. Bert only by the merest chance missed having to write about it for his paper. He sought her out at once; she had gone to a hotel there in the city, where she lived openly as the mistress of the other man. 'What are you doing, Bert, hanging around this town?' she had asked him point blank. 'I want to be near in case you need me, Helen,' he answered humbly. She gazed at him with those eyes that, according to his account, still retained their innocence—though it's hard to believe they hadn't by then acquired a trace or two of calculation. 'It's gone a long way beyond that,' she said coldly. 'I won't need you again.' He tried to take her hand. 'I can't let you go this way, Helen!' he cried. 'Let me go? You sent me,' she told him.

" 'What was the use?' he said to me. 'I thought of the old days—they seemed old already; and when I looked at her, I couldn't realize that there had been any change. But it seemed pretty evident that she had quit caring. So I left her—but I couldn't go away.'

"Some months later, she went in a yacht for a cruise among the South Sea Islands. The cruise was a long one; it ended, for her, in a quarrel at Honolulu, as a result of which she changed her second man for a third, and took up her abode in that glorious island of the Pacific where everything but happiness is supposed to wither and die in the magic sun. In the course of time Bert heard the details, folded his tent and followed her. But almost as soon as he landed in Honolulu she was off on another tack; for by now she had settled into the stride of her career.

"So it went, year after year, from Honolulu to Shanghai, from Shanghai to Hong Kong, and down the coast to Singapore; a term in Calcutta, another term in Batavia; a year on the West Coast, Lima, Iquiqui, Valparaiso, she never resting, and he following in due time. It's hard to imagine what her life must have been during this pilgrimage; for now we know that she loved him, too, and that her heart likewise burned in the fires of hell. Pride, pride, what anguish will be borne in thy name! She of course had grown into a strong, clear-headed

woman; only strength could have carried her so
far. But he must have managed things very badly.
I haven't a doubt that the thought of him constantly
at her heels, the sight of him now and then in her
wake, making hard weather of it, spurred her to the
course that she had chosen. No woman respects a
man who can't solve his own destiny.

"How they finally came to Australia, I don't
clearly remember. They must have been there some
time; he spoke of Sydney, of Newcastle, of Brisbane,
and of Melbourne, where he saw her for the last
time. 'I met her face to face one day,' he said.
'She looked a little tarnished—as if things had been
going downhill with her. I suppose I told her so; I
wasn't in the mood to dodge facts that day. She
was angry at my comment—I don't blame her. But
I tried to make up for it the next moment—show
her what I really meant, how glad I would be—that
is, that it rested with her to change everything. I
asked her if I mightn't come to see her; she answered that it wasn't difficult to gain access to her
apartment. All the while she was looking me over
with a sort of amused scorn. Then she said something that was quite unnecessary. She said I didn't
look as if I had the price. . . . That woke me up.
I realized suddenly, fully, decisively, how impossible it was to keep on. Impossible! . . . By
chance, I'd been talking about Anjer with Captain
Roach that very morning. He was sailing the next
day, bound up this way, and I came along with him.
I went with Roach to Batavia, for he knew that the
consulate had been abandoned. Reardon leased me
the bungalow. So here I am. I've got a little money,

enough to live on. And God's been good to me—
I've found a measure of peace. Now you have come
along—I think I'll be all right. . . .'

" 'Yes, this certainly was the place for you,' I
temporized, struggling with irritation at the mess
he had made of existence. I couldn't but recognize
the inevitability of what he had told me; but my
heart kept asking, why is it necessary for men to be
so selfish, so helpless in the face of results clearly to
be foreseen?

" 'Exactly,' he agreed with my spoken word.
'This land had taught me a great lesson. I'm getting back my grip . . . more than I hoped. . . .'
He stopped abruptly. Again I had the feeling of
something withheld, of something missing from
the story. I awoke to the fact that, notwithstanding all he had told me, his present spiritual
status remained unexplained. Quite obviously he
had recovered his grip—but how, and why? It
wasn't in keeping with the rest of the hidden years.
And of course I didn't believe my own platitude on
the influence of the land.

" 'I mean, I'm getting back my self-respect,' he
said. 'I'm really thinking of going home. The past
begins to look like a sort of joke—a horrible, fantastic joke; but I shall quit loving her now. Try to,
anyway. I've learned. . . .'

"I wondered what it could be that so puzzled me
about the case. After I'd gone to bed that night—
it was nearly morning—I lay awake for a long while
trying to think the problem out. Why had he lost
his self-respect, in the beginning? Because she
wouldn't love him? I thought I knew him well

enough to recognize this as the correct answer; he belonged to the unhappy company of men who can't support life when the ego is denied. But she had sent him away, at last, with a lash of the whip, with scorn that even his tried humility couldn't brook. How the devil, then, had he recovered his self-respect? Self-respect was a matter of human relations; it couldn't be drawn out of the air.

V

"While I tossed on the bed, vainly trying to piece this broken logic together, I heard someone moving on the opposite side of the house. Bert and I were alone in the bungalow. He, too, had been kept awake by the excitement of our meeting. Soon he began pacing softly up and down the far side of the verandah. I was debating in my mind the wisdom of going out to have another smoke with him, when his footsteps seemed to leave the porch and sink into the grass. In a moment I heard low voices outside, a little distance from the house. I couldn't make out what was being said. Suddenly I thought that someone must have come with a message from the ship. I jumped up and ran to the window.

"My window opened on the patch of moonlight across which I'd come earlier in the evening. He stood there now, as if waiting; and, before I could speak, a woman came toward him with a gliding, crouching step, starting out of the very shadow where I'd paused to hear his song. As she drew near, he held out his arms; she quickened her pace,

like a jungle deer, and flung herself on his breast,
uttering low, native cries. 'You are safe? You will
not go?' she asked breathlessly. 'Safe?' he asked,
bending above her. ''Have you been watching?'
She looked into his face with a glance of infinite concern. 'The man stood beside me, as I was about to
call,' she said. 'I would have killed him, but I saw
that you were warned.' 'Thank God!' he exclaimed.
'You should have known—and gone away.' She
drew her arms about his neck. 'I could not go!' she
cried. 'I had to see you!' 'Hush!' he said. 'Speak
lower—you will wake my friend.'

''She used perfect English, though her language
was picturesque. 'Your friend? Who is your
friend?' she asked fiercely. 'In all the time that
you have dwelt here, no ships have waited, you
have had no friends come. Who is your friend that
comes in a great ship, unknown and unbidden?' He
smiled down at her. 'Dear heart,' he said, 'he is
more than brother to me, and I have not seen him
for many years.'

''She shrank away from him. 'Ah!' she cried.
'Then he will take you—you will go?'

'' 'No, not yet,' he told her. 'Not, perhaps, for a
long time.'

'' 'But you will go?' she persisted. 'Some day
you will not be here—and, for me, the sun will fail
to rise, and the moon and stars will grow cold, and
all light will die—and you will not be here!''

'' 'I have told you, dear, it must be so,' he said.
'You knew it long ago.'

''Again her arms clasped him. 'No, no!' she
cried. 'I cannot let you! You are mine! Stay here.

It is a fair land—and am I not fair?' She touched
her breast. 'You will not look at me!' she said.

" 'I dare not!'

" 'Then look!' she whispered.

"I saw him take her in his arms. So he had found
. . . this, beyond what he had hoped. Another wave
of irritation at his heartlessness swept over me. I
turned away angrily—then paused a moment, considering the true nature of the phenomenon that had
appeared before me as if out of the sky. I felt that
he hadn't sought this new entanglement. No, but he
evidently had accepted it. Yet the woman had furnished the motive force, literally had flung herself
at his head. Nonsense!—why be a prudish ass? It
wasn't in the least a matter of morals; why persist,
then, in viewing it in the moral plane? Incurable
habit of conventionality, never so strong as when we
strive to be unconventional! Here was a meeting of
instincts and elements, a transaction in lucid terms,
according to a simple formula. It was a phase of
God's excruciating biological experiment. She
wanted him alone, and had taken her way to get him.
He was receptive, for he wanted love. Could she
have awakened love in him, he would not have denied it. Failing that, he would be forced to seek
elsewhere. In the meantime, why repulse divine
experience? . . . But the shocking callousness of
the experiment! While he dallied, detached and
unconcerned, his life had been refreshed as if at a
fountain of vitality. His heart sang with the knowledge that she loved him; he was happy, whole, and
conscious of his power again. He'd said that he had
recovered his self-respect—a curious choice of

words, in view of the occasion; but now I understood what he had meant. . . . This had been her
priceless gift to him.

"A quick exclamation outside drew me again to
the window—could you fellows have kept away? He
was trying to disengage her arms from about his
neck. 'It cannot be!' he said decisively. 'It is impossible! So, to save greater pain, I will go at
once.'

"She clung to him desperately. 'I do not understand,' she cried.

" 'Dear heart,' he answered, 'I have seen too
much, and failed too miserably, to want the spell to
fall on you. All that I touch turns to ashes; whoever enters my life is cursed with my own pain.'

"She gazed deeply into his eyes. 'I am not
afraid,' she said. 'It is for this I love. For what is
past, I have no memory. To-day lives, to-morrow
we carry with us like a child unborn, but yesterday
is dead. What do you seek? Love? Have I not
given you all?' She threw out her arm in a sweeping gesture. 'My love will never fail!' she cried.

" 'I prize your love above all else,'' he said.

" 'What do you seek?' she cried again, springing
away, confronting him with a savage crouching
intensity. 'Faith? Happiness? Peace? All are
here. My people will honor you, for I am noble in
the hills. What do you seek? Ask, and I will give!'

"He leaned toward her, held her at arm's-length,
returned her gaze. I heard him give a sigh.

" 'It is because you do not love!' she said quite
low. 'Before Allah, am I not fair? Why have I
not your love? Look—we are alone. See how I

hold you, feel my heart here, behold my eyes—ah!'
Her face was close to his. 'If love lay in your heart,
you could not stand thus,' she whispered.

" 'Stop!' he cried. 'You cannot see . . . '

" 'I cannot see, my eyes are dim with love!'

"He thrust her away suddenly, as if in fear.
'Listen,' he said in a dead voice. 'For many years
I have followed a woman who would not love me.
To the ends of the earth I have followed her, until
I am weary, and heartsick, and must forget. I have
left my home, I have forsaken my friends. But now
I must return. Dear heart,' he said, 'if I were
young and full of hope, I would not stand here idly,
I would stay with you. But I have nothing left to
offer. An old heart — broken — a brain without
fire. . . . "

" 'I will make well the heart, and fire the brain!'
she cried.

"He swayed toward her, met her in a brief embrace—then broke away. She gave a little cry.
'You will not?' she said. 'I cannot ask again.'

" 'Dear, it is not to hurt you . . .' he began.
'Why won't you understand?' He covered his face
with his hands. 'Oh, God, why can't I make you
understand?'

"She pointed toward the house. 'It is because
your friend has come,' she said fiercely. 'Never
before have you been as to-night. Never before
have you refused me. He brings you memory, and
now you think of home. I should have killed him
when I stood at his side!' She fell back a step, a
savage figure, magnificently tall. 'So—you have
chosen,' she said. 'This which I offer, you throw

down. What is it that you seek? What will you find? Is love so strong in your land, are nights like this, is happiness so deep? In convent-school I learned otherwise.' He put out his hand; she drew away like a wild creature. 'No! It is done,' she cried.

"A moment passed. He stood irresolute, the plaything of fate, while she devoured him with her eyes. Then, with a swift motion, she left him standing in the grass, and ran toward the shadow. He didn't follow. She must have turned at the border of the jungle; I couldn't see her clearly, but she seemed to make a violent gesture, and the moonlight struck sharply on a bracelet that she wore."

VI

"Bert spent the following day with me aboard the ship; I had decided to remain another night in Anjer. We found much to talk about, but didn't approach the incident outside my window that morning; although I'd felt certain that he, not suspecting my awareness, would broach the subject. In fact, I more than once adroitly guided the conversation in this direction; but his mouth was closed. This gave me both alarm and satisfaction; at least, he took the affair with the seriousness that it deserved.

"Late in the afternoon, as we sat here under a little patch of awning spread from the spanker boom, we sighted a small bark to the westward, coming up the straits. She'd just appeared beyond the lower point, some three or four miles distant.

Watching her idly through the glass—I had a powerful telescope—I seemed to find something familiar about her; and a little later, when she had drifted another mile nearer, I suddenly recognized the craft. 'That's Halsted, in his little packet,' I remarked. 'Her name's the *Senegal*. You must have seen her before, if you've been here over six months. He makes two trips a year.'

"Bert took the glass from my hand. 'I can't remember,' he said, after a moment's scrutiny. 'Ships all look alike to me. Where has she come from? You seem to know about her.'

" 'Why, Australia, of course!' I exclaimed, suddenly remembering his own point of departure for Anjer. 'You must have seen this little bark in Melbourne, if you were familiar with the waterfront. Halsted runs a sort of packet service from there to Singapore.'

" 'Halsted, Halsted,' said Bert. 'No, I think I've never met anyone of that name—certainly not there. Look, Nichols, he seems to have run into a strip of calm.'

" 'Yes, and that strip of calm will spread until it covers the straits,' I answered. 'I know the box he's in—he's just about an hour too late. There's a nasty current off the point, with a tide-rip on the ebb. He'll drift away from us for several hours, then slip back in the night, when he picks up the land breeze.'

"After supper we went ashore. I planned to sail in the morning, but would be down the China Sea again in three months' time. Bert had promised to make his arrangements in the meanwhile, and to

leave Anjer with me on my return. I'd urged him
to come at once, and would have waited a day or
two longer, but he wouldn't listen to it. It was
another calm, hazy evening, with no wind on the
water, but a faint languorous breeze among the
palms. We sat on the verandah planning the future,
if you please; he seemed to want to talk about the
world, and I felt it best to encourage the inclination.

" 'Well, old man,' he said at last, 'I've got to turn
in. I'm weary to the bone—didn't sleep well last
night, at all. This has been an exciting time for
me, you know.'

" 'Go ahead, and leave me here to finish out my
smoke,' I answered. 'I'll be all right—I know my
way about.'

"To tell the truth, I welcomed the opportunity to
sit for a while alone, in the midst of the luminous
night, close to the land. Perhaps I might achieve
the hint of a solution; I was baffled and pained by
the tremendous vital difficulties I'd observed. The
wind had risen; it swept down the hillside in a solid
breath of sweetness, softly clashing together the
broad leaves of the palms. Halsted, it occurred to
me in a wandering moment, would now be creeping
up under the lee of the land. I drew my chair to
the edge of the verandah. The scene of the previous
night stood vividly before me; I couldn't keep my
eyes away from that region of heavy shadow, where
she stood at my elbow undecided whether to kill me
or let me go. Suddenly I started; was there a movement in the shadow? I watched it narrowly—and,
by Jove, in a moment she actually materialized there,
as if in answer to my thoughts; advanced, became

substantial, and moved into the moonlight, coming swiftly in my direction. I remained seated, chained to my chair. She came to the railing and put her hand lightly on my arm, as if administering caution. Her eyes were level with mine.

" 'I must see you,' she said in a repressed voice. 'I have waited for him to go.'

" 'Me?' I exclaimed, for my first thought had been that she'd mistaken the figure on the verandah. 'What do you want of me?'

" 'Like you, I am his friend,' she answered simply.

" 'Yes? . . .' I parried. Face to face with her, I saw how beautiful she was. She had the golden Malay skin, dusky, full, smooth as dark marble; across her brow she wore an ornament of ivory and carved blackwood; her breast was bare in a long slit, shadowed like the face of a quiet pool. The moonlight revealed her, the jungle stood at her back; and through her hand on my arm I felt the blood of the East, rushing like water in the hills after a tropic rain.

"I stood up abruptly. 'All are his friends,' I said. She lifted her eyebrows. 'Has it been thus?' she asked with meaning. I nodded, marvelling meanwhile at her admirable directness; a woman pure as diamond, true as steel. She lived, like light, in instantaneous collimation. 'Yes,' I said; 'he has found many friends.'

"She pondered the fact. 'But none have loved him with the heart?' Was it a question, or a statement? 'Many,' I answered, 'but none gained the answer.' 'None?' she asked, searchingly. 'You

know, and I only can repeat what is true,' I said.
'His heart is given to one who wears it on a chain
for play.'

"She trembled at the thought. 'Where is she?'
she demanded. I told her that I didn't know. 'Not
. . . home?' she asked. 'Not there? . . .' She
stretched out a hand vaguely. 'Oh, no,' I said,
relieved to be able to speak an open word. 'Then
it is not for her that he goes?' she cried, pathetically
relieved. 'No,' I said again. She leaned toward
me, as if to make a critical examination. 'Why have
you come, to change and take him from me?' she
asked bitterly. 'I came by chance, without knowing,' I answered. 'It is the hand of destiny.' Throwing back her head, with a passionate gesture she
flung an uplifted arm across her eyes. 'Is she so
beautiful?' she cried in a low voice, like one plead-
ing with fate.

"I heard a slight movement behind me, and
whirled, to find Bert standing in the door. He gazed
from one to the other of us in troubled silence; then
crossed the porch and stood beside me at the rail.
She heard his step, and turned, a superb figure, her
uplifted arm still shading her eyes.

" 'Nichols, I'm awfully sorry . . . ' he began
weakly.

" 'Ah!' she cried, her arrow-like candor tearing
the veil he would have dropped. She went to him
swiftly. 'All day I have wandered in the hills,' she
said. 'All day I have thought of your choice. I
have asked the forest, why? and the mountains,
why? and the great ocean, why? I have held up my
hands to the white clouds, to the sun of life and wis-

dom, asking why, why? Now I have come to you
—and him—to ask you, why? My Love,' she said
softly, 'I think it is that you do not understand, and
your words fall without knowledge. You are the
light of life to me, and the breath of the body. I
cannot live alone. You have taken my heart from
my breast, and now would carry it with you to a
strange land, where it would perish and die. But
these are words—you cannot mean them. You will
not go. See how I hold you fast!'

"He gazed at her in trepidation. 'It is decided,'
he said. 'When the ship returns, I am to go.' 'Then
I shall follow!' she told him. 'I shall go with
you . . . home.' He snatched his hands away. 'Oh,
no, you can't!' he shouted. 'It isn't what you think.
'Blind one,' she answered, 'would I not be near
you?' He started violently; she took his hands
again. 'Then stay with me, here in my land, which
waits for us alone. Stay with me in these nights
that never end!'

"He sighed profoundly. 'It would soon be
over. . . .'

" 'When it had ended, we could die,' she whispered. 'I would gladly die thus, having lived for a
time. Stay with me till love grows cold!'

"He pushed her off like one dazed and distracted.
For a long while he stood perfectly motionless.
'Stay!' she whispered once more. 'Be quiet—let me
think,' he said. She pressed against the railing.
'Look down!' she said. 'To-night we live—but there
may be no to-morrow!' While she was speaking,
clear and sharp across the water came the rattle of
a falling anchor-chain.

"He seemed to stiffen where he stood. His face in the moonlight looked sterner than its wont, set in the struggle that came hard to him. 'No!' he cried in a loud voice. The word seemed to echo among the palms, a tragic whisper of universal negation. She gazed at him a moment in naked terror—then tottered and sank slowly to the ground, uttering little stifled cries. I saw him leap the railing and kneel beside her; but I didn't wait for more. I'd stayed too long already; and what was coming would be harder than what had gone.

"It must have been fully an hour later, after I'd lost the path and threshed around in the jungle until I was tired out, that I succeeded in regaining the bungalow. Bert was sitting on the porch, alone. I dropped into a chair beside him. 'Too bad, old man,' he said, observing the state of my white linens. 'It was decent of you, though.'

" 'Yes, we're a decent breed, aren't we?' I snapped in reply. 'Anyway, let's not balance a heart against an hour of discomfort and a suit of clothes.' He turned his head and looked me over. 'I can't say that I blame you,' he exclaimed. 'But honestly, old man, I think she will forget.' 'I don't,' I said. 'Did you?' He winced, but I went on angrily. 'You ought to know better by this time. You've had a double experience now—the chaser and the chased. . . .' 'Hold on, Nichols!' he interrupted. 'You're getting unpardonable. What would you have me do? Do you want me to stay here and live with her?' 'No, I don't!' I shouted. 'I merely want a revision of life and human nature—no one to be unhappy, no love to go unrequited, no heart to be thrown away.' He laughed. 'I'd like that, too,' he said.

"The silence lengthened between us, as we gazed across the placid harbor, thinking our own thoughts. In the brilliant moonlight, every object in the roadstead was plainly discernible. 'I see your friend has arrived,' said Bert suddenly. 'He's anchored pretty close to your vessel. By Jove, that must have been his chain. . . .' 'It was,' I answered, musing on the fortuitousness of events that shape our lives. 'Now he seems to be getting a boat into the water. Where are your night glasses?' In a moment Bert brought them to me. Aboard the new arrival there was an unaccountable flurry, but I couldn't make out the scene below the rail. In a short while, however, a boat appeared out of the shadow there, and swam toward us through the bright moonlight. 'I wonder why he's coming ashore, at this time of night,' I murmured. 'Can't imagine,' Bert replied. Soon we heard the chunking of oars in the rowlocks, and two or three quick commands. The boat was nearing the beach. She passed for a moment behind the point of the jetty. Now she had reached the landing. A confusion of voices broke out, loud and jarring, pitched in a key of anger and violence. Then, cutting the stillness like a knife, came a sudden sharp cry.

"My heart leaped into my mouth. 'My God, did you hear that?' asked Bert, breathlessly. 'Keep still—it sounded like a woman's voice,' I said. We leaned across the rail, straining our eyes, but couldn't see what was taking place; the landing lay too close under the trees. After the cry, an absolute

silence had fallen. This lasted a full minute. Then
a man's voice started up, the same angry, jarring
tone: 'Give way, boys!' Almost immediately, we
heard the sound of the oars again.

"The unexpectedness of the occurrence had held
us spellbound; we stood gazing at each other like
two wooden images. Then, in the same instant, we
found our voices, began to confer hurriedly, and
started on the run for the center of the verandah,
where a broad flight of steps led down to the jetty
path. At the head of the path we both halted as if
transfixed. Some one was coming up from the landing. The moonlight plainly showed it to be a
woman. She advanced slowly, stopping now and
then, staggering as she walked. When she drew
nearer, we could see that she was hatless and empty-
handed. She walked like a somnambulist, gazing
fixedly on the ground before her, now and then holding out a hand as if to feel the way. At the last
turn of the path, she stopped and raised her head.
Bert, at my side, made a low strangling sound. Evidently discovering us, she started forward again.
Her face was quite terrible. All hope seemed gone
from it, like the face of a suicide I once saw; her
eyes stared at us blankly, and she clutched with one
hand at the bosom of her dress.

" 'Who is there?' she asked brokenly.

"Bert left my side and flung himself toward her.
'Helen!' he cried. She would have fallen, but he
caught her in his arms. 'Helen!' he said again, with
his face close to hers.

" 'Bert?' she asked in eager fearfulness. Her
low voice seemed to tear the heart. She gazed at

him long and deep, while desperation turned to wonder in her eyes.

"For the second time that evening I fled the scene of life's amazing hazard. This time I hurried down the path with all haste, making for the jetty; by shouting, I would be able to raise the ship and have a boat sent ashore for me. As I glanced back at the corner, I saw Bert help the woman up the steps. I thought I heard her sobbing; but, in a moment, I realized that the sound came from another direction. Off among the trees, in the heavy shadow, some one was uttering smothered, choking cries. I broke into a run. The ways of the land were getting too damnably complicated altogether; I wanted to surround myself with a safe strip of water again.

VII

Nichols reached for another cigar. "And that's the way he found her," he went on. "For it wouldn't be true to say that she had found him; until the moment in front of the bungalow when he took her in his arms, she hadn't dreamed that he was there.

"I heard the final chapter of their romance while we were going up the China Sea; I'd waited for him, after all, and had taken them both north with me. After Bert had left Melbourne, she had missed him, and had awakened to the realization that she'd driven him out of her life. So she discovered what it meant to her, what she'd been doing, and bowed before that law which through any wrong keeps the

heart pure and the spirit ready to fulfill itself. She
had determined to follow, but couldn't locate him.
Some said he was in Singapore, some in Hong Kong;
the concensus of many vague rumors, however,
agreed that he had gone north into the China Sea
region. It was familiar ground to her; she had
friends there, and sources of information. She'd
always known of Halsted's packet service; the next
time he came around, she had taken passage in the
Senegal for an indeterminate trip up the coast.

"Unfortunately, Halsted also knew of her. He
was a beastly sort of character. The moment they
got outside he grew familiar, and soon was making
forthright approaches. She was the only woman on
the vessel; the other passenger was an elderly man,
to whom she couldn't hope to look for protection.
She, of course, was a woman of experience, as capable of protecting herself as is humanly possible; but
there are limits to the power of the mind over brute
force, when passion is engaged. Make no mistake—
her aversion to him was virginal, and nothing could
have induced her submission.

" 'I took my revolver on deck one morning, to
show him my marksmanship,' she said. 'I shot a
bird off the end of the spanker gaff. Then I got him
one side, and told him what I would do. I told him
that I would constantly be on the watch, and that I
would shoot him dead if he came near me. It was
the only way—but I knew he was a coward.'

"So this was the situation on board the *Senegal*
—on the one hand defiance, on the other balked and
fermenting desire. Halsted watched her as a cat
watches a mouse, trying to catch her off guard.

Throughout the afternoon while they had been coming up the straits, even while my glass had been looking them over, the silent battle had been going on. The presence of the land had filled her with nameless apprehension. Then they had run into the calm; in this condition, the supper hour had arrived. She had waited on deck until she thought the others would be nearly finished; when she entered the forward cabin, she saw that she had waited too long. The mate and the old gentleman had gone on deck forward; Halsted sat there alone. She had to pass him to reach her seat. As she attempted to slip by, he rose suddenly and crushed her in his arms. The Chinese steward in the pantry turned his back on the scene.

" 'My hand fell on a table knife,' she said. 'I fought him with it—succeeded in cutting him badly about the hands. The blood frightened him; he had to let me go. I've never seen a human being in such a dreadful rage. He swore he wouldn't keep me on board 'n hour longer.'

"The rage had persisted; as soon as the sails had been furled, after dropping the anchor, he had put a boat overboard and bundled her into it, bag and baggage—well he knew that she was in no position to make trouble for him. She had thought of trying to attract the attention of the other vessel, but finally had decided that she would better take her chances on land. She had supposed there were white people ashore; at the landing, where her things had been pitched at her feet, she had asked Halsted the way to the settlement. When he'd told her brutally what an abandoned place it was, she'd suddenly lost heart. It was then that we had heard her cry out.

" 'Go up to the consulate bungalow,' Halsted had told her. 'See the lights? Somebody must live up there.'

"So she had climbed the hill, trusting to luck, which already had arranged the scene. It might have been vastly different, you know. Suppose she had found him with the native woman? Well, suppose it—the renunciation merely would have changed hands. Inexorable formula!—for them, one or the other; for him, heads I win, tails you lose."

VIII

Nichols went to the rail, and stood for some time in silence, facing the land. "And I have seen the other," he said slowly. "It was about a year later that my course led me again through Sunda Straits, and I arrived at Anjer on another evening of moonlight and stillness and awakened memory. After the anchor was down I ordered a boat set overboard, and went ashore in the late evening to revisit the bungalow. As I went up the path, the shadows seemed to start and move about me, and a wandering breeze stirred the palm trees with a quick rustle as of departing feet. I found the wreck of a rattan chair standing on the verandah, pulled it to the railing, and sat there a long while facing the oval of grass flooded with moonlight, the fixed set, as it were, where the actors of this unseen drama had stalked through their extravagant business and said their futile words.

"Nothing had changed; it seemed as if I had left the place but yesterday. I turned to the heavy shadow where I had seen and heard her last, the shadow that must have marked the end of a hillside trail; and it wasn't surprising to me, but only natural, to see her standing there once more, her form drawn back as if from a sight she didn't dare behold. In a moment the tense figure moved. She walked like a tiger, with a cruching step of absolute grace, cautious yet unafraid. Crossing the oval, she came directly to the railing. I got up hastily, in excitement and alarm; and we faced each other without speaking for quite a period.

" 'You? . . .' she said at last in a low voice, drawing back. Her hand tightened on the rail. She was regally beautiful.

" 'For what do you wait?' I asked, striving to be calm.

"She threw down her arms with a violent gesture. 'A word, a message!' she cried. 'Can you tell me nothing? Has he come?'

" 'He is far away,' I answered.

"She put her hand on mine. 'You are his friend,' she said. 'I do not blame you now; I see that it rested with him alone. But keep nothing from me. Has he sent no word by you?'

" 'He does not know that I have come,' I said.

" 'Ah, I have waited, night upon night!' she cried. 'Whenever ships stop, I have waited here—in darkness, in rain—always!—thinking to see you, or that

he might come, or that a message. . . . Will he not
come? Tell me!'

" 'He will never come,' I said.

"She drew her hand away, and stepped back
sharply. Her voice rang out, fierce with hate. 'He
was a child. The woman took him! Tell me,
why? . . . '

" 'The woman was his wife,' I felt obliged to say.

" 'Enough!' she cried. Her form became rigid,
as if every muscle were stretched to the point of
breaking. Suddenly she relaxed, and turned to me
for the last time.

" 'He is happy?' she asked quietly.

"I nodded—for the moment I couldn't speak.

" 'She loves him?'

"Again I nodded.

"Her voice caught at the next question, but ral-
lied bravely. 'He loves her?—you are sure? . . . '

"I cursed myself for having come—but there
could be no kindness in sustaining the delusion. 'I
am certain,' I answered. 'He never will tire of her.
He loves her better than all the world.'

"She gave a quick cry, like one who has received
a vital wound. Before I could recognize the significance of the moment, she had moved swiftly into the
open. For an instant she stood with arms outstretched; but not until the dagger flashed above her
breast did I see what she held in her hand. When
I reached her she'd fallen in the rank grass, and life
had gone.

"And that's the way I left her, a figure very beautiful, crouching low as if to spring, the tall grass
closing over her, the mystery dissolved in mystery.

Aha!—these high spirits, this gruelling difficulty of
life. But she, you'll note, had solved the difficulty,
had met it boldly and triumphantly, with the master
stroke that levels fate itself to the dust. As for the
others, they had solved it, too, though not so keenly,
had triumphed, though not so magnificently—had
gone away, had found their home, were happy, for a
little longer. . . . What did it signify?''

MOMENTS OF DESTINY

I

For two weeks the ship had been hove-to off Cape Horn, bucking a black sou'wester that seemed only to gain strength and persistence as it blew. Day after day brought the same story, without a hint of change; the adverse weather seemed fixed for all time. It was as if they had run head-on into a wall of wind and water, as if a gigantic hand had reached down out of the sky to bar their way around the tip of the continent.

Fred Williams, the first mate, lunged aft along the weather alley. The gale screamed steadily overhead in the mizzen rigging; the ship staggered as a fresh squall struck her. He looked up to find Captain Chandler standing at the corner of the house.

"A fine prospect, Captain. It's blowing harder than ever this morning."

"Yes, I believe it is." Captain Chandler spoke with unusual quietness for so young a man. "We may as well make up our minds to a long spell of it. Let the ship take her medicine. There's nothing to be done till the wind changes."

"It's collision that I am worrying about, Captain. I've never sailed in a finer sea-boat than the *Resolute;* she's good for anything they care to send. But this infernal blow has collected quite a fleet of ships already, sir. I counted eight sail o' vessels in sight at dawn this morning, all hove-to. When we come around on the other tack, we'll strike back into a perfect nest of 'em.''

Captain Chandler nodded gravely. ''Right you are, Mr. Williams. Well, that's our business. Beginning with to-night, you'd better have a man in the slings of the fore yard, in addition to the double lookout on the forecastle-head. Relieve him every hour. And have our own sidelights reported every quarter hour. I'll try to keep on deck myself as much as possible in the night time.''

The mate drifted forward, while the captain paused a moment at the corner of the house, gazing across the bleak expanse of the Antarctic Ocean. Even in the narrow sector that his eye happened to rest on, there was a ship in sight, hull down in the murk and spray on the weather quarter. Her bare spars, carrying only the three lower topsails, leaned sharply out of the smother, like the masts of a vessel sunk on some hidden reef in the open sea. Other ships were scattered along the horizon; they appeared and vanished through the driving squalls, sometimes standing out for an instant with startling clearness against the ragged fringe of the sky. It was the season of long nights in those low latitudes. Williams was right; the abandoned waters of Cape Horn were getting dangerously populous.

His own ship handled herself sweetly, as she always did. The long curves of the *Resolute's* handsome hull eased over the seas with a reserve of buoyancy, in spite of the heavy cargo under hatches.

Captain Chandler, standing clear of the house and swaying his body to the violent heave of the deck, watched her performance with approval. He couldn't but be proud of his vessel. He liked to feel that she was his property, every stick and timber of her, that nothing in ordinary luck and reason could take her away from him. That was something, at any rate.

He took a few turns to the stern rail, walking easily on practiced sea-legs that anticipated every motion of the vessel. A low, leaden sky, turning almost to black in the west, hung on the sea, letting the daylight filter through in broken patches. Stretches of wild water were thrown suddenly into high relief, only to be as suddenly blotted out by the lashing rain. A dismal, hopeless day. Captain Chandler quickened his pace, his oilskin coat rattling like a suit of armor, as the scene closed in on him. Before he knew it, he was fathoms deep in the memory that always lay in wait for him now; walking the quarter-deck with grim, frantic energy, like a man running a race with destiny.

He might have won her, if Steve Goodall hadn't got in the way. God, how he loved her, even yet! His body shivered with passion as he paused at the stern rail to think of her, of her alone, her face, apart from the other fancies that crowded his mind. He saw it clearly—the fine eyes, with a touch of sadness, as they had looked at him when she had sent him away; the mouth, with its strong curves and maddening allurement; the woman herself, so lovely, so infinitely desirable, and now so utterly unattainable. He turned away sharply. At moments like this he felt on the point of flinging himself into the sea.

Perhaps she always had cared more for Steve Goodall than for anyone else. But Steve had been away from home so constantly, on foreign voyages —three or four years is a long time at the age of twenty-five; and Eben Chandler knew that there had been nothing definite between them. He had felt, when he arrived home this time to fall desperately in love with Hope Thatcher, his sister's closest friend, that she had forgotten Steve in a certain measure, that the coast was clear for him. She had responded, had let him show his love. She had been learning to love him, slowly and secretly, as women will.

Then Steve had arrived, home from a voyage around the world with a good record and an engaging personality; and the old relentless battle for a woman had begun. But it was quickly over. Hope wasn't the girl to doubt her own heart, or throw life away in sentimentality and unavailing sacrifice. She was too brave and true for that—and thus the more desirable. Steve's presence had reawakened her girlish love for him; she had made the choice without hesitation, and had told Eben exactly how the matter stood.

So Steve had won, apparently without half trying, and he and Hope were to be married at the end of the next voyage. To Eben Chandler, still fighting over the lost battle on his quarter-deck, it seemed impossible to admit it; the cup had been snatched from his lips too recently for him yet to have reconciled himself to fate. How was life to be endured, without the happines that he had only begun to know?

It certainly couldn't go on in this fashion. Day after day, and night after night, the loss pursued him, tormented him. There seemed to be no use in trying to live. He was beginning to neglect his ship; hadn't thought of the danger of collision, for instance, until Williams had reminded him of the situation. Perhaps he wouldn't care if the ship were to be lost at any moment, sinking him along with his dead hopes. Time, they said, would heal such wounds. Well, let time pass, then, as quickly as possible; he had need of some ministration. Unless he soon found a different outlook, he felt that he would go mad.

What an unaccountable thing it was, this choice of love. If Steve hadn't appeared, the whole case might have gone the other way. Damn him!—luck always followed Steve Goodall. This voyage was another illustration. Steve, in command of the ship *Orion*, had sailed for San Francisco two weeks ahead of the *Resolute*. He had probably reached the Horn before the black sou'wester had set in; had rounded the Cape, no doubt, with all sail set, and now was swinging merrily northward in the Pacific, while the *Resolute* threshed out her heart and spoiled her passage in the grip of the gale. To him that hath shall be given.

Darkness had fallen. The mood of revolt temporarily had worn itself out. Captain Chandler stopped at the weather rail, waiting for the mate to come aft. No use to blame Steve—no use to blame anyone—just an ordinary turn of life. But was it?

He couldn't forgive, not quite yet, couldn't restrain the bitterness in his heart. His mind felt weary and adrift. Why had Steve turned up, to spoil life for him? It might just as well have been otherwise.

The mate drew up beside him in the gathering gloom.

"I'm going below for a while, Mr. Williams. Be sure and have the side-lights reported. She lies nicely now. Call me at once if you sight anything."

II

How long he had been sitting on the cabin couch, staring straight ahead at the lee wall of the room, he could not remember. Long enough to go over the whole tale once more, to dwell on the face of his dreams, to realize with frenzied heart the appalling emptiness of the life that lay ahead. Long enough to revive acutely, as his physical weariness began to pass away, the mood of revolt and bitterness.

Through this mood, he became dimly aware of confusion on the deck overhead. A faint hail from forward; a loud answering shout from the quarter-deck. Heavy steps along the alley—some one running. A hoarse, wild crying in the waist of the ship. A hand at the door of the after companion—a voice drifting down, a frantic summons:

"Captain! On deck, sir! Big ship under the lee bow!"

He leaped to his feet, shaking himself like a man emerging from deep water. In a few strides he was up the companion, and had reached the lee rail.

Leaning forward, he peered intently into the night. The glow of the cabin lamp still blinded his eyes. Holding the rail, he ran forward and leaped to the main-deck. Abreast the main rigging, the mate's hand fell on his shoulder.

"A point on the lee bow, sir. She's close aboard. There!—see her green?"

Captain Chandler swung himself to the top of the bulwarks, hanging on by the main rigging. Then he caught sight of it—a tiny point of green light, lifted high in air as the *Resolute's* lee rail sank to the level of the water. As he watched it, the vague outline of the vessel herself, little more than a shadow against the blackness of the night, loomed on the crest of a great wave. He fancied he could make out her tall forefoot, stripped to the keel as the wave passed under.

A ship hove-to on the opposite tack. Coming toward him almost head-on. If he fell off, he might pass to leeward of her. The *Resolute* carried steerage-way, but would respond slowly. No time to lose. If the other ship likewise fell off, collision would be inevitable. If she were going to fall off, the order already would have been given, and nothing could change it. Rules of the road made little difference in such a pass; perhaps the other ship was unmanageable. All depended on what she was going to do.

These thoughts passed like lightning through Captain Chandler's head as he watched the green light closely, trying to make out if it were changing its relative position. Then a torch suddenly flared up on the forecastle-head of the oncoming vessel. The tall forward spars, the narrow belly of the lower fore-topsail, the lurid glare above the overhanging bows, leaped without warning out of the night, and stood poised in the surrounding blackness like a gigantic and terrible apparition.

"My God, she's almost on us!" screamed a thin voice from the main-deck.

"Shut up!"

In all the ship, these were the only words spoken.

To Captain Chandler, the lurid scene a couple of ship's lengths away was more than an apparition. He clutched the rigging behind him with a grip of iron. Something seemed to snap in the very center of his being. The man holding aloft the torch on the opposite forecastle-head was Steve Goodall. The wild light fell full on the tall figure standing alone at the knight-heads of the laboring vessel. No mistake—the attitude, the outline, were characteristic —Eben Chandler knew them too well, even at that distance, in the midst of that inferno. The ship, too—he began to recognize her features. It was Steve Goodall, in the *Orion,* lunging toward him out of the night.

In the brief moment of the flaring of a torch, Eben Chandler had encompassed the whole situation.

He knew, now, that the other man had no intention of falling off—knew it intuitively, through the message of the torch. Steve was an able sailor, a man of sound judgment; and this, in the crisis that confronted him, was the correct decision. Too far athwart the *Resolute's* hawse to save himself by falling off, it was his duty to hold his course, luffing if possible, and passing responsibility for action to the other ship. And Eben Chandler could clear the

Orion yet, he saw, if he gave the word to put up the *Resolute's* helm. If he didn't give the word, now, immediately, the ships would come together; and neither man nor God could stop them.

Well, why not? Finish it up, here and now, the last round of the contest. He was ready. Let them both render their accounts, in a tragedy of the sea. Let them sink together, success and failure, and nothing left to show. . . . Was it this—or was it the instinctive knowledge, not consciously admitted even to himself, that he stood the better chance in a collision, that as the ships lay and as they would come together, the *Resolute* would deal the *Orion* a ramming blow along the starboard side?

Why was he waiting, this irretrievable span, this moment of destiny? Was he considering the discovery that the failure to act could never be brought home to him in its real guise, that it would be attributed only to momentary indecision in a crisis where no one could have been certain of his ground? His mind was a mass of fire. Fragments of memory kept bursting through the pattern of his thoughts— vivid snatches of past scenes. He seemed to be spanning vast distances, receiving unimaginable impressions. He trembled as if in the throes of violent transmutation. All that it meant, appeared before his eyes like a panorama—all that it might accomplish, an awful gamble, a horrible and devouring temptation.

Even the mate, on the main-deck at his feet, could never know. The captain lost his grip—usually quick of decision—inexplicable—tight place, though —only an instant—no question of blame. So would run the opinion of the nearest expert, a man confronting the same situation.

Wait a little longer. . . . Yes, it was Steve, beyond the shadow of a doubt. Ruined his life. Always lucky. Married next year. . . . A little longer.

All this passed in a fraction of time, while the vessels were advancing half a ship's length toward each other. Then the torch went out. Pitch darkness swallowed ships and men.

"Captain Chandler! Are you there, sir? There's only one chance. . . ."

"I think she was falling off, Mr. Williams."

"No, sir! No, sir! We must put the helm up!"

Silence. A little longer . . . a little longer . . .

"Captain Chandler! For God's sake, sir!"

"Put the helm hard up!" The captain had found his voice at last; the roar carried above the noise of the gale. Several men started aft, shouting wildly. "Helm hard up! Helm hard up!" In the lead, the mate stumbled up the steps and dashed along the alley. He was crying like a child. "Oh, my God, it's too late now! Helm hard up, there! Oh, damn you, hurry!"

With the same instinctive precision which had marked his every movement during the instantaneous crisis, Captain Chandler leaped lightly to the main-deck, gained the weather bulwarks, and hurried aft. Abreast the mizzen rigging in the weather alley he paused, wrapped an arm around the sheer-pole, and turned forward again, ready and waiting.

Over his shoulder he heard Williams struggling frantically at the wheel, gasping and cursing. A

heavy squall had flattened the ship down to her lee
scuppers. He tried to make out if she were beginning to answer the helm—tried to estimate the
remaining margin of safety, but it was impossible
to estimate time itself. The moments seemed inter-
minable. He felt as if hours had passed, as if a
lifetime of anguish had suddenly descended on him
with the weight of inexorable retribution. What
had he done?—what had he done? Had he gone mad
—or had he deliberately tried to kill his rival?
Before his eyes, floating rapidly past in the heart of
the night, appeared the face of his lost love—
appeared, gazed at him steadily, and was gone.
No, no, not that! . . . he wasn't a murderer. Before God, he hadn't meant. . . . It wasn't yet too
late. This squall would knock her off—there would
be time. . . .

The *Resolute* began to lift on a long sea. As she
rose forward, her bowsprit seemed to be ripping out
the pillars of the sky. Directly under her bows, but
a little to windward now, a second torch flared. It
disclosed a great ship prostrate before them, her
waist presented to receive the blow that was coming.
Under the impact of the squall, the *Resolute* had
fallen off nearly enough to swing clear. Her jibboom was stripping the other ship's mainmast.
Yards were falling like trees in a forest, gear was
snapping like a volley of musketry. A wild crying,
like the voice of a distant mob, streamed through
the gale. Suddenly the jibboom carried away, leaping into the air like a live thing, and taking with it
the fore topgallantmast.

Then the *Resolute* came down on the sea. A terrific crash rent the storm. The shock that went through the ship seemed as if it would tear her asunder. Top hamper from all three masts crashed to the deck. A horrible splintering and grinding rose forward, where her bows were battering at the exposed flank of the other vessel. The two ships swung together, pounding heavily, their yards clashing like rapiers, carrying the battle into the sky.

Captain Chandler ran forward, dodging the falling debris, and swung himself into the weather fore rigging. The evil spell was broken now; the instinct of self-preservation had done its work and lost its power. He looked down into a narrow mill-race of boiling water that opened between the ships as they rolled apart. Again their ponderous sides crashed together. Above his head the fore topmast went over the lee rail, while almost at the same instant the fore yard fell at his feet across the bulwarks, sparing him miraculously. Directly opposite, in the side of the other vessel, yawned a great hole through which the ocean was pouring. Thirty feet of her starboard side seemed to have been bodily crushed in at the waterline.

The second torch on board the *Orion* had gone out; the rest was to be a voice in the night—a voice he knew.

"Ship ahoy! What ship is that?"

"*Resolute*—Eben Chandler. Is that you, Steve?"

"Yes. . . . Eben, I'm done for!"

Captain Chandler leaned far to windward, funneling his hands. "Try to jump aboard when we come together. . . . I may be done for, too!"

No answer. Something was happening aboard the

other vessel. Confused shouting broke out again. A moment passed. A great wave came, sundering the grip that the ships had on each other; they drifted rapidly apart. Before Captain Chandler's eyes the *Orion* slowly vanished in the darkness to windward. The shouting along her deck became mingled with the roar of the storm. Suddenly the hail came again, far away, but astonishingly loud and clear, as if a channel had been opened for it through the elements:

"I'm sinking, Eben! . . . . Tell her, *'Never mind.'* "

Dropping to the main-deck, Captain Chandler crouched in the lee of the bulwarks and covered his face with his hands. He was sobbing violently. A man running aft stumbled against him.

"Captain! What is it, sir? Are you hurt?"

He leaped up savagely, throwing off the mate's arm. "No—I'm all right. Have you been forward, Mr. Williams?"

"Yes, sir. She's badly stove. I can't make out how bad. The bowsprit is gone clean at the knight-heads."

"Sound the pumps, and let me know what you get."

"Yes, sir. . . . What's the matter, Captain. Have you been struck?"

"Nothing has touched me. I am perfectly all right, Mr. Williams. I'll wait here."

The mate hurried aft. Captain Chandler leaned against the bulwarks, burying his head in his arms. He couldn't go forward, not yet—couldn't bring himself to look at the damage under the bows. He wanted this moment, a moment alone . . . to think, to realize. . . . A murderer?—a murderer? It was over now; the matter stood between himself and God.

When Mr. Williams came back with his report, he found the captain apparently recovered from the shock.

"She seems to be making no water, sir. Must have struck with the overhang, as she came down on the sea. It seems incredible that her stem isn't injured. But she's a wreck forward and aloft. . . . You think the other vessel? . . ."

"Gone with all hands."

III

Once in the southeast trades, they began to make up some of the time lost off the Horn through storm and collision. The gale had blown itself out the day after the tragedy; then a spell of unusually favorable weather had set in. The *Resolute* was badly crippled aloft, but her hull had emerged from the crash perfectly sound. Passing ships offered assistance, but it was not needed. They rigged her up themselves, sending aloft the spare spars that a well-found vessel carried. In the meanwhile, a slant of easterly weather took them around the Horn and well across the zone of variables in the South Pacific.

For some time the officers noticed nothing strange in Captain Chandler. The work of rigging up the vessel in an open seaway occupied all their attention. The captain himself was a fiend of energy, driving the crew day and night, planning and contriving ten tasks for every one completed. Had they known what lay behind his ceaseless activity, they would have been alarmed. In spite of the constant demands on his craftsmanship, the labor was largely automatic; his real thoughts were engaged in other business. They roamed far, adrift in the universe, relentlessly going over and over a record that had closed. By day, he managed to conceal this deepening abstraction; but alone on the quarterdeck at night, lost in the hollow arch of wind and sky, in the immensity of the elements, he gave himself up without check to the awful consciousness that his heart held. At times he would cry out suddenly, or halt at the rail in an attitude of close attention. During these weeks, the man at the wheel often had a weird tale to tell in the forecastle; but it took some time for the rumor to find its way aft.

Thus they had reached the trades, the extra work had let up, leisure had returned along with tropical skies and quiet days. With leisure, the terrible burden on Captain Chandler's mind had increased by leaps and bounds. Only a moment—but he had deliberately waited; and that moment had carried death on its wings, death to a whole ship's company. He had known exactly what he was doing; he recognized it clearly now. A different nature temporarily had mastered him; but this was no excuse. He had waited, when he knew better, when waiting was a crime. He had committed murder. No one else knew.

He began to keep to the cabin more and more,

especially in the late afternoon and early evening, when the mates were likely to be aft. Hour after hour he sat motionless in the big chair beside the chart table, often refusing to go out to supper, apparently failing to notice the steward when he came in on tiptoe to light the lamp. A profound change gradually was taking place within him, a remarkable enlightenment. Many things that heretofore had seemed obscure and meaningless were now growing very plain.

Sometimes, in these long silent evenings, Steve Goodall would come in to talk things over. He would sit down on the sofa, laughing in his jaunty way, apparently much amused at the situation.

"Why did you do it, Eben? Did you really think that you could get me out of your road that way?"

"God knows, Steve. I guess I didn't think at all. I loved her too much, to be able to think. Can't you understand?"

"Loved her, or loved yourself? Which was it? But of course I understand. Only, you see, don't you, that you can never have her now?"

"I see more than that, Steve. But it rests with me alone. I must be my own judge in the matter."

"And your own executioner?"

"I haven't fully decided yet. I must take the ship in—maybe take her home. I'll determine later what the right thing is to do."

Sometimes, too, Hope would come in for a moment, bringing with her a fresh odor that seemed to sweep through the cabin like a breath of land-breeze. She wouldn't sit down—would stand for a moment, gazing at him with a look of pity harder to bear than hate or condemnation, and always speaking the same words.

"I loved him, Eben. I told you that I loved him. I chose freely. Did you expect this to change my choice?"

These were the occasions when the helmsmen would be startled to see the captain rush out of the after companion like a man pursued by terror, flinging himself into the open air with spent breath and staring eyes.

The rumor had come aft now. Mr. Williams tried to scoff it down, but his own mind was troubled. In his night watch on deck, he couldn't very well help hearing disquieting sounds through the cabin windows. Once or twice, without being observed by the crew, he had crept to the skylight to see what was going on below; but all that he could make out was the captain sitting in the big chair and talking to himself, now and then making slight gestures, as if he were not alone. Williams began to fear that the terrible experience off the Horn had broken the Captain's nerve.

There was the question of eyesight, too. Or was it eyesight? More than once lately, on deck with him at night, the captain had plucked his sleeve and drawn him to the lee rail.

"Mr. Williams, isn't that a vessel on the lee bow?"

"Where, sir? I don't see anything."

"There, there! Close under the lee bow? Don't you see her?"

"No, sir. Nothing there."

"Nothing there? . . ." Whenever this happened, Captain Chandler would lean across the rail, gazing wildly off into the night; then, with a muttered exclamation, would turn and go below.

One night, in his watch below, Williams was awakened by a violent commotion on desk. Men were running about, yards were swinging, quick orders were being given. He rushed on deck to find the ship in stays, with everything flat aback. At first he thought that she must have been caught by a sudden shift of wind.

"What's up?" he demanded of the second mate.

"God knows, Mr. Williams! The captain came on deck, and I went forward. I saw him run to leeward. Next thing I knew, he had her flat aback, with the helm hard down."

Williams hurried aft. Instinctively, he knew that he would find Captain Chandler in the lee alley.

"What is it, Captain?"

"My God, Mr. Williams, we were almost on top of a big ship! I caught sight of her close under the lee bow, standing toward us. What's the matter with our lookout, anyway?"

"Have you seen the ship since you came into the wind, Captain?"

"No. She must have gone about herself and stood away on the opposite tack. See if you can pick up anything with the night glasses."

The mate took the glasses with a heavy heart. Well enough he knew that nothing was to be seen. Then he went forward to straighten the ship on her course again. When the sails were full and he found time to come aft, the captain had gone below.

IV

One morning a couple of months later, the *Resolute* stood in from sea toward the Golden Gate. Picking up a pilot inside the Farallones, she closed with the land rapidly, heeling to a steady breeze that seemed to sweep directly off the heights of Mt. Tamalpais.

After a few vain attempts to engage the captain in conversation, the pilot drifted forward, joining the mate on the forecastle head, where they were busy getting out the anchor. Fort Point was coming up under the lee bow; he wanted to keep a close watch of the vessel. With the tide at ebb, the reef on the point ran out a considerable distance; they might not be able to fetch clear on the present tack.

"What's the trouble with your old man, Mr. Mate? He's a morose customer—would hardly open his mouth to me."

"Our experience off the Horn was pretty harrowing, as I told you. It seemed to take the starch out of him. He's been, as you might say, brooding over it ever since. I suppose he feels responsible."

"You don't say? Nothing worse, I hope?"

"Oh, no. He's in perfect shape otherwise. But it was a dreadful accident—enough to stagger any man's nerve."

Mr. Williams let his eyes rest with a look of heartfelt relief on the approaching land. He himself was worn out with anxiety and loss of sleep; for the past two months he had kept the captain constantly under surveillance. The necessity for doing this without arousing the other's suspicions

had made the task doubly difficult. At no time had
Captain Chandler's condition warranted removing
him from command; yet Williams had seen clearly
that all was not well with him. So it happened that
he still was in complete charge of the vessel on the
day of their arrival. The worried mate thanked
Providence that, with the pilot aboard and the ship
already entering the Golden Gåte, the voyage at last
was safely over.

The *Resolute* swept forward at an eight-knot clip
as the sea smoothed under the lee of the land. The
fresh breeze, flurrying down from the heights above
the harbor entrance, shifted to the northward in a
five-minute squall, long enough to luff her past Fort
Point with a safe margin. The harbor of San Francisco, with many ships lying at anchor, began to
open up beyond the shoulder of the town. Almost
immediately, however, the wind jumped to the
westward, heading the *Resolute* off against the
strip of shore between Fort Point and Telegraph
Hill.

"Now we'll have some quick work," exclaimed the
pilot, as he watched the ship's head fall off inch by
inch. "Does she handle cleverly?"

"The *Resolute* never missed stays in her life,"
answered the mate. 'You can depend on her to come
into the wind like a schooner yacht."

"Then I'll allow her to sag in pretty close. It's
a bad place here, but the longer we hold this tack,
the better position we'll be in when we go about.
There's the spindle on Anita Rock; see it, a little on
the lee bow? But the reef runs well outside of the
spindle. Well, it's good to have a real ship under

you; the last vessel I brought in was built for a scow.''

While this conversation went on forward, Captain Chandler, who had been pacing the quarter-deck in moody silence, taking scant notice of the ship's progress or the appoach of land, stopped suddenly, went to the port rail, and gazed with fixed attention across the empty reach to windward. For a sailor, the action was unaccountable; nothing was in sight on the water there, while all the interest of the moment lay on the starboard side, where the shore-line was rapidly coming up under the lee bow. But no one noticed him, or saw the wild expression in his eyes.

On the forecastle-head a tense silence had fallen.

"How far does the reef run out?" asked Williams anxiously, as the ship picked up her heels in the freshening breeze.

"Oh, quite a way. It's deep water almost to the edge of the rocks. We won't be able to squeeze by; but we can hang on a little longer.

A little longer. . . . All unknown, they were approaching another moment of destiny.

At last the pilot whirled in his tracks. "About ship!" he shouted, passing the signal to the captain with a wave of his arm. He and the mate started aft together.

Crossing the main-deck, they began to realize that the ship's course had not changed. The captain hadn't yet given the order to the helmsman. The *Resolute* held on unchecked, racing toward the danger that could not be approached any closer.

As the realization struck them, they both broke into a run, shouting frantically.

"About ship! About ship! Put the helm hard down!"

Captain Chandler stood in the port alley, clutching the rail with a desperate grip, gazing intently on the weather bow. His eyes flamed with the light of madness; he seemed like a man in the throes of a tremendous emotion.

"In a minute, Mr. Williams. We aren't clear yet."

"Aren't clear? We'll be piled up in a minute, sir! Put the helm down, there!"

"No, don't do it!—do you hear? My God, Mr. Williams, we can't luff into the waist of that big ship! *We aren't clear yet!*"

"What ship?" cried the pilot, staring to windward in amazement.

"There, on the bow! I've been watching her a long time."

Williams didn't stop to look. He tried to get past Captain Chandler and reach the wheel. The helmsman, puzzled by the confusion of authority, had completely lost his head. For an instant the mate and the captain struggled together in the narrow space.

"Captain, let me go! You'll lose the ship, sir. Put the helm down, there!"

"No, I say! Stop, Mr. Williams! Not yet! *I won't do it a second time!*"

While they struggled, the pilot scrambled to the top of the house, ran aft, and seized the wheel. He whirled the spokes madly. The ship came into the wind with a rush that seemed like a conscious effort

to escape her doom. But it was too late. With a
grinding shock, she took the outer ledge—crashed
on, staggering and pounding, while again gear
rattled from aloft and spars went over the side.
When she settled to rest on the point of the reef,
her bottom had been knocked out from stem to stern.

V

Two weeks later, another ship stood in from sea
toward the Golden Gate. She seemed to carry an
extraordinarily large company; men were scattered
everywhere along her bulwarks, while half a dozen
officers paced her quarter-deck. Even her captain
shared his side of the deck with another man.

"Well, Captain Goodall, here you are at last.
The land must look good to you, after such a close
call. If ever a crew escaped from the jaws of
death . . ."

"Yes, we really haven't any right to be alive,"
laughed Captain Goodall. "Who would believe that
boats could live in such a sea? But if the *Orion*
hadn't gone down almost beside your vessel, it might
have been another story; I wouldn't have cared to
be in the boats many hours, under those conditions.
How we got them overboard and kept them afloat,
and how you managed to pick us up without losing a
man, is all a mystery to me. I wonder what happened to Eben. Pilot, has the ship *Resolute* been
reported here?"

"The ship *Resolute?*" The pilot, who had been
listening to the conversation, showed his amaze-

ment. "Was it the *Resolute* that ran you down off Cape Horn, Captain Goodall?"

"Yes, the *Resolute.* What do you mean? Has anything been heard of her?"

"There she is." The pilot pointed to the south shore of the harbor entrance, where the tall spars of a wreck, leaning sharply offshore, had opened to view behind Fort Point.

"What, the *Resolute?* Ashore there? How did it happen? When did she come in?"

"She went ashore two weeks ago, Captain—a total loss. This Chandler, who was master of her, piled her up in perfect weather, as they were coming in. He had gone crazy, it seems, but no one knew of it. He thought there was another ship on top of him, and didn't come about in time. She struck the rocks full tilt, and knocked her bottom out. I remember, now, that they were saying he'd been through a terrible experience off the Horn."

"Poor Eben!" exclaimed Captain Goodall. "They think this experience was responsible for his condition? Too bad, too bad. Why, he wasn't in the least at fault; it was one of those collisions that can't be avoided. I suppose he thought we were lost, and the fact that he had sunk us preyed on his mind. Do you know what has happened to him, Pilot? Is he still in San Francisco?"

"A hopeless case, sir, I understand. They had to take him away."

CAPE ST. ROQUE

I

"FOR a long while, I had been greatly interested in the work of Lieutenant Maury," said Captain Forbes. "Lieutenant Maury!—a name to conjure with, in the palmy days. We Yankees were wonderful seamen, and clever, remarkably clever, at trade; but we hadn't many geniuses to be proud of, leastwise, in the seafaring profession. There were Donald Mackay and Lieutenant Maury, dreamers both, in a class by themselves, although they dreamed along very different lines. Mackay dreamed of ships, and Maury dreamed of passages; Mackay dealt with the curves and lines of a vessel's hull, while Maury dared to tackle the charting of the elements. And both, in their different fields, created a new regime.

"At the time of which I'm telling, Maury's fame was international; the whole seafaring world, the world in which we lived and moved and had our being, acknowledged its indebtedness to his well-grounded and practical vision. For wasn't he the man who had saved time for us on every passage, who had cut the corners of our courses to a minimum, who had shown us where to go and where not to go, where to find the wind we wanted and where it

271

couldn't be found; the man who had systematized
the sailing routes of trade? We'd largely been
going it alone, before his day, every man for himself and the devil take the hindermost; exchanging
experiences, of course, and spinning the intermin-
able yarn of the sea; but in the actual choice and
shaping of courses, keeping within the limits of a
conservative tradition.

"Forgive me—you belong to a world that has forgotten how to sail. The crossing of oceans under
canvas isn't as you suppose. The steamship lays
her course from port to port, or from shoulder to
shoulder of the continents in a straight line, regardless of the winds; and, quite unconsciously, you think
of the sailing vessel as doing the same. You think
she strikes as straight a line as possible, taking the
winds as they come. Nothing could be farther from
the fact. The winds of the ocean lie in zones, and
the trade winds that blow unfailingly around the
world forever, are the key to the whole plan. The
sailing master's problem, on a given passage, is to
avail himself of all the fair wind he can find; to
avoid the adverse zones, to place himself sufficiently
to windward so that the trades will not be against
him, and, in general, to do as little beating to windward as possible. Thus it happens that few ocean
crossings can be made in a direct line under sail;
while the majority of them are negotiated in a series
of legs and angles, of crooks and corners, that to a
landsman would seem like going around Robin
Hood's barn.

"So the knowledge of these zones of wind, and
how to handle them, was all-important to the sail-

ing master. Yet it's a fact, as I have said, that sailors for all the centuries of nautical endeavor had been largely going it alone; that is, the data of ocean conditions had never been assembled and worked out according to a scientific plan. The trade winds were utilized, of course, and certain other courses had been traditionally established; but nothing was proved and known, and the tendency was to exaggerate dangers and difficulties, to refrain from making experiments, to seek safety in the longest way around, and to accept custom as the inevitable. In short, the sailor was ignorant, superstitious and credulous; he never forgot, and never learned. He was a Bourbon, too.

"For instance, sailors for centuries after Vasco de Gama had been in the habit of rounding the Cape of Good Hope eastward bound with the land held close aboard. That region off the blunt toe of the African continent was the beastliest stretch of water to be found from Land's End to the Eastern Passages. The winds were tricky there, and seemed always to be ahead, while the notorious southers, the worst gales of that latitude, drove everything afloat against a long lee shore; the Agulhas Banks shoaled the water, raising a sea that was a proverbial terror among sailors; and the task of rounding Africa under these conditions was a bitter struggle often lasting many weeks on end. It was the desperate nature of this passage that inspired the story of The Flying Dutchman, the allegory of the man who, for his sins, was consigned to beat off the Cape of Good Hope forever, never to return and never to get around.

"Yet ships had to pass from the South Atlantic to the Indian Ocean, and that was the way it always had been done. Who would have dreamed of running south in the Atlantic to the latitude of 45°, six hundred miles below the tip of Africa, and there of swinging to the eastward and crossing the Indian Ocean in that low latitude; that is, of cutting a tremendous half-circle around the Cape of Good Hope, leaving it as it were in the lurch, so that the course seemed not so much the rounding of the cape as it meant the sailing of a thousand extra miles through empty seas? But this is the course that I've always followed, as a commonplace of nautical knowledge; and the secret of it is easy to explain. In the latitude of 45° you've crossed the zone of variables that lies below the southeast trades, and reached the 'roaring forties,' where a gale of wind is blowing almost continually from the west. When you've reached this zone, you haul away to port and run before the gale; day after day you reel off the miles, often scudding under three lower topsails, the main-deck flooded with the tops of green seas. You could circle the world in this latitude, never changing your course, carrying the same gale, if Patagonia didn't intervene. These are the 'westerlies,' where you 'run your easting down.' You use them as long as you want them, then swing north and leave them to blow on their eternal way. You turn north on the eastern margin of the Indian Ocean, striking up for the Straits of Sunda. You have rounded the Cape of Good Hope without having come near it or known anything about it; you have been hurled like a bullet along the miles, where

the sailor of old beat and floundered on the Agulhas
Banks, wearing out his heart and his ship together.

"The 'westerlies' had been discovered before
Maury began to scan the seas; although, even in my
day, many masters could be found who refused to
run so far to the southward, to go out of their way
for nothing, as they expressed it. Maury changed
all this. He set us busy investigating our own calling, put us to school to him, and knit the race of
seafarers into one great family. In the course of
years he had thousands of ship masters contributing
to his meteorological data at Washington, keeping
daily logs for him at sea, sending him from ports
at the far corners of the world his little printed
charts on which they'd recorded their just-completed
passages. This material he painstakingly worked
over and put into shape, giving us the benefit of a
thousandfold broader experience than we could have
gained by word of mouth from our contemporaries;
giving it to us clearly and practically, each fact in
its proper bearing, with the authority behind his
statements of a romantic vision and a scientific mind.

"He led us on, too, urged us to try new routes, inspired us with the zeal of adventure and exploration
and discovery—the breath of genius blowing away
the heavy old fog of conservatism. We justly were
proud of him; and the light he gave us disclosed a
new and fascinating aspect of the sea. There was
joy, real boyish fun, hidden away in what we had
been brought up to consider a prosaic phase of our
calling. To play with wind and weather, to run a
race with the elements, to be armed with knowledge,
and supported by the consciousness of power; to

wrestle with this whirling ocean globe, and now and then, through skill, to get a fall out of it—why, we were only beginning to find out what it meant to be a navigator.

II

"I had been master of the ship *Wandering Jew* for twelve years, in which time I'd made ten round voyages to the China Sea in her. New York to Singapore, Hong Kong, or Shanghai, with an occasional half cargo for Amoy or Foochow, and one voyage to Japan thrown in for luck; a leisurely couple of months at anchor in eastern roadsteads, loading general cargo; home again in a little over a year: this was the way of it, the finest traffic ever known. During those years, Maury was making especial efforts to cut down the run from New York to the Equator on the outward passage—the first leg of the journey, which if sailed in anything like hard luck was sure to ruin the outward voyage.

"There was a fixed tradition for covering this leg. Sail, if possible, on a westerly gale, and run an east course nearly to the Azores, through the variables; then turn square south and enter the northeast trades, much as if you were coming out of the English Channel, planning to strike the doldrums in the neighborhood of 25° west longitude. This was in order to place yourself to windward before taking the northeast trades; and this, in turn, was in order to be in a position to enter the southeast trades well to windward; and this, again, was in order to escape being caught to leeward on Cape St.

Roque, the shoulder of the South American continent. In the last analysis, the Brazilian Current
lay at the bottom of our wide angulation. This current, you know, runs northward from Cape St.
Roque along the South American coast, until it loses
itself in the Caribbean Sea. It was an established
platitude of the sea that, for a vessel caught to leeward on the corner of Brazil, there was no hope of
beating to windward against the sweep of waters
there. She would have to stand back into the open
Atlantic, re-enter the northeast trades, and try the
operation over again. Moreover, the Sargasso Sea,
through which we would have been obliged to pass
on a straighter course to the Line, was generally
believed to be a place of strange and baffling calms,
an infernal region from which escape was difficult.
Yes, this old legend persisted, even in my day, a
relic of the Spanish navigators; I've known masters, otherwise well informed and efficient sailor-
men, who no more would have crossed the Sargasso
Sea than they would have shipped the devil for
first officer.

"Maury raised the whole question. He didn't
deny the existence of the Brazilian Current, or claim
that it would be advisable for ships to sail on a
straight course from New York to Cape St. Roque.
He did, however, contend that the traditional run
to the Azores was unnecessary, that we safely could
cut our angle in the North Atlantic in half; and that
even if we did get caught to leeward on Cape St.
Roque, with a smart ship and ordinary ability it
would be no killing matter. As for the Sargasso
Sea, he ridiculed the superstition, assuring us that

we'd find the northeast trades blowing across those waters as strongly as anywhere else within their zone.

"The incident began in New York, where I once again was loading for the China Sea. Blake, in the ship *El Capitan,* and Shepherd, in the *Sea Witch,* two able men and handsome vessels, were loading alongside me, and would be due to sail at about the same time. We all were bound to Hong Kong.

"On our last night beside the dock, I had them both on board to supper and spend the evening. After a while, we fell to talking of Maury and his theories. Shepherd was a man of my own age; Blake was a vigorous ancient, a captain of the old school. A warm argument developed; the old man Blake was scornful of new-fangled notions, and banged his fist on the table.

"'I've been to sea for fifty years,' he shouted. 'I've crossed the Line in the Atlantic a hundred times. How many times has this fellow Maury crossed it, I'd like to know? Huh—Maury! Handle a rowboat nicely, I've no doubt, on a quiet river; but now it's ships and oceans he's playing with. Leave it to a landlubber to solve our difficulties for us. I'll use my own experience, thank you, when it comes to crossing the Line.'

"'Hold on a minute, Captain Blake. Lieutenant Maury is a capable seaman, and has come up through a good training; he's no landlubber. The Navy——'

"'Yes, the Navy!' Old man Blake exploded at the word. 'These young Navy sprouts—capable seamen, you call them? Capable dancing-men and tea-drinkers! A handsome spectacle they make, now, don't they, pretending to show a merchant captain of fifty years' experience how to sail his ship? They'll want to dress us up in gold stripes and brass buttons pretty soon.'

"I turned to Shepherd. 'Where do you stand in this argument?' I asked.

" 'Betwixt and between,' he said. 'I expect there's plenty of wind in the Sargasso Sea. But the last time I met it, the Brazilian Current was no slouch of a proposition, let me tell you.'

" 'Got caught down there, did you?'

" 'Caught? I was stuck off the mouth of the Amazon for four of the longest weeks I ever put in. I was master of an old three-masted schooner, my first command; we were bound from Boston to the River Plate, with a deckload of lumber half way up the lowermasts. The old *Jabez Cushing*—I'd as lief try to beat to windward in a dishpan. We fetched to leeward everywhere; and of course we finally landed on the shank of Cape St. Roque, plumb in the middle of the Brazilian Current. Down there, the southeast trades blow steady and strong— nothing but southeast trades, for ever and ever. And underneath your keel, the water's slipping away in the same direction; slipping away to lee- ward without a sign or sound, as if it was pulling you into some infernally deep hole where the bottom had dropped out of the Atlantic Ocean. It runs, like the wind, steady and strong—never a slack, never a spurt, never a blessed change. There we beat in the old *Jabez Cushing*, sliding off sidewise like a crab. At first, I had a notion the current would be less inshore; in we stood, till we sighted the coast of Brazil. No difference—sixty miles a day, it was running there; and the next day, farther offshore, it was running sixty miles; and the next day, sixty miles. Beautiful weather, a beautiful wind and sky, a beautiful smooth sea; but all rushing away, and slipping away, and sliding away, with nothing in heaven or earth to hold yourself by.'

" 'How did you finally come out?' asked Captain Blake.

"Shepherd laughed. 'I threw the deckload overboard in a heavy squall, then came about and stood back through the doldrums into the northeast trades. I was ninety-seven days from Boston to the River Plate, a celebrated passage in its day.'

"Well, now, see here,' I interposed. 'First, you allowed yourself to get caught too far to leeward; no one advocates fetching the mouth of the Amazon. Second, you had a clumsy vessel; you couldn't have made a decent passage in her under any conditions. With the *Sea Witch* it would be a different story.'

" 'Yes, the *Sea Witch* can sail. But, I'll have to confess, the bare memory of that Brazilian Current takes the starch all out of me. I wouldn't run a chance of meeting it again.'

" 'Do you mean to tell me, Forbes,' broke in the old man Blake, 'that you would dare to put the *Wandering Jew* into the Brazilian Current, and beat her around Cape St. Roque?'

" 'No such idea,' I answered. 'But I'm not so thundering afraid of the Brazilian Current, that I'll go around the north of Ireland to get away from it.'

" 'All right, all right,' he chuckled. 'We'll be on hand to welcome him, Shepherd, when he comes in

through Lymoon Pass—eh, Maury or no Maury.
And when we're slipping down through the southeast trades, we'll think of him back there, beating
away on the shoulder of Brazil. He needs a dose
or two of his own medicine.'

III

"Two days later we sailed on the tail of a westerly blow, the three of us together. The ships were
evenly matched, and for the first day it was a running race, with main topgallant-sails set and the
honors even. But our courses were like three sticks
of a fan; Captain Blake, true to his colors, held
away hard to the northward; I followed the southerly stick; and Shepherd's course lay in between.
Next morning the *El Capitan* was hull down on our
port beam; at noon I lost sight of her. The *Sea
Witch* outsailed us a trifle, and was in plain sight
that evening when darkness fell, broad on our port
bow. But at dawn of the second morning, the horizon was deserted. That day the westerly wind fell
off, dying out altogether in the late afternoon. The
evening and first part of the night were calm.
"Then came a breeze from a little to the northward of east, a fresh breeze, dead ahead, with signs
of blowing up a gale. I put the *Wandering Jew* on
the port tack and let her go to the southward, keeping the royals set. The sea was fairly smooth. I
wondered what the other ships were doing. This
east wind would be a puzzler for old Blake; he swore
that he never permitted himself to make a mile of

southing till he was ready to enter the northeast trades. He would be fetching Greenland on the starboard tack. Shepherd probably would compromise —would take the port tack, and shorten sail. I laughed to myself, and let the vessel go as fast as the weather would allow.

"Day after day the wind blew from the eastward. Now it was east-by-north, now it was northeast-by-east; now it forced us down to reefed uppertopsails, now it permitted us to set the royals again; but all the while it was sending us off to the southward, where we didn't exactly want to go. We were making a splendid run, and it wasn't the southing itself that I minded, but only the fact that it had come too soon. Why, we scarcely were fetching to windward of the Bermudas, and would enter the northeast trades. . . . Lord, when I thought of the northeast trades, it gave me a turn! We wouldn't be able to fetch clear of the Windward Islands; we would hit the Brazilian Current on the nose; we easily might land to leeward of the Amazon. But such a smashing breeze, such a glorious run.

"It was testing my faith, that east wind; it was bound that I should fairly face the question. After a while, I hesitated. Well enough to have theories, and to believe in them; but Maury in his most extravagant moments wouldn't have advocated such a course as this. My chief mate was bitterly skeptical; he went about decks with a long face from day to day, shaking his head as he looked to windward, and sighing deeply over the noon observation. But something urged me to keep on. At about that time, the wind headed us up a notch or two. Why not beat to windward in the lower part of the northeast trades, if I saw then that I was certain to be caught on Cape St. Roque?

"Next morning I came to a decision. I went on deck and called the mate.

" 'Set the three skysails,' I said. 'I'm going to hold this tack till we enter the trades.'

" 'Well, Captain,' he answered, 'I haven't seen Barbadoes for several years, but I always liked the place.'

" 'Cheer up!' I told him with a laugh. 'You're a doubting Thomas now, but you'll soon sing another tune, as they all do when someone has carried them by the corner.'

"I had one consolation—if the other two ships had struck the same easterly spell, they still would be beating far to the northward. My beating might come later. There was a decided advantage, it seemed to me, in doing this beating at the end of the leg instead of at the beginning; with Cape St. Roque close aboard, I would be able to see just how much beating to do; while off a couple of thousand miles they would be liable to do too much of it, for fear of doing too little. On the other hand, back in the zone of variables, they probably had met with a change of wind; while in the trades, it would be a certain beat for me till I fetched clear.

"We slipped into the northeast trades in 30° north and 60° west, right in the middle of forbidden ground; luffed to a southeast course, and struck off bravely with a fresh breeze. I drove the *Wandering Jew* hard, and jammed her for all she was worth; she was a splendid vessel on the wind, could head within

six points, and log twelve knots in this position
under the three sky-sails. I picked out the four best
helmsmen forward, and had them do all the steering. Every inch that I gained now, was as good as a
mile on the shoulder of Cape St. Roque.

"Meanwhile I pored over Maury's records.
There was one report that particularly interested
me; a long letter written by a Captain Spaulding, in the clipper ship *Ivanhoe*. Sailing from New
York for San Francisco, he had determined to try
the shorter route to the Line; had run into a spell
of easterly weather, and had let her go to the southward; had found the trades light and easterly, had
lost them early, had spent a week and a half in the
doldrums; and had fetched far to leeward on the
Brazilian coast, where he'd put in a couple of miserable weeks of beating. Only the unusual smartness
of his ship had made it possible for him to beat
through the Brazilian Current and win his way
clear.

" 'I am able to inform you, sir,' Captain Spaulding had wound up his report, 'that I tried your
new route for what was in it. I shall keep my chart
for a curiosity. I blew away two old suits of upper
sails, and wore out several coils of good Manila
braces. The yards wouldn't stop swinging for a
month afterward. Whenever I bring the ship close
to the wind now, she wants to tack. I hope to get
her straightened out in a voyage or two.' And in a
postscript he had added: 'I would like to show you
that Brazilian Current some time.'

"It was characteristic of Maury that he'd put
out such an adverse criticism from a man of prom-

inent standing. He wanted us to read both sides, and make up our own minds. This liberal method was a revelation to me; for, as the days went by, I realized that my best information, if not my chief encouragement, came from Captain Spaulding's record. I saw that whereas he had stumbled over the northeast trades, I was finding them fresh and northerly. Holding them wonderfully, too; I scarcely could believe my luck. We carried the trades to the Equator without a break, crossing in 35° west longitude. It was a handsome run to have made close-hauled; in ten days we had covered some twenty-five hundred miles. Seventeen days out from New York we crossed the Line. But 35° west longitude!—I'd never before ventured such a meridian. Cape St. Roque bore due south of me, the Brazilian Current ran between, and the southeast trades were waiting to catch me on the bow.

IV

"That day we lost the northeast trades; I knew the southeast couldn't be far away. I felt confident that we had dodged the doldrums. Our whole chance now depended on the direction of the southeast trades—for they vary widely near the Line. They came that night, from southeast; not so bad as it might be, but not good enough. The next morning, however, they shifted a point to the eastward; toward night they headed us up another point. The second mate, a perfect helmsman, steered throughout that day; at eight bells in the dog-watch

I took the wheel myself for the night. The sea was as smooth as a millpond, with a bright moon and a gentle breeze; I kept the weather leech of the mizzen sky-sail lifting, and could feel the ship beneath me eating her way into the wind. Another day and another night we held the port tack, clawing to windward, the second mate and I doing most of the steering; on the following morning the Brazilian coast was in plain view on the lee bow.

We had edged past Cape St. Roque, but the corner at Pernambuco was going to catch us. I had no coast charts of the region, and daren't approach the land any nearer. So we came about at noon, and stood away on the starboard tack that afternoon and night. Next morning we came about once more on the port tack; and before nightfall picked up the land to leeward, saw that we were clear of the last corner, and let the *Wandering Jew* fall off a little free. The trades increased, the ship settled down to her business, and we were flying along the second leg of the passage.

"After that, we couldn't seem to stop. We ran from the southeast trades directly into a spell of westerly weather; in the 'roaring forties,' a single gale swept us across the Indian Ocean; before we could catch our breath, we were back again in the southeast trades. We passed Anjer sixty-five days out from New York, and caught the southwest monsoon in the Java Sea. In seventy-seven days from the date of our departure, we raced through Lymoon Pass and anchored in the harbor of Hong Kong. Needless to say, neither the *El Capitan* nor the *Sea Witch* had arrived.

"We had been at anchor a solid month in Hong Kong, and had discharged the last of our cargo, when Shepherd brought the *Sea Witch* in one day. He had thought that he was making a banner passage; had found a report of me at Anjer, but had felt it to be an impossibility and put it down as a mistake; and wouldn't believe my story till he had seen my charts and verified the date of my arrival.

"A week later, the *El Capitan* came nosing in. I took my charts of the Atlantic Ocean, called at the *Sea Witch* for Shepherd, and we were alongside the newcomer in my sampan before Captain Blake had let go his anchor.

"'Well, well,' he said, as he met us at the gangway. 'You both got here ahead of me, after all.'

"'Yes,' said Shepherd. 'I arrived last week. But Forbes, here, is loading for home.'

"'Loading for home!' The old man Blake whirled on me. 'When in thunderation did you get in?'

"'Five weeks ago,' I told him. 'I was seventy-seven days from port to port.'

"His jaw dropped as he looked at me. 'Give me your charts,' he demanded. He spread them out on top of the after house, glanced down my track, and gave a long whistle.

"'You see how the theory works out, Captain Blake,' I said. 'The easterly spell that we met off the Coast was just a slant for me. I stood to the southward, and didn't give up the port tack till I came about off Pernambuco. What were you doing in that easterly spell?'

"'Beating,' he answered grimly.

" 'Where were you—let's see—on the twenty-fifth of April?'

" 'Beating.'

" 'You hadn't left the variables on that date? You hadn't entered the northeast trades?' "

" 'No.'

" 'That was the day that I passed Cape St. Roque.'

"The old man Blake brought his fist down with a crash on top of the charts. 'I'll try it!' he shouted. 'I will! I'll be damned if I don't! Surge old spunyarn!—seventy-seven days!' "

"The next time I met him, three years later, he had tried it; and was an enthusiastic supporter of all theories put forward by Lieutenant Maury, at the Hydrographic Office in Washington."

A FRIEND

I

On the other side of the world, in China waters, the old New England sea captain and I sat on deck one evening and talked of home. The lights of Hong Kong rose like a breaking wave at the base of the Peak; the breeze suddenly fell still, as if a curtain had been drawn between the ship and the land. He told me a story of himself, a story as old-fashioned as a family portrait or a dress of purple poplin laid away in camphor wood.

"Have you ever catalogued your friends?" he asked. "A man finds a host of them, going up and down the world, fellows we enjoy talking with, and hearing about, and seeing now and then; all the great company of those we've met on common ground. There are the ones we've known intimately, the ones we've eaten and drunk with, sailed with, played with, lived with; there are the ones who have liked us in the past, and followed us, and served us, and seen us stripped, as you might say, down to the ground. They filled our lives once; we couldn't have conceived of leaving them behind. And now where are they? We've lost sight of them; they are forgotten. They haven't lasted—or we haven't lasted, which is much the same thing. We even can't recall some of their names. And the strange thing about it is, we don't miss them. We see that they were transient guests in our hearts; they didn't touch the depths, they didn't come to stay. . . . But there are a very few, known to us always, perhaps not always thoroughly understood; and after years have passed by, and the quick youthful flames have become ashes, we discover that in some unaccountable way these few have remained with us in a secret chamber, emerging now and then with tried and constant affection, like fixed lights on a horizon of wheeling stars.''

He paused for a moment. ''Will Staples and I grew up together in an old ship-building and sea-faring town,'' he went on slowly. ''You know the town; you've seen its name in gilt letters on the sterns of ships in every Eastern port. We all followed the sea there, and had for generations. Will's grandfather and mine had been pioneers in the coasting and West India trade. His father was a successful retired ship master; mine was unsuccessful and still at sea. This marks the difference between our families; but it was no difference to us as boys. Will had everything a boy could ask for, the best of everything—guns, boats, skates, fishing rods, bats and balls (no one used a padded glove in those days—I caught behind the bat with a skin-tight glove); but he shared it all with me. He'd have shared a great deal more if I would have accepted it; but I was touchy and proud.

''In fact, pride was about my only asset in boyhood—pride, and athletic ability. I was a good

fighter. I even whipped Will once, at the beginning of our friendship. After that we fought in
pairs, and many a stiff battle he and I won against
the Down-Towners; we lived in the East End. Then
he reached the age of thirteen—he was a year the
older—and suddenly outgrew me physically in a
season; shot up into a big strapping youth, while I
always remained small. He assumed the rights of
protector—anyone who was my enemy, was his
enemy; and as I was continually at swords' points
with someone over a real or imaginary insult, he had
his hands full most of the time. Looking back, I can
see in him during those adolescent years the
predominating traits of the character he later developed; loyalty, honesty, frankness, self-confidence,
generosity, and all combined with tact and insight,
for he treated me squarely, in a way that didn't
hurt or lessen me. You recognize the difficulty,
don't you? It's sufficient to say that never for an
instant did he try to make me his fag. We came
through boyhood shoulder to shoulder, with perfect
understanding and no illusions about each other.

"We went away to the same school, and roomed
together. Our boys didn't go to college then; they
had two or three years at what today would be
called a preparatory school, entered a ship's forecastle at the age of sixteen or seventeen, worked up
to the quarter-deck in the next few years, and commanded a vessel when they were twenty-one. At
school, we continued to be friends through the most
tremendous and distrustful period of youth; we
even grew more intimate, as we successfully negotiated the bigger relationship. Our instincts devel-

oped together; we estimated the new world with
the same eye. We were clean fellows, I'm glad to
remember.

"There were rocks, too, on which we split—girls,
for instance. He always had been a great girl's
boy, perhaps because he was so much of a boy's
boy; later he became one of those men who exert a
powerful attraction over women. I was a boy's
boy, too, but of a wholly different nature. As early
as school days, my heart was attached to one girl, the
one that I finally married. I was too serious about
it for my own happiness. But Will was a free agent,
courted half a dozen girls at once, and cut a dashing
figure. That made the girls love him all the more;
and it made me admire him against my will. I was
his room-mate; it couldn't help meaning much to
me, to have him the leading spirit of the school.

"He might have had anyone for a chum; there
were rich fellows in school, and clever fellows, and
fellows with plenty of dash and recklessness, while I
was quiet and morose, quick of speech and independent of action. I never toadied to him; but we liked
each other. Yet sometimes I used to wonder why
he clung to me; and once, in a moment of dissatis-
faction with myself, I broached the subject.

"'Why, didn't we come here together?' he
answered with a puzzled look—his psychological
processes were not so complicated as mine. 'You
don't want to break up, do you, Skeet?' They used
to call me Skeet, short for mosquito, because I was
fiery and small.

"'Of course I don't,' I said. Then I went on to
remind him of my unimportance in school affairs, of

how his money had furnished the room, of how most
of the things in it were his. . . .

"He stopped me short. 'Aren't you as good a
ball player as we've got on the team?' he demanded.
'Can't you lick anyone in school but me? What are
you talking about? Why, God damn it, I love
you!'

" 'But I'm not in your ring,' I insisted perversely.

" 'Shut up, you fool!' he yelled at me. 'And
don't be so sensitive. You scared me, for a while.'

"I remember the time they tried to keep me off
the ball team. In those days it happened that most
of the fellows who played ball were well-to-do, perhaps because the expenses of the team were borne
by the players. I worked nights and Sundays at
manual labor in order to earn enough to pay my
share. That spring, without consulting Will, they'd
planned to go on sailing trips to all the neighboring
towns (the school was on a river), and play a series
of games with the town teams. Every trip would
mean a wild time; they naturally wanted a congenial
crowd, and black-listed my name. Will, however,
they couldn't do without; he was their star pitcher.
But they hadn't dared to consult him, on account
of me.

"One evening he inadvertently found out about
the plan. He went at once to the captain of the
team—I've forgotten the fellow's name—told him
exactly what he thought of him; and they fought it
out by moonlight under the window of the Precep-
tor's room, while the good old man wrung his hands
and expostulated with them from the sill. The captain was the older and heavier boy, but Will could

fight like a wildcat, and righteous anger made him irresistible. I was sitting alone in the room, innocent of what had been going on, when suddenly he burst in, swearing and half-crying, with one eye blackened and his nose running a stream of blood. He wouldn't tell me anything about it; threw himself down on the bed, and refused to speak a word. By and by a few of the baseball crowd came to the door, intending to propitiate him. Without moving, he told me not to let them in. They tried to push past me; Will leaped from the bed, grabbed a baseball bat, and attacked them like a madman.

" 'You dirty skunks!' he shouted after them down the corridor. 'We'll settle this tomorrow.' Then he came back and stood in front of me. 'I won't have it!' he cried. 'I'll leave school first. If they think they can turn that kind of a trick. . . .'

" 'What's it all about?' I asked.

" 'They're trying to give you a dirty deal, Skeet,' he said. Explosively and incoherently, he told me enough to understand the row. Then I was mad with him. I began to give him a terrible blowing up; the bare idea of his fighting my battles in public —shaming me that way—what in hell did it matter, anyway? But in the middle of my tirade, I stopped and became confused. His hurt look had warned me; I went to him instead and put my arm around his shoulder.

"There were many long, quiet evenings that we spent together, when the sober mood that hovers over boys got hold of us. We would lie for hours on the bed, talking of right and wrong, of love, of ambition—yes, very much of ambition. The world looked big and rosy to us, and in our hearts we felt the power to achieve. Will knew exactly what he wanted; I knew what I wanted, too, but wasn't so willing to talk about it. I can hear him yet, lying beside me and planning our careers. 'We'll both have ships, and be successful, and earn a lot of money,' he would prophesy. 'We'll each have a wife and family; then we'll retire, and build ourselves houses, and we'll have boats, and horses, and dogs, and everything we want.' He would reach over and pat me on the arm. 'You wait, Skeet, my boy, and we'll show them how it can be done.'

He didn't leave me out of the future, either.

II

"My father died at sea in the spring of my sixteenth year; in the space of a day, when the news arrived, I became the head of the family. We had no means; it was necessary for me to buckle down to life at once. I left school, and shipped before the mast in a vessel commanded by a cousin of my father's. I never liked him, and he never liked me. So that career of mine got a bad start; for my relative did nothing to further my advancement, and a good deal to hinder it, as it lies in the power of a shipmaster to make or mar a green lad's reputation. Equipped with a nature violently independent, I was chained by circumstance to an early course without independence; I daren't leave the ship I was in, for fear I wouldn't find another. The money was needed at home.

"I lost sight of Will, and several years went by. Now and then I would write, now and then I would get a letter from him; but it soon appeared that our friendship wasn't the corresponding kind. He followed me to sea in a couple of years, sailing from the first in one of his father's vessels; and at the age of twenty-one, in normal fashion, had taken his first command. At twenty, I still was a second mate when he became a captain. Then the old bark *Hudson,* in which I'd sailed ever since starting on the sea, was lost on the coast of Australia, and we were lucky to bring our lives out of the wreck. I soon found another berth, but it wasn't promising; I hadn't succeeded in placing myself in line for sound advancement. Friendships and influence were all-important on the sea. Gradually I came to believe in my own ill-luck. My disposition, too, was against me; I was too sensitive, too proud. I said what I pleased, and made enemies instead of friends. I rose to a mate's billet easily enough, in the course of the ⌐ext two years, for my worth and ability as an officer couldn't be questioned; but the next step upward, from mate to captain, seemed farther and farther away.

"Just at this time I met Will Staples again. It happened in Pisagua; he arrived one afternoon, and we were due to sail the following morning. He had been captain of the *Challenger* for a couple of years; I was mate of the *Solferino.* As I watched him round to and anchor in his fine ship that afternoon, a mood of desperate revolt came over me. I didn't want to see him—hoped he wouldn't come near me. The chip on my shoulder fairly quivered with the desire to be knocked off. I thought of him with anger; all the old intimacy seemed gone. No man was my friend just then. He was a captain, I was a mate; a gulf lay between us. To meet him would only be uncomfortable. I knew, however, that he was aware of my present berth, for I'd recently written him. And in my heart of hearts, I suppose I knew that when he found the *Solferino* was in port, he would come at once to see me.

"He came that evening. I caught sight of him sitting in the stern-sheets of his boat before he drew alongside. By the time he'd stepped over the rail, I had vanished forward. The captain met him, took him aft and down below. I hadn't indulged myself in a glance at him; but when I thought he must be out of sight, I looked aft to see him standing at the head of the companion, evidently trying to locate me somewhere on deck. He had grown into a fine figure of a man; the air of confidence and command hung about him. I cursed under my breath. God, if he should send for me to come to the cabin! He had too much sense to do a thing like that; but now that I'd seen his face again, there was a great ache in my heart that seemed to be eating up the bitterness. I came aft and went to my room, for no better reason than to be a little nearer him.

"I hadn't been long below, when someone knocked on the door. 'Come in!' I snapped. The door opened, and Will stood there grinning at me.

" 'What kind of a game is this to play on a fellow?' he demanded in his old impulsive way.

" 'No game at all, *sir*,' I said in a nasty voice.

'I was busy forward when you came aboard, and couldn't very well leave.'

" 'Oh, were you?—couldn't you?' he said, a sudden flush mounting to his face. Then he threw back his head with a quick toss, as if to snap a bad mood away.

" 'I didn't suppose you'd care to see the mate,' I persisted absurdly.

" 'Shut up!' he roared at me. He came in and closed the door firmly; then crossed my little room, and put his hands on my shoulders. 'It's been a long time since we've seen each other,' he said. 'If you want to spoil it by fighting, I'll go away.' I tried to look him in the eye, but my lip suddenly was trembling. He gave me a vigorous shake. 'Skeet, you're a bigger fool than ever!' he exclaimed. The old nickname tore my heart like a knife. Pain and disappointment and memory came on me all at once; I threw myself on the bunk and broke down. He sat besides me, with his hand on my back. 'I didn't know it was as bad as that,' he said.

"After a while we began talking. He had had disappointments, too, I learned; but he was getting ahead, while I was standing still. He swore at me when I reminded him of this. 'How old are you?' he asked scornfully. 'Anyone would think, to hear you talk, that you were a worn out old man. Your life's all ahead of you yet!' I knew it—but it did me good to hear him say so. I was in desperate need of encouragement; the loneliness of a sailor's life at times seems unendurable. Gradually, as we talked, the years were swept aside, and we were

chums again. Thoughts that I'd buried, and others
that I'd forgotten, revived in my heart; hopes,
dreams, aspirations, the stuff of ambition that was
in danger of being soured in me too young. He
asked about the girl that I was going to marry; I
told him that she still was waiting. 'I guess she'll
have to keep on waiting,' I said. 'That's what
makes life so hard.'

"He touched my arm. 'But she's glad to
wait—I know her,' he said. 'That ought to make it
easy.'

"His words seemed to break through a great
cloud that hung over me day and night. 'It
does, it does. . . .' I admitted. 'It would be all
right, if I could see where I was going. But
now. . . . Lord, Will, you've done me a lot of
good!'

" 'It does me good, just to look at you, you little
fighting cock!' he cried. 'You're the only fellow
who ever stuck by me through thick and thin.
That's why you hurt me so like hell tonight, when I
came aboard.'

" 'I was sick . . . heart-sick,' I told him.

"He nodded rapidly. 'The same old boy,' he said.
'Why do you make yourself suffer so?'

"We fell to talking of school days; while he was
telling me what had happened to the different boys
and girls after I had left, the captain of the *Solferino* came through the forward cabin hunting for
Will. I asked him in; he sat on my trunk and
smoked in silence, while Will and I yarned away like
a couple of boys. The etiquette of the ship was
broken for a while; I felt on an equal footing with

them. The same freedom would have been impossible, had I been asked into the after cabin. As he listened, I could see that my captain was gaining a new respect for me. A couple of hours passed swiftly, every minute of the time adding strength to my spiritual rehabilitation. Then they went away, in the same free and easy fashion. Later, at the rail, I said good-bye to Will for another term of years. That night I lay awake a long while, eager with happiness and anticipation. The world seemed a better place, the battle of life more worthy, the chances more favorable. I had got back a friend.

"We sailed early the following morning; I didn't see Will again face to face. But he was on deck when we crossed the *Challenger's* stern, waving his hand and watching us through his glasses. 'Good luck, Skeet!' he shouted across the water, oblivious of the listening crews. I gave the first laugh of sheer pleasure that had been vouchsafed me for a long time. I could even sing out, 'Good luck, Captain!' without thinking of the word.

For months my heart was lightened by the memory of that evening. Maybe the inspiration lasted longer than I know. My spirit had been on its last legs when he appeared; another shove, and I might have started on the down-hill journey that ends in disaster. Who knows? Our lives are turned by the weight of a feather; by events unnoticed and unrecorded, by things so easy to do yet so often left undone. Who has influenced you most by saying least? That man is your friend.

III

"Two more years passed by; I heard that Will had left the sea, had married a girl we both knew at home, and had gone into the shipping business in New York. He didn't write me the news. I know the reason now—he wanted to wait till he could make me a definite offer; but at the time my morbid sensitiveness conjured up another cause. I imagined that at last he wanted to drop me. Well, said I, there isn't an easier person to drop on the face of the earth. So I proceeded to drop myself. Whenever I'd arrive in New York, I deliberately would refuse to look him up or send him any word.

"My own affairs, in spite of the season of encouragement, had taken no turn for the better. The *Solferino* was a splendid ship, but I had committed an error of judgment in staying by her. From voyage to voyage I'd continued to go first mate, on the promise of an eventual command from her owners; but I had neglected to inform myself of the business standing of these owners. They suddenly went into bankruptcy, just as the *Solferino* was due to arrive in New York; instead of getting my command, which I'd hoped for at the end of this voyage, I found myself on South Street without a berth, and with a record of having been mate too long.

"Life indeed was passing; I had wasted nearly five years in the *Solferino*. All the boys who had started out to sea with me, had left me hull-down astern; it's a serious thing when a grown man begins to call himself a failure. My temporary revival of spirits so long ago in Pisagua had died and been buried in the fruitless years, and I was bitterer and more discouraged than ever before. Had I been in a normal frame of mind, I would have gone at once to Will. But the chronic malady of my ill-luck made this the most impossible thing in the world for me to do. Subconsciously, I must have known that he hadn't changed toward me; but I was the prey of an acutely conscious ego, and subconscious truth hadn't even a ghost of a show to make itself heard. Easy enough to look back, from the vantage point of age and wisdom, and condemn my moral perversity, which I called pride; but to deal with the present, the actual mood, the devil himself, is quite a different story. It's a damned sight harder to live life now, than to analyze it afterward.

"I stopped at a hotel on the water-front where all seafaring men used to put up; by day, I made a desultory search for another ship, but when night came around, I walked the Battery, or locked the door of my room and paced the floor. I felt like the top boards of a deckload after a long voyage, all warped and twisted. I couldn't afford money to waste on amusements; mother was ill at home, and my younger brother had to be kept in school—the same school I'd attended a century or two before. The girl I loved as faithfully as ever—she was a woman now—was still waiting. Indeed, it wasn't easy—my anxieties and disappointments were real. I would have given the world to run home for a brief visit; but I had to find a job at once—find myself first. Besides, I couldn't have stood the questions I'd have been asked on the streets at home.

"One evening, as I was smoking a pipe in the only

chair my room afforded, there came a loud knock at
the door. I got up irritably, forgot that it was
locked, fumbled a while with the key, cursed my
caller roundly, whoever he might be, and at length
got the door open. Outside in the corridor stood
Will Staples, the same grin on his face that I'd seen
that evening in Pisagua.

" 'Hello, Skeet,' he said, holding out his hand.
'I've been thinking of you all the afternoon. I want
to spin a long yarn with you.'

"I shook his hand—but I felt angry with him for
having looked me up. He came in, and sat down on
the bed. Now for a curtain lecture, I said to myself; well, let's get it over with as quickly as possible. But no, he hadn't a word of reproach to utter;
his tact that evening plainly was inspired. For see
what a ticklish place he'd projected himself into;
he had to tread on eggshells, at the same time main-
taining a firm step and an air of nonchalance. He
chose, wisely, not to beat about the bush; didn't ask
about my affairs, didn't refer to home or friends.
He had come to make me a business proposition.
He knew of a ship that would be available, and stood
ready to lend me the money to buy a master's interest in her. It was the chance that I had been
waiting for.

"A perfectly unreasonable antipathy to the plan
rose and swelled within me, took complete possession of me, like the mania of a disordered mind. I
refused his offer point-blank. I felt that I couldn't
take his money or his patronage.

" 'All right, Skeet,' he said at last. 'You know
best.'

" 'Don't think me ungrateful, Will,' I answered, finding the decency to be apologetic. 'The fact is, I've about completed a deal to go into another ship, and I can't drop out of it.'

" 'What ship is that?' he asked.

" 'I have to keep it to myself,' I said. 'When it's settled, I'll come around and tell you all I know.'

" 'Good enough, Skeet!' he exclaimed. 'I'm glad for you—you deserve the best. Don't forget, now, that I want to hear about it as soon as you're free to tell.'

"You may have been thinking that, if he were such a friend, he should have done something for me in a material way long before this. If so, I've failed to make the story clear. I wouldn't have allowed him to help me; and he knew it. You must remember the custom of that town from which we sprang, its social texture, its dominating principles of life and activity. You must bear in mind the stringent ethics of the sea. To have made my advancement under Will's ægis would have tarnished my position and destroyed my self-respect. Will could go forward under the family ægis with full propriety; but it was my task to win success single-handed, unless my family could help me. He would have done anything in the world for me; it must have been a bitter cross to him that we couldn't share ships as we used to share fishing rods, that the silly conventions, formed to protect a selfish society, had branded us with the mark of pride and shame. But heretofore he had known the world and me too well to make me an offer. He could help me only by remaining true to an ideal.

"What I had said to him about a ship was part truth and part lie. I had that very morning heard of a little bark with a master's interest for sale; but until the words had passed my lips, the notion of buying into her myself hadn't entered my head. Where would the money come from? But when Will had gone out that evening, it came over me with a rush that I'd have to make good my word. Well, why not? Why not tackle a big task as well as a little one? Other fellows did it. But I would at last have to button in that famous pride of mine. There was a distant branch of my family living in New York, people of wealth, who for some reason or other had turned a cold shoulder to my father, who never had taken an interest in me or disclosed a knowledge of my existence, and whose doorbell naturally hadn't felt the touch of my hand. But I would go to them now. Pacing the floor of my room, in a moment of sudden impulse, I tacked ship and stood into uncharted waters. I congratulated myself on my decision; I was a man of spirit, with plenty of fight left in me still. . . . It isn't strange that I overlooked the thankless office of a friend.

"Luck took a flip in my direction. I forced myself to call for the first time on my New York relatives; and couldn't believe my senses when I found them agreeable and even delighted that I had come. The estrangement between our families had been another of the mistakes of life. In the library after dinner, over our cigars, my business proposal met with a favorable reception; I asked for the first loan of my life, and discovered that it wasn't such a mean predicament as I'd supposed. Next day I talked with the owners of the little bark, and won their confidence. In a week's time I'd given my note, received and handed over my money, and was master of the bark *Ella*, of 800 tons register, painted white with a fancy gilded billet-head and a round stern—the only round stern I've ever seen on a down-east sailing vessel.

"I rushed immediately with the news to Will Staples, for now I could talk to him as man to man. He was overjoyed, as much, perhaps, at the change in me, as at the accomplished fact. He insisted that I go home with him that night, to see his wife—I'd known her as Grace Porter—and the two children. But I hadn't time; the bark was loading in Boston for the River Plate, and I wanted to leave for home that afternoon. I threw bitterness and disappointment to the wind, and went home in an ecstacy of good spirits, in a hurricane of love. It was summer; the town seemed more beautiful than I remembered it. The woman of my choice met me in just the way I wanted; we were serenely happy, happier than a month before it would have seemed possible to be. Mother was growing old; but when I talked with her, she showed me that my life had been worth while. My brother came home from school to see me, a strapping lad, full of the news of youth, charged with an unblunted enthusiasm; I swore an oath that his ways should be easier, if I could manage it. Thank God, I told my betrothed, we wouldn't have to wait much longer. One trip to the River would clear things up; when I returned we would be married. We made many plans, as people will when they're in love; the world grew big and rosy again, just as it once had seemed in an ideal picture—just as it always might be, if we could leave it alone.

"For a while, luck sat on the end of my spanker boom, as the saying is. We had a high figure on lumber to Buenos Ayres; out there, I chartered her for home at a paying rate on hides and wool. The little bark was a beauty, sailed like a witch, and took me to Buenos Ayres in forty-five days. We left for home with every prospect of making a four-months' round trip, quick work and excellent business.

"We had reached the vicinity of Fernando de Norohna on the homeward passage, when, one night in the middle of a howling squall, the air thick with rain and the vessel racing through it at a twelve-knot clip, we were run down by a big iron ship, travelling at the same rate on the opposite tack, and literally were cut in two. I caught a glimpse of painted ports, and noticed that she had four masts, but nothing more. We barely had time to throw a boat overboard; the ship that had rammed us, had immediately disappeared in the murk and confusion. Maybe she couldn't find us, maybe she escaped intentionally, or maybe she herself was badly injured, and went down. At any rate, we never saw her again.

"Our experience was dramatic and interesting, but I am telling you a story of the heart; it's enough to say that the little bark was gone. You know how much she meant to me, what years lay behind the getting of her, what hopes I'd built on the insecure foundation of this tiny wooden engine afloat on the deep. Well, here I was, suddenly cast into a boat in the midst of a tropic squall, with my foundation gone from under me. The squall passed, the sea grew calm, stars came out thickly; I covered my face to think. It was a terrible blow. The ship was insured, but I'd hardly be able to redeem my note with the proceeds. For the rest of it, more misery—more waiting and wandering. How had we ever dared to plan?

"Morning dawned at last; we shaped our course in the general direction of Pernambuco. That day we fell in with a steamer bound from Rio to New York; she picked us up and brought us home. Even in less than four months, the voyage was over; I had risen on the top of one wave, only to be swamped by the next.

IV

"The steamer docked at Red Hook in Brooklyn; I went to the foot of Atlantic Avenue and took the ferry for New York. I stood at the bow of the ferry-boat, watching South Street grow nearer—the familiar haunts, the piers crowded with shipping, the air full of the sound of life and activity. It was all waiting for me, to hear my story, to laugh, and then to smite me again.

"I had affairs that demanded immediate attention; was busy the greater part of the afternoon, so busy that I hadn't time to think. But at length I'd done all that I could that day. The sun sank lower, the air grew cold and frosty; it was mid-winter, and a penetrating north-wester was blowing. I went to the deserted Battery and stood for a long while at the sea-wall, facing the river and the wind and the setting sun. The gale didn't touch me—I was beyond physical sensation. All the thoughts that had been beating at my door throughout the afternoon, all the thoughts of the past two weeks, gathered together and came on me swiftly, as memories do when you stand beside the dead body of someone you loved. This was the finish. I saw it like a picture spread across the shafts of the sunset, and gazed at it with unwinking eyes. I was in debt and stranded, without a future, without an acceptable past, standing alone with the city behind me and the bay at my feet, like a man isolated in the toils of a terrible nightmare. What was the use of a true heart now? Then, without warning, the face of my love seemed to appear before me; the scene widened, like a rapidly moving panorama, and I saw in a single glance a vast accumulation of events, a fantastic jumble of forgotten impressions. Suddenly blindness fell on my eyes; something snapped in my head, and I lost track of what I was doing.

"I came to myself on South Street, at the foot of Coentes Slip. Evening had come, the gaslights were flaring in the wind, a flurry of snow fell from a low cloud. Several hours had passed unaccounted for. I felt sick and cold and hungry—but where should I go? Will Staples? Impossible! I no more could have gone to him than I could have begged for bread on the street corners. Why go anywhere? The evil thought kept pressing on me, returning insidiously; but I firmly thrust it aside. That wasn't the way to meet the issue. To a hotel room, then, and stare at the four walls? The idea seemed insupportable. Walk the streets? I was staggering already.

"I pushed open the door of a saloon, and entered a noisy, beer-smelling room. Men lined the bar, most of them sailors and petty officers. I knew two or three faces, saw them turn to me, light up with drunken recognition, detach themselves from the crowd, approach. . . . I wheeled at the door, and fled for the open air. Anything but tipsy sympathy! I wandered on, and by and by I brushed against a woman. The touch thrilled me. It semed to me that if I only could hold a woman in my arms, the crisis would solve itself in some unimaginable way. Don't think me unfaithful—it was a passing sensation merely. I had no intention, and stood in no danger of acting upon it. My love would have understood.

"A moment later, a man ranged up beside me, and took the bag out of my hand—I'd been carrying it unconsciously. I whirled on him, drew back my fist to strike—and saw that it was Will.

" 'I've just been down to the hotel, Skeet,' he said. 'They told me that you hadn't come in yet.'

" 'Well, you've found me,' I answered. 'Give me back that grip.'

" 'No,' he said. 'I'll carry it. Where are you bound?'

" 'To hell!' I cried wildly.

"He uttered an oath. 'Not yet!' he said through his teeth. 'Not by a damned sight, Skeet. You're coming home with me.'

" 'I can't do it,' I growled. 'I mustn't. I don't want to. For Christ's sake, leave me alone!'

" 'Grace came all the way to the office this after-

noon,' he went on as if I hadn't spoken. 'She had
seen an account in the morning paper of your arrival, and wanted to make certain that I had heard
the news. She said I must bring you home to dinner.
She's been getting things ready, Skeet, and it
wouldn't do to disappoint her.'

" 'You're making that up,' I snarled. 'You want
to play on my feelings.'

"For answer, he slipped his arm in mine. 'I'm
not making it up,' he said. 'But I want you like the
devil, if that's what you mean.' Resistance suddenly died out in me; I followed him to the ferry
like a truant boy.

"The ferry-boat was deserted; it must have been
after eight o'clock. We sat stiffly side by side in
the dimly lighted cabin. Over my broken spirit
swept alternate waves of anger and penitence, of
mutiny and remorse. The black mood was leaving
me, but I fought to hold it. In my mental chaos, I
conceived the notion that it was a weakness to accept
help in an internal battle; if I myself couldn't con-
quer, then I deserved to lose. Will didn't attempt
to talk with me. My mind wandered; it occurred to
me that the hour was late for him to be in the city.
How had he happened to meet me at the end of
Coentes Slip? It wasn't on the way from his office
to the ferry . . .

" 'Will, how long have you been looking for me?'
I demanded.

"He glanced away. 'Some time—a little while,'
he answered shyly.

" 'You've been running all over the lower end of
New York, ever since office hours!'

" 'I was afraid for you, Skeet,' he said. 'I've never been so damned scared in my life. I hadn't heard the news till Grace brought it. I reached the insurance office just after you had gone out. They didn't know where you'd gone. I went to the office of your owners; they hadn't seen you since two o'clock. Then I ran down to the hotel, but you weren't there. It was dark and cold, and it scared me. I've been on every pier between South Ferry and Fulton Street. I've been all over the Battery. At last I began going into barrooms to inquire of the loafers. It was in one of them that I got track of you. A man said you had gone up the street. Then I found you. Where have you been hiding all this time?'

"I reached out and grasped his hand; he returned the grip firmly. 'I don't know,' I said. 'I can't remember. Let's not talk about it any more.' Throughout the rest of the ferry journey we sat in silence, our hands gripped tightly together between us on the seat.

"Will lived on Ninth Avenue in Brooklyn, abreast the park. Grace met us at the door, when we at length arrived; she'd been greatly worried at our delay. The last time that I'd seen her, she had been nothing but a girl. She was a beautiful woman now, the wife for Will in every day. With a glance at him, she came straight to me; took both my hands, and kissed me like a sister.

" 'I'm sorry it had to happen,' she said with a directness that startled me but somehow didn't give me pain.

"I held her off to look at her. 'Grace Por-

ter! . . .' I said aloud, but I was talking to myself; what I was thinking couldn't have been put
into words.

"'Yes, Skeet, the same tomboy Grace,' she
flashed. 'Now run upstairs with Will, and wash as
fast as you can, and hurry back to dinner. You
must be starved, the both of you.'

"They lived quite formally, for those simple
times—kept a couple of servants, I believe. But it
was a home dinner that appeared before us. Such
biscuits!—they were like puffs of feather; I wouldn't
dare say how many I ate. Such chicken, such vegetables, such lemon tarts! I asked about them, and
learned that Grace had gone into the kitchen and
made the biscuits and pastry with her own hands—
in my honor, she said. It touched me so deeply that
a tear dropped in my plate. She was throwing
about me the atmosphere of home. She cared.

"We talked of the old days when we had been
young together; we had a gay time of it, laughing
over half-forgotten episodes. Grace seemed to realize that my barriers were broken—or was it that she
assumed a woman's license? Early in the meal, she
asked me pointed questions about my betrothed; I
discovered that the two kept up an infrequent correspondence. She knew more than I did about
affairs at home; all of her news was exactly what I
wanted to hear. It was as if my dear love sat with
us at the table. I saw the fabric being woven,
appearing out of the air; as the meal went on, I
opened my heart more and more to them, because
they understood. I was myself again, for the first
time since the disaster.

"After dinner we went upstairs to the third floor, where Will had his smoking room, and sank into deep leather chairs. Grace got cigars for us, and lit a match for me, and tucked a little pillow behind my head. Then she stood looking me over for a moment. Suddenly, acting on one of her characteristic impulses, she took my face between her hands and shook it slowly from side to side, as if administering punishment.

" 'You're a stubborn, contrary, grown-up child!' she said. 'You deserve to be spanked—licked, I suppose you'd call it. Why have you stayed away so long? If you could know how Will has missed you! Skeet, it was a cruel thing to do.'

"I gazed at her wide-eyed, and kept on shaking my head after she had let it go. I couldn't answer her question. There was no answer. Now that the ice was broken, I saw no sane excuse, no valid human reason, why I had stayed away. What had possessed me? Where precisely had lain the difficulty? And now she'd accused me of cruelty. True enough! I hadn't thought of that. The world is cluttered up with the cruelties of pride.

" 'It wasn't to hurt him, anyway,' I said at last. 'And you're wrong in one point, Grace. I have been licked for it—God, you can't imagine the lickings I've taken! But I deserved them, as you say.'

" 'Never mind now,' she cried gaily. 'We've got you at last, and nothing's been harmed or changed.' She held out a hand to me. 'Come upstairs a minute, Skeet—there's something I want to show you.' The babies, of course! I cursed myself for an unmannerly boor; I'd forgotten all about them.

'Will said I wasn't to do it,' she whispered, as we went out the door. 'He said it might disturb you—but I know better.'

" 'My dear girl,' I answered humbly, 'if you can forgive me for not asking. . . .' She put her hand in my arm as we went up the stairs.

"They lay in two little cribs, a boy and a girl, real babies. I could see at a glance how healthy and handsome they were. Something was wrong with the clothes about their necks; she bent over each one in turn and made it right.

" 'Aren't they beautiful?' she asked rapturously.

" 'Beautiful!' I repeated. I wasn't thinking of the babies at all. I was thinking of my life, a harsh life spent among men on the empty sea, a life of embroilment and brutality, so foreign to all this that it took my breath away. I wondered if I ever would be worthy, now, to attempt this purity. But how I wanted it! I stood above them in anguish, lost in the old aching dream of love. Was she aware how much it hurt me, after all? I think she was—and bless her for it. Women are very wise.

"She took me back to Will, and left us alone together for the rest of the evening. But when it was nearly midnight she came in again, still dressed, and told us it was time to go to bed. 'Come, Skeet,' she said. I saw that I was to go with her. These matters, I felt, were being done according to a careful pre-arrangement; or else Will was leaving everything to her. We chatted light-heartedly while she turned down the bed for me and fussed about the room; my secret amusement was a pleasure in itself, for I knew what she planned to talk to me about.

She reached it fairly soon, taking the subject head-on, as was her habit. Making a pretense of busying herself at the bureau, but now and then facing me, she told me plainly that it was time for me to marry. I stood beside a window, hanging my head, while she explained the situation as I never had seen it before. I must give up my intense and self-centered attitude. I must come to a decision, and act upon it. I must marry my love, and let her help me. It wasn't fair to keep her waiting so long.

"I may have seemed taciturn and gloomy to her; but secretly I was elated. I offered no objection to what she was saying; the sterner she made her commands, the better I liked them. When she had gone, I rushed about the room like a man demented, flinging off my clothes and humming the snatch of a tune. Life with its boundless flood was sweeping me along. I stood in front of the glass and looked myself over; thank God, I could say that I had kept my body clean. For a moment I gazed at the white linen sheets in trepidation—then boldly plunged into them. But sleep was far away, and I didn't want to find it. My blood ran too keen with happiness, to wish for any change.

"I'd been lying there some time, with the moonlight streaming through the window, when the door opened and Will came in. In his pajamas—he'd formed the habit out East of wearing them, as most seafaring men did—he looked not a day older than the boy I'd roomed with in school. 'Asleep yet?' he asked. I laughed. 'God, no!' I said. 'I never shall sleep again.' He crossed the room and got into bed with me. 'Grace has been telling me what she said

to you,' he chuckled. 'I think she's right, don't
you?'

" 'She seems to be one of those people who generally are right,' I answered. 'It's a dangerous
quality, but I'll have to admit she handles it well.'

"The talk we had, with our arms around each
other, lasted a long while, and ranged from pro-
fundity to triviality with the lightness that's born
only of joy. It put the finishing touches on my
recovery; the free communion of words seemed to
let down the pitch, to relieve my heart of an intol-
erable pressure, and the health and affection that
sprang from his very presence, that came to me out
of the feeling of his body close beside me, were a
pure gift of human divinity. This is the mystery
simple but forever unexplainable, the power that all
may wield. This is the core of life, without which
all our handsome enterprises are only a hollow
mummery.

"So they left me that night, with my life changed
again. Yes, saved, perhaps—as I looked back to the
end of the afternoon, I realized that it had been
touch and go. With sanity, I could have fought it
out; but I shuddered to recall that my mind had lost
its reckoning. Who shall command the ship of life
when mind, the master, fails? But now I walked my
quarter-deck again. . . . I went to sleep almost
before Will had closed the door behind him. I slept
dreamlessly, slept like a log; and awoke late, in a
room full of sunlight and color and cleanliness, to
hear his voice shouting up the hall.

" 'Turn out, you lubber, and yet your grub!' he
called.

V

"And that's the story—there isn't much more to tell. I went with Will to the office, and put myself in his hands. He had a ship ready for me, a big ship, a better ship than I'd ever hoped to command. Within the next month I had hurried home, had married, and had sailed with my wife in this fine vessel. My life, that I'd thought to be failing, had just begun. All that you know of me, my years, my position, my reputation, have happened since that time; so that it often seems, as I look back, that the early period must have belonged to the record of another man. Luck has pursued me, in many bewildering guises— the same luck, I suppose, that once nearly drove me to destruction. Or was it my error, the fierceness of my egoism, the implacability of my pride? . . . Well, I've learned better now, I hope. I've learned what's true or false, what's worth while and what's of no avail. I've had few friends, from choice; but one friend has come with me through desperate occasions. He stands firm, while the world drops away."

BALLAD OF MASTER MARINERS

How we have longed for the sea, for the life that is
   over,
  Wind, and the lift of the swell, and the sun-lighted
    foam;
Bred to a ship, with white canvas towering above
   her,
  How we have longed for the sea, our love and
    our home.

Many the years that have passed since we saw blue
   water,
  Waste of the gale-driven south where the alba-
    tross flies,
Down in the Westerlies, watching the wave on each
   quarter
  Follow us, send us, outrun us, to where the wind
    dies,

Cut off in the trough of the long and desperate
   surges
  Rolling the open, pitiless reach of the Horn;
Vistas of gloom, ere our sea-worthy vessel emerges,
  Lunging before it, into the eyes of the dawn.

Many the years since we felt the Gulf Stream's
   anger,

Homeward bound, and the home-coast on the lee,
Done at last with the tropic's stealthy languor,
  Stun'sails pulling, driving her in from sea.

How we remember ships, and the lore of their
      sailing,
  Learned in youth, in the life that was hearty and
      true,
Breathed with the breath of the salt wind, clean and
      unfailing,
  Born of our ardor, all that we ever knew.

How we remember their grace in an open seaway,
  Part of the wave, and part of the thundering
      gale,
Holding five points to the wind, making scant lee-
      way,
  Eating to windward under a press of sail;

Joyful and buoyant vessels, proudly careening,
  Lightly and swiftly stepping the dance of the
      wave,
Clouds of canvas aloft, and tall masts leaning,
  And forefoot shouting the challenge, loud and
      brave;

Swirl of waters astern, in the wake out-reeling,
  Crash of wave upon wave beneath the bows,
Seas far flung, to the great ship's heavy heeling,
  Shouldered and broken seas, as she strongly
      plows;

Murmuring high aloft, through the air wind-scoured,
  Whistle and grind of yards on the swaying spars,
Mournful whisper of shrouds, and ever, forward,
  Roar of the straining sails against the stars;

And under our feet the body leaping and yearning,
  Swing and drive of the deck, and the ship's good
    will,
Love for the sailor's love, outbound, returning:
  How we remember—how we are sailing still.

Ships that carried us hence, with a priceless cargo,
  Youth, and the high career, to win and prove,
Lying dismantled under time's embargo,
  Never to feel the sea beneath or the wind above;

Bones of ships on the shores they passed so proudly,
  Outworn hulks in the streams they graced of yore,
Silence forward, where the forefoot sang so loudly,
  Stunted spars, where the press of canvas bore;

Courses lost, that we ventured to discover,
  Islands lone, that welcomed the passing sail,
Channels filled, where our keels ran freely over,
  Stirring dangers, a pleasant fireside tale;

Only a few of us left, to care and remember,
  Never again the wind-swept wave to roam;
Days gone by, and lives burned out to the ember:
  How we have longed for the sea, our love and our
    home.